Charise Mericle Harper

BALZER + BRAY
An Imprint of HarperCollins*Publishers*

Balzer + Bray is an imprint of HarperCollins Publishers.

For information address HarperCollins Children's Books, a division of HarperCollins Publishers, 10 East 53rd Street, New York, NY 10022.
www.harpercollinschildrens.com

Library of Congress Cataloging-in-Publication Data
Harper, Charise Mericle.
Dreamer, wisher, liar / by Charise Mericle Harper. — First edition.
pages cm
Summary: Ashley's summer is filled with babysitting, letters to her best friend at camp, and a wish jar filled with secret revelations that help her understand her mother in a whole new way.
ISBN 978-0-06-202675-0 (hardcover bdg.)
[1. Babysitting—Fiction. 2. Magic—Fiction. 3. Wishes—Fiction. 4. Mothers and daughters—Fiction.] I. Title.
PZ7.H231323Dre 2014 2013008222
[Fic]—dc23 CIP
AC

Typography by Dana Fritts
14 15 16 17 18 CG/RRDH 10 9 8 7 6 5 4 3 2 1
❖
First Edition

For my mother and daughter—
I wish we could be twelve together.
Just for a day.

chapter one

Joy

I'm not great with dates, but April 16 isn't hard for me to remember. It was the last perfectly happy day of my life. When your world is suddenly upside down, it's easy to remember the last day you were standing right side up.

The sixteenth was a school day, and pretty much a regular one, except for when Mr. Lester, our teacher, got the phone call for an emergency meeting. I don't know what kind of emergency meeting needs an English teacher, but Mr. Lester seemed excited about it. He had his stuff packed and was gone in seconds. A few kids were sure we'd get to go home early, but of course that didn't happen. Instead, Ms. Wooten, the school psychologist, came down to substitute. She was surprisingly organized; she introduced herself and then said, "I'm looking forward to this, so let's get started! I want you all to make a list of the joys of your life." Everyone groaned, but there was no choice.

It took her a while to explain what she wanted us to do, and mostly I wasn't paying attention, but I was glad I heard her say, "Use nice handwriting, because we are going to be hanging these up in the hall." I don't know if she was warning us on purpose or not, but a list that hangs on the wall is very different from a list that lives in your binder.

THE JOYS THAT I PUT ON THE HALLWAY LIST

- Friends
- Reading
- Pizza at Fannucci's
- Riding my bike
- The internet
- Good TV
- Pie

THE JOYS THAT I DID NOT WRITE DOWN ON THE HALLWAY LIST

- Lucy, my best friend in the whole world
- Eating cereal without milk
- PJ Walker books
- Eating and thinking about food

chapter two

April 17

How do you tell someone the worst news of her life?

If you are Lucy's mom, you take the someone to her favorite restaurant, Fannucci's, wait until dessert, and then, when the someone's mouth is full of apple pie and ice cream, you say, "Ash, Lucy doesn't know how to tell you this, but at the end of the summer we're going to be moving to Oregon."

At first I felt really bad about spitting pie into Lucy's mom's cappuccino, but later, the more I thought about it, the more I decided she deserved it.

Her one sentence ruined a lot of stuff for me—my

friendship with Lucy, Fannucci's, summer, the state of Oregon, and now even just thinking of apple pie kind of makes me gag.

April 17 was two months ago.

It was the last time I was filled with joy.

chapter three

Truth

I didn't know this before, but sadness can be perfect. Today Lucy left for summer camp.

If things were perfect, there would have been thunder and lightning, tree limbs crashing to the ground, a freezing cold wind, and sirens howling in the distance. Instead it was partly cloudy, T-shirt weather, and there was an ice cream truck across the street chiming out an annoyingly cheerful song. It was decidedly not perfect. The world's outsides and my insides did not match up.

Lucy and I were in the school parking lot, not saying much, mostly shuffling our feet in the gravel. The little stones around us were bunched into piles, and my new white Converse sneakers were dirty and gray. But I didn't care. It felt right, my shoes matching my mood—grimy and dark.

The camp bus was parked off to the side. It was the exact same bus we rode to school every day, except for the piece of cardboard in the front window saying CAMP RED OAK. This first good-bye was only for a month; the next one would be forever. I tried not to think of this as a practice run for the real thing, but it was hard to ignore.

Three weeks from now I was going to join Lucy at camp. That would be our last month together before Lucy moved to Portland. FOREVER. It was like two stepping-stones into an abyss—lonely, happy, and then nothing.

Lucy's parents were waiting with us, but off to the side—invisible if I twisted my head to the left. I didn't want to see them. I hated them. This was new, but it was their fault—I didn't feel guilty. If they changed their minds and let Lucy stay, I could love them again. It was that simple. But it wasn't going to happen.

I wanted it to be just Lucy and me. I didn't want them standing there watching us. Even though they were silent, I could read their thoughts, and it was distracting.

Lucy's mom was thinking, *Oh, how cute, the two girls are saying good-bye.* Lucy's dad was the opposite. He looked at his phone, sighed loudly, and shifted Lucy's bag from one hand to the other. I knew what he was thinking too. He wanted out of there. He caught my eye and smiled. I could read his mind: *What's the big deal? You'll see each other in a few weeks.* I scowled and ignored him.

They were both wrong! This wasn't cute, and it wasn't temporary! This was earthquake-rumbling-tornado-swirling-tsunami-coming serious! At least for me; I didn't know about Lucy. Sure, she'd miss me, but still, she was probably excited, too. Why not? Camp, even without a best friend, was going to be fun.

"Ash, let's promise to write every day," said Lucy. "I want to know everything I'm missing."

She was being nice, trying to make me feel better, but I was staying here. Nothing fun was going to happen to me. She wouldn't miss a thing. Instead of going to camp, I was babysitting for the first month she was gone. Mom had made me one of her deals. Her deals were always the same: "You listen, and I'm going to tell you what's going to happen." There was no give-and-take. So now I was babysitting some seven-year-old kid who I'd never even heard of before. It was completely unfair! For me there'd be no zip line rides, no water skiing, no rock climbing, no sleeping under the stars, no anything! What was I going to write about? Playing hopscotch with a seven-year-old?

"Maybe every second day," I said. "And we should do postcards. You're going to be way too busy to write whole letters."

Lucy looked at me like I had just said something mean, but I wasn't being mean; it was the truth. I'd looked through the camp guide. Camp was a busy place. Okay, maybe I was being a little mean, but I couldn't help it.

"All right," said Lucy. She sighed. "Postcards, but I wish we could email. Stupid camp!"

"Yeah, STUPID CAMP!" I said it too, but mine was louder and meaner—I meant the "stupid" part a lot more than she did.

Lucy's "stupid" was because Camp Red Oak didn't let campers bring computers, cell phones, or anything electronic with them to camp. Going to Camp Red Oak was like being zapped back in time—not all the way to the dinosaurs, but more like 1985 or something, which was a lot less interesting. The camp motto was "Trees Over Technology," and they were serious about it. Campers were only allowed to write letters—no exceptions, not even to parents. Someone hadn't thought this through very well, because a lot of trees were being killed just so everyone could send home paper mail. Lucy said she was going to bring that up at some point. Maybe organize a protest—save a few trees and get to use email. Anyway, this dumb letter rule was Lucy's reason for the "stupid." It was a good one, but it wasn't mine. Mine was longer—I had a list.

Before the bus left, we hugged, we cried a little, and I tried not to think too much about what was happening. Lucy got on the bus. She waved, I waved, and then she was gone. I didn't want to, but I couldn't help it. I cried—a lot. It's good I knew the way home, because it's really hard to see where you're going when your eyes are like Niagara Falls. And it's even harder when your hair's hanging down to hide it.

By the time I got home and walked up the back steps, I was done—all dried up. I still felt bad, but the crying part had stopped, and now I was hungry. That was a surprise. I wasn't expecting that. I looked in the fridge for a snack. I liked yogurt and applesauce, but today they seemed wrong. I needed something hard and crunchy. I picked out a granola bar, and with each bite I thought about my stupids. The crunching made it easier to get through them. Yogurt wouldn't have been the same. With yogurt I'd have been stuck at the top, wallowing in loneliness.

chapter four

My Stupids

<u>HERE ARE MY STUPIDS</u>

- Lucy leaving
- Mom making me babysit her friend's kid for three weeks
- Having face blindness and not being able to recognize people
- Being lonely and alone

The last two kind of went together, like peanut butter and jelly.

Weird problem + alone = unhappy forever

It was a sad sandwich.

Prosopagnosia—that was the peanut butter, and it was stuck with me forever. It was invisible, it was stupid, and I could hardly even pronounce it. Plus it was something no one had ever heard of. Whenever I tried to explain it, I could tell that people thought I was making it up. And I couldn't blame them. If someone told me, *If I see you tomorrow and act like I don't know you, it's only because my brain doesn't work right and I won't recognize you,* I'd think they were crazy too.

Finally I was done eating and feeling sorry for myself. I picked at the last few crumbs and rolled the wrapper into a tube. I looked through it, pretending I could see Lucy. What was she doing? I imagined her on the bus, heading to camp, all alone. How did that feel? I crumpled up the tube. I didn't want to know, but it was too late; I was already thinking about it, and now I felt guilty.

I'd started my good-bye to Lucy three weeks ago. It was my plan. Each day I made myself see less and less of her, so that now, on the day she was really leaving, it wouldn't be as bad. It was like giving up sugar—you start slow and build it up—only I wasn't quitting food. I was quitting Lucy. But it had been a mistake, because now that today was here, I still felt terrible. The good-bye hadn't been easier at all. Today was the worst day ever.

And there was more; those five times she had called last week, I had lied on purpose. I wasn't too busy to talk. I was just grumpy.

Angry and grumpy.

Jealous and grumpy.

Selfish and grumpy.

Worried and grumpy.

Sad and grumpy.

Grumpy is like ketchup—it goes with a lot of things.

This was a lot to make up for, and too much to write on a postcard. Plus, it wasn't fair. It might make me feel better, but it wouldn't help Lucy. And she was probably already sad anyway.

She wasn't a camp kind of person, but there she was on the bus, heading off into the woods. Lucy's parents were going to Oregon for the summer to fix up the new house, so the choice had been go with them to Oregon or go to camp. Lucy had picked camp, because of me. We were going to spend the last month of summer at Red Oak together. It was something I should have been looking forward to, but it was hard to be really excited about it. It seemed more like a final countdown to total unhappiness—the last thirty days until I lost her forever. How can you look forward to that?

I had to find something else to do—a distraction. I needed to feel better before I wrote to her, so it could be a happy, positive letter; she deserved that.

chapter five

Escape

Our house is small. Normally I didn't care about that, but today I did. Every time I moved, Mom and Dad were there, close by. And every time I passed Mom, she smiled and gave me the look.

I hate the look!

THE LOOK MEANS:

- Do you want to talk?
- I feel bad for you.
- I know how you feel.
- Can I help?

The look is uncomfortable. And no, she can't

possibly know how I feel.

Normally I wouldn't go hang out in the basement—mostly because it's dirty and filled with junk—but today I made an exception. It was an escape from the look, and from a potential Mom-talk, and I was definitely not wanting one of those. There was an armchair down there; I could just sit in it and listen to music or something. Mom might follow me upstairs to my room, but she'd never come down to the basement. The basement was safe because it was filled with too many unfinished projects she wanted to ignore.

Mom's a Freecycle addict—which really just means junk addict. Freecycle is this organization that works like a garage sale, only it's on the internet, and everything is free. Mom's a subscriber, which means she gets hundreds of emails from strangers describing junk they want to get rid of. Things like "I have a set of blue dishes with painted llamas on them—anyone want them?" If Mom decides she needs the llama dishes, she emails the person back, and they put the llama plates on the curb for Mom to come and pick up. I don't like thinking of Mom as one of those garbage-picker-type people, but the truth is, she loves junk. The more stuff she has, the happier she is.

At the beginning she tried to get me excited about it, but I only went once; it's not my thing.

Mom's favorite part of the whole thing is sorting everything out; she says it's like treasure hunting. That's not how I look at it, but I just nod and agree with her—it's easier that way. She puts her favorite stuff into the basement, and everything else goes into the garage. So the garage is a disaster; it's hard to even move in there, but Dad doesn't care—he just parks on the street. He says it's nice for Mom to have a hobby, but mostly I think he's supportive because it's a lot cheaper than if she went shopping.

Once in a while Mom gets inspired and gives something a makeover—that's how I got my zebra-patterned nightstand; it's supercool and I love it—but that doesn't happen very often. Mostly stuff just sits in piles waiting to be noticed.

I grabbed my headphones and disappeared downstairs. I was right about the chair; it was in front of the workbench—not a normal place to keep an armchair—but it was clean and junk free, so I was happy. I turned on the light, pulled out my headphones, and was just about to sit down, but then I changed my mind. There were nails and a piece of wood on the workbench, and just seeing them started a thought in my head. A second later, that thought turned into a project. *I could spell Lucy's name on the wood with the nails.*

I'm not afraid of hammers, and pounding the nails was fun, especially when I made a direct hit and the nail pushed deep into the wood. After about ten minutes I had spelled out the *L*, the *U*, the *C*, and half the *Y* of Lucy's name. I held the wood out and studied it. It looked pretty good.

Four more nails and I'd be finished. I searched the workbench, but there weren't any left; I'd used them all. I knew Mom had more. A long time ago I'd seen it—a jar of nails and screws. I scanned the basement. Finding that jar was not going to be easy. There were boxes stacked everywhere, and in between the boxes was random junk—chairs, pipes, clothes, wood, really anything you could imagine. It was chaos and in no way organized. I walked over to the sink and found some rubber gloves. If I was going to dig around, I definitely wanted hand protection.

<u>THE JUNK I FOUND</u>

- Old plastic cups and lots of forks—probably hundreds! Why so many forks, I have no idea.
- A box filled with wire, string, and plastic

farm animals. Weird.

- A glass jar with the word WISHES written on a pretty label. Pretty dirty—I was glad to have the gloves on.
- A small box filled with screws. Almost right, but not quite.
- A large jar filled with nails. Exactly what I needed.

It was amazing that I found the nails so fast. They weren't a perfect match, but once I hammered them in, you could hardly tell they were smaller than the other ones.

I put the wood on the edge of the workbench and sat down and studied it. What would I think if I were seeing it for the first time?

Would I like it? Was it cheesy?

Yes. No.

Was it fun?

Yes.

Would Lucy like it?

I knew the answer to that. She'd love it. I could send it as a surprise, instead of a postcard. Maybe she'd hang it up in her cabin, near her bed or something. I smiled. These were happy thoughts, but they didn't last.

It's not always easy to be in control of your

thinking. Sometimes even when you are having fun, your brain can still mess things up. There I was, happy one second, and the next, completely sad. It was like being struck by lightning. You can't ignore lightning, and mine was a bolt of worry.

With Lucy gone, how would I recognize people?

It's not easy to overcome a weird problem, but Lucy had helped me do it. If I didn't know someone, she'd quickly whisper a name or say, "Don't worry—we don't know them." It had worked perfectly, and with her there, I'd almost forgotten I wasn't the same as everyone else. But now things were going to be different. And this kind of different was not going to be good.

I could have sat there for hours feeling sorry for myself, but I didn't. Maybe it was because "worry" and "wishes" both start with *w*, or maybe it was just because I was desperate, but whatever the reason, I got up, put the gloves back on, and went to find the jar with the word "wishes" written on the side of it. It was my new hope, and suddenly I wanted to believe in magic.

chapter six

Wish Jar

The jar itself was nothing special—probably just an old mayonnaise or pickle jar, but I couldn't tell for sure. The lid didn't have any writing on it; that would have helped. There was something inside, little white things. At first I thought it was packing peanuts or popcorn, but when I brushed off some of the dirt and looked closer, I could see that it was paper—tiny balls of crumpled white paper. But none of that mattered, because what was most interesting was the label on the front. It was a rectangular red frame highlighted in gold, and inside the frame, against a cream-colored background, was the word WISHES in golden writing. It was beautiful and elegant. That's why I'd remembered it. Fancy label and crummy old jar—they didn't fit. I looked at it closely and made my own wish: *Be magic.* It was impossible, a fantasy, but it's what I wanted more than anything, so I held on to them both—the thought and the jar. I was desperate.

I carried the jar back to the chair and sat down, but only for a second. I jumped up again. I needed something else. After a quick search of the workbench I was back in the chair, a pair of safety goggles in my hand. I cleaned the lenses on my pants and pulled them on. It was ridiculous, but still, better safe than sorry. I was hoping for a wish-granting genie—the friendly kind, but you never knew; it could go the other way too. It could happen—I'd seen it on TV; there were grumpy genies. I leaned forward, grabbed the hammer off the bench, and put it next to me on the chair.

I shook off the rubber gloves and very slowly rubbed the side of the jar. My fingertips tingled, my ears pounded with my heartbeat, and suddenly everything seemed far away. It was just me and the jar. If this had been a movie, the audience would have been watching an extreme close-up of my hands. And the music would be tense. Supertense. I unscrewed the lid.

If this had been a movie, the audience would have been disappointed, and maybe even wanting their money back, because even though I had done everything right, nothing happened. It was just me, sitting in the basement, holding an old jar. I slumped back into the chair. Had I really expected that to work? I waited for a second, dumped all the paper balls out onto the floor, and stood up. I wasn't giving up. There was a pen and a notebook on the bench. I ripped a page out of the notebook and then, in my best printing, so there would be no mistake, wrote down my number one wish.

I Wish That Lucy Stays Here

After saying "please" about twenty times and "come true" about thirty times, I kissed the paper and dropped it in the jar. I twisted the lid back on, set the jar on the floor, and waited for the magic to begin.

The longer you have to wait for magic to happen, the less you end up believing it's going to work.

Minute one—"This is so exciting!"

Minute two—"Any second now."

Minute three—"Huh."

Minute four—"Maybe I did something wrong."

I checked the lid to make sure it was tight and gave the jar an extra shake.

Minute five—"This isn't going to work."

Minute six—"Maybe another minute."

After you've been waiting for a long time, you might have to get up and go to the bathroom, or do something else in another part of the house while you continue to wait.

Lucy's mom called just as we finished up dinner to say that Lucy was fine and that she'd made it to camp. After that, I was pretty sure the wish jar was not going to work.

I helped Mom clear the table and load up the dishwasher. When we were done, I told her about the name sign I'd made for Lucy.

"Oh, Ash!" she said. "That's fabulous! Amazing!"

She was being way too enthusiastic, probably relieved that I wasn't in my room sulking, feeling bad, and crying. But she was wrong; I was still sad. In fact, her thinking I was okay made it worse. Didn't she know how I was really feeling? Couldn't she tell? But Mom didn't notice; she smiled and kept talking.

"Can I see it?" she asked.

I nodded and went downstairs. Since I was down

there anyway, I tried some last-minute stuff with the jar, just in case. It's not easy to give up on a dream.

THINGS THAT MIGHT MAKE MAGIC WORK

- Spin around three times while holding the jar.
- Shake the jar for two minutes while saying, "Come true, come true, come true!"
- Rub the jar and say, "Genie come out!"
- Rub the jar and say much louder, "Genie come out!"
- Open the lid and say, "I command you to come out!"

THINGS THAT PROBABLY WON'T MAKE MAGIC WORK

- Call the genie stupid and lazy.

In the end I was probably just lucky that I didn't break the jar. Mom would have been mad about broken glass all over the floor. Working with magic was exhausting. I gave up and collapsed into the chair. What was I thinking? Of course it hadn't worked. I opened the jar, took out my wish, and shoved it into my pocket. A few minutes later all the paper balls were picked up, and the jar was back in a junk box. I sat in the chair, disappointed, but not devastated. I hadn't really believed it would work anyway. I pulled Lucy's sign off the workbench and looked at it. Mom would gush over it, I knew that; maybe it would make me feel better.

I ran up the stairs full of fake energy.

"Hey Mom! Look, here it is." I held it out.

Mom walked over and took it from me. "Oh, Ash, Lucy will love it," she said.

I smiled; it was exactly what I wanted to hear. Maybe I was feeling better.

"How are you going to send it?" asked Mom. She didn't wait for an answer. "Did you know that the post office can mail that just like it is? All it needs is a stamp."

I turned the sign over and thought about what Mom was saying. I could paint a note and the address on the back, and then mail it like a postcard—only it would be a wooden postcard. I liked that idea—it was exactly what Lucy and I had promised each other, only cooler.

"Do you want to watch TV with us?" Mom pointed to the living room.

Dad was watching something I wouldn't like; I could tell by the gunfire. If I went in there, Mom would make him change the channel to make me happy. Then Dad would be grumpy and I would feel guilty. It was too much mood shuffling.

I shook my head and said, "I think I'll go upstairs. I'm pretty tired."

Mom looked disappointed, but she didn't say anything. She smiled, nodded, and walked toward the sirens—I guess the good guys were coming.

I wasn't sad to leave Mom and Dad; I wanted to go upstairs. There was something up there I'd been saving, just for tonight. It was PJ Walker's new book, *Have Mercy, Percy*. It was under my mattress, somewhere in the middle of the bed. I'd done that on purpose, so I wouldn't cheat and start reading it early. PJ Walker was my favorite author. I'd read all her books. I wished she wrote faster, but she was slow—only one a year. I'm not a big fan of mysteries, but hers were different. They were smart and funny, and usually if I paid attention, I could figure them out before the main character did. That was my favorite part. I couldn't wait to start this new one. I had it all planned out—one chapter a night, no matter what. It was like being on a diet, but with a book.

Nighttime is the worst for sadness, but PJ Walker was going to save me—literally. I was going to fill my mind with her story so there would be no room for anything else. The book had nineteen chapters—that was almost three weeks of reading. After that I didn't have a plan, but I'd worry about that later. I studied the cover. There wasn't much to it—just a picture of some broken glass on a table, and in the distance a small furry thing on the ground. You couldn't really tell what it was, but my guess was a squirrel. PJ Walker had a thing about squirrels. All her books had squirrels in them—not as main characters, but still, they were there, scurrying around in the background. It didn't matter; I'd find out soon enough. I stretched out, fluffed my pillow, and opened the book. This was going to be the best part of my day.

chapter seven

Dream

It was nine p.m., and I was standing in the kitchen, reading a cereal box and eating handfuls of Crunchy O's. I'd rather have been reading my book, but I'd breezed through the first chapter superfast, and I didn't trust myself not to read more. I'd shoved it back under the mattress, but still, it was safer to leave the room.

Now that I was fortified with vitamins, I was thirsty. After cereal I like to drink a cold apple juice, but we didn't have any in the fridge. There was only cranberry juice, and I hate that stuff.

Mom and Dad were still watching world

destruction in the living room. But the humans were putting up a fight—at least it sounded that way. I stuck my head out in the hall and added to the noise.

"I'm going to the basement to get juice!" I shouted, but there was no response—my voice was drowned out by explosions. I thought about trying again but decided against it. I wasn't scared of the basement.

As soon as I got to the pantry shelves, I could tell that Dad was the one who had unloaded the groceries. The heavy apple juice bottles were on the top shelf, and the not-heavy toilet paper was right in front of me, at perfect grabbing height. There was no way I could reach the apple juice without standing on something. Suddenly I remembered the box where I'd put the wish jar. It wasn't a normal cardboard box; it had wooden sides. It was strong, and if I was careful and put my weight mostly on the wood, it would hold me.

I found it and dragged it to the shelf. Apart from the wish jar, it was filled with bags of fabric and wooden spools. I emptied it and turned it upside down. The trick was not to stand on the bottom of it—that part was just cardboard. I stepped up onto the wooden sides and wiggled a little. It was strong. I felt safe. I took a deep breath and then slowly and carefully reached up for the apple juice. As soon as I pulled the bottle from the shelf, I knew I was in trouble. Sometimes, in the second before something bad happens, your brain can sense what's coming. It's not enough time to change anything, only to be superaware, and suddenly everything can seem like it's happening in slow motion.

A second later I was on the floor—hurting, but not broken. My knee was throbbing. I looked up at the shelf. I was lucky; the whole thing could have fallen right on top of me. I shivered just thinking about it. Other than the broken box under me and the plastic apple juice bottle a few feet away, nothing seemed out of order, but then suddenly I noticed the wish jar. It was lying in the middle of the floor. How had it gotten there? Was it broken? I stood up and hobbled over to check. It was fine. But my knee wasn't; it was killing me. I needed to sit down. I dragged myself over to the chair, put the jar on the floor, and pulled up my pant leg. I was expecting a large welt, bruising, maybe even blood, but there wasn't anything. It was just a little red. It was crazy, but I was almost disappointed; I wanted it to look as bad as it felt. I leaned back in the chair. I needed a rest before I tried to climb back up the stairs to the kitchen.

I nudged the wish jar with my toe, leaned over, and picked it up. The little paper balls jiggled. I shook the jar, and they spun around, like snow in a snow globe. But they couldn't float; a second later they were still, clumped together into a white mountain at the bottom of the jar. What were they? Why were there so many? I opened the jar, picked one, unfurled it, and flattened it out against my leg. Unfolded, it was just a skinny rectangle of paper, but there was something written on the other side. A faint outline of blue swirls, dots, and dashes showed through. I turned it over and read the words.

I Wish Ashley Wouldn't Ignore Me

WAIT! WHAT? THAT'S ME! WAS THIS ABOUT ME? I was confused. Suddenly my body was tingling—my toes, my fingertips, everything—and a second later it was over. It took me a minute to recover. I rubbed my eyes and looked up.

Surprise!

Shock!

The basement was gone. Instead of sitting in the chair, I was outside, sitting on the ground in the rain! And it was *daytime*! This couldn't be real. I stood up and shook my head. It was a dream; it had to be.

Two girls were up ahead, walking toward each other on the sidewalk. I had a million questions.

Where am I? What happened? Where's my house?

Why am I here? What's going on? Who are you? Suddenly I froze; I had three new thoughts, and the last one I couldn't keep inside. It came out of my mouth in a scream.

It can't be! I'm dead! "I'M A GHOST!"

The girls didn't stop, or even look my way—they hadn't heard me. I *was* a ghost. The one with the short blond hair smiled at the one with the long brown hair. When they passed she said, "Hi." The dark-haired girl stared straight ahead; she didn't respond. Maybe she couldn't see her? Maybe the blond girl was like me. Maybe she was a ghost too! I ran to catch up to her.

"Excuse me! Can you help me? Where are we? What's going on?" My voice got louder and louder as I tried to get her attention, until finally I was screaming.

"HEY! BLOND GIRL! STOP WALKING!"

But she didn't. She looked straight ahead like she hadn't heard me. She was almost running now. I stopped following her. No, she wasn't like me; she wasn't a ghost. Her hair was soaking wet, and mine was perfectly dry.

"WHAT'S HAPPENING?" I yelled. But there was no answer. I stood there watching the girl until she disappeared. I couldn't be. I didn't want to be. Was it true? Was I dead? I shut my eyes and dug my nails into my palms, trying to make them hurt.

"WAKE UP! WAKE UP! DON'T BE DEAD! DON'T BE DEAD!" Suddenly there was a jolt, a zap, a sting, but not like from an insect; my whole body hurt. Was it death?

There wasn't time to think—someone was calling me.

"ASH! Are you okay? I heard shouting." I recognized that voice. It was Mom.

I looked around; I was home—back in the chair, back in the basement. I was alive! Mom was at the top of the stairs calling down to me. I wasn't dead! YAY!

I dropped the wish and ran upstairs. What had just happened? It had seemed so real. I was confused. Was it the jar, or the wish? I didn't want to be near either of them. Mom was waiting for me at the top of the steps.

"What about the apple juice?" she asked.

Stupid! I'd left it downstairs. I wasn't going back down there.

I shook my head. "I decided to have water instead—healthier."

I pushed by Mom and walked to the cupboard to

get a glass. My throat was suddenly dry; it was hard to talk. My heart was racing, and my hands were shaking.

Mom followed me. "Is everything okay?"

I filled the glass with water and took a sip. "I think I fell asleep in the chair and, uh . . . had a dream." I didn't want to say more. It was all too weird.

Mom shook her head. "Oh, sweetie, I bet you're tired. It's been a . . ." And then she stopped.

I knew she was looking for a word that would describe my hard-impossible-stressful-emotional-devastating day, but I didn't help her. Instead, I stood there pretending I had no idea what she was talking about.

Finally she just gave up and said, "Okay, well, try to get some sleep."

chapter eight

Reflection

Reflection is when you do serious thinking about things that have happened. I had a lot of thinking to do. What had happened in the basement? Was it magic? A dream? I lay down on my bed to try to figure it out. Serious thinking and beds do not go together. The next thing I knew, Mom was shaking me by the arm to wake me up, and it was morning.

"Ash, wake up! Hurry. Claire will be here in ten minutes. Her dad called. They're coming a day early."

My brain felt fuzzy. I jumped out of bed. I had to get dressed. I staggered to my dresser and suddenly remembered the basement. It made me shiver;

I pulled on sweat pants and a sweater over my T-shirt. The doorbell rang just as I was brushing my teeth. I finished up and spit in the sink. On the way downstairs I went over the list of things Mom had already told me about Claire:

- Seven years old
- Needs lots of attention because of her mom
- Is an only child
- Likes fashion

It wasn't a big list, but Mom had said she'd tell me more before Claire got here. Now that she was here, it was too late for that. I guessed I'd find out more on my own. When I got to the last step, I could see that the front door was open. I walked over slowly and stood next to Mom.

"Are you sick?"

Those were the first words Claire said to me. She was standing in the open doorway looking in. A man, probably her dad, was hanging back. He was younger than Dad, but more tired and kind of grungy looking. He reminded me of the people on those TV shows who go off into the wilderness with only a tent and the clothes on their back. I glanced at Claire—no, she didn't look like she'd been camping. He saw me staring and nodded. I looked down, embarrassed.

"Do you think you might be sick?" asked Claire.

I looked up, forced a smile, and shook my head. Why was she asking that? Maybe I had toothpaste on my mouth. I wiped it and checked my hand. No, it was clean.

"There was a girl in my school who was sick, and she had to wear sweaters and scarves all the time," said Claire. "We had to be nice to her. It was a rule."

Mom leaned toward me. "Are you feeling okay?"

Now everyone was staring at me; suddenly I felt hot. Why was I wearing this outfit? It was the middle of summer.

"I'm fine." I waved my hand in front of my face and pulled off my sweater. "I forgot it was summer."

Mom still looked worried, but Claire seemed relieved. She smiled at me. "Oh, good, because when you have an illness, you mostly have to do quiet things, and I like moving around better."

Mom frowned, looked down, and shook her head, like she was trying to jiggle the pieces around to make them fit. We all stood there uncomfortably for a few seconds.

"Ash, that's Mr. Bardwell, and this is Claire." She

smiled and patted Claire's shoulder.

Claire held out her hand and repeated her name. I nodded, and we shook hands. I looked over at her dad; he didn't move from where he was standing, but he gave me a half wave. Suddenly Claire turned, ran back to her dad, and gave him a quick hug. A minute later she was standing next to me, her big panda bag by her side. Mom motioned for me to pick up the bag and take Claire inside. She closed the door behind us so she could talk to Claire's dad in private.

"I couldn't wait to get here," said Claire. "I made a whole list of stuff we can do." She pulled off her backpack. "Do you want to hear it?"

I shook my head. "Uh, maybe later." I was still sleepy, and not a big fan of other people's lists. Plus, this whole thing was too sudden. I wasn't ready to be babysitting.

"Why did you come a day early?" I asked. "Was there some kind of emergency?"

Claire fiddled with her backpack. "Daddy has to work. He's pretty busy." She looked up and smiled, but I didn't know her yet, so I couldn't tell if it was a real smile or not.

Mom opened the door and came back in. I thought Claire's dad might come in too, but she closed it behind her. I guess he was gone.

Mom tapped Claire on the arm. "How about some breakfast. Are you hungry?" She was using her super-friendly voice. The one she uses for pets.

"What are we having?" asked Claire. "I hope it's pancakes."

Mom smiled. "Perfect—let's have pancakes!" I followed them to the kitchen.

I was thinking three things: I forgot that Mom had that voice, pancakes did sound good, and Claire dresses kind of stylish for a seven-year-old. I couldn't remember the last time Mom made pancakes. We used to have them all the time, but now we didn't. I don't know why. I still liked them. It's funny, endings are different from beginnings—beginnings are easier to remember.

"Do you want to help me crack the eggs?" asked Mom. For a second I thought she was talking to me, but she wasn't; she was looking at Claire.

"I love cracking eggs," said Claire. "My mom taught me." She leaned over the sink to wash her hands. Mom helped her reach the soap. For half a second I could almost imagine it was me and Mom standing there. We used to do the exact same thing. Suddenly I had the feeling that Claire's visit was going to be a big trip down memory lane. I watched Claire with the eggs—she could crack them with one hand. How did she do that? I was almost envious, but I caught myself.

"Wow, Claire, you're good at that." I stepped closer to see if there was any shell in the bowl. There wasn't. "How did you learn that? Is your mom a chef or something?"

Mom gave me a look, but I couldn't read it. I ignored her.

Claire threw the shells into the garbage. "My mom was good at making breakfasts," she said.

"Do you always have big breakfasts?" I asked. I was happy with how things were going. It's not always easy to talk to a seven-year-old, and I wanted her to like me. Especially since we were stuck together for three weeks. Claire cracked another egg.

"We used to have special breakfasts all the time, but now that my mom's gone, we don't anymore. Sometimes Daddy takes me out for an egg sandwich, but I like pancakes and other stuff better."

It took a few seconds for me to understand what she was saying. That can happen when someone surprises you. I looked over at Mom for help. But she didn't give me any—she was shaking her head. What did she mean? Slowly my brain put the pieces together.

Her mom gone + Mom shaking her head at me = OH, NO! Something happened to Claire's mom. Did her mom die?

Suddenly I felt sick. I shot Mom an angry look. Why hadn't she told me?! What was I supposed to say? I wasn't ready for this. Mom leaned over and gave Claire's shoulder a squeeze.

"We're so excited that you're here having pancakes with us," she said. "It's an extra-special treat, right, Ash?"

Mom was patting Claire's shoulder but looking at me. I had to say something.

"I CAN'T WAIT FOR PANCAKES! PANCAKES ARE GREAT! I LOVE PANCAKES!"

It was too much enthusiasm, but I couldn't help it. I was relieved. And then I was sweating—burning up—crazy hot. Who wears sweat pants on a summer day?

"I'll be right back." I pointed to my legs. "I need to put on some shorts."

Mom mumbled something, but she had her head in the cupboard looking for syrup, so I couldn't hear it. I gave Claire a wave and ran upstairs to change.

The second I stepped into my room, I gulped for air. I hadn't noticed it, but I'd been holding my breath all the way up the stairs. I flopped onto my bed and stared up at the ceiling. I just wanted to lie there quietly, resting, thinking of nothing, but that didn't happen. Within seconds, thoughts were spinning in my brain:

Claire must be so sad.

Could I help her?

How did her mom die?

How would I feel if Mom died?

Suddenly there were too many thoughts. It was uncomfortable and confusing. I forced myself off the bed and got changed.

There is a song I know with the words "You came into my heart with candy-coated sweetness." I don't like the song that much, but for some reason it was stuck in my head. Maybe that's why it happened—why I made the promise. I stopped in the middle of the stairs on my way down to the kitchen. I put my hand on my heart, and in a whisper I said, "I promise to be sweet to Claire, for as long as she is here." I'd never made a promise like that before—hand on heart, out loud for the universe to hear; it felt important.

There's a difference between the promises you say in your head and the promises you say out loud. The out-loud ones are harder to break.

chapter nine

Pancakes and Old People

I love pancakes, but I'm not so sure about old people. I guess they're okay. Claire loves both. When I got back downstairs, Mom and Claire were sitting at the table. Claire looked up.

"We're waiting for you." She pointed to a plate of pancakes at the visitor's chair. It was Lucy's spot, where she used to sit when she came over.

Claire was in my seat; it wasn't a big deal, but it was different, and somehow that made me uneasy. I sat down and stole a look at Mom. She's a terrible actress, so if she was mad, I was going to know right away. She glanced at me for a second, half smiled, and picked up her fork.

"Let's eat," she said. "I'm hungry."

Claire stuffed a forkful of pancake into her mouth. Suddenly I was hungry too. It's hard to stay worried while eating pancakes. After a couple of bites I felt much better. Maybe everything was going to be okay. As soon as we finished eating, Claire got her backpack and took out the list she'd been talking about.

She waved it in the air. "It's called 'Summer List of Things to Do.'"

I tried to read it, but she was moving it around too much. It looked pretty long.

I reached out my hand. "Can I see it?"

Claire flattened it tight against her chest.

"No looking!" She shook her head. "I'm only going to tell you one thing a day. That way every day can be a surprise." She looked at me and waited to see if I was going to be as excited as she was. I nodded and forced a smile. Here we were only an hour into her visit, and I was already working to keep my promise. I didn't say anything, but I hate surprises. It's probably because of my face blindness. When your days are filled with uncertainty, added surprises aren't really a bonus.

Claire took my smile as a yes and let out a squeal.

The list and I were not going to be friends. I could tell that already.

Claire peeked at the list again, swung her hand in the air, and shouted, "Number one thing for today! Do crafts with old people!"

"WHAT?" I didn't mean to shout, but I couldn't help it. I was startled. I wasn't expecting crafts with old people. I thought she'd say pool, park, or playground—something like that. What did "crafts with old people" even mean?

"Like Grandma and Grandpa?" I asked. "They don't even live near here." I looked at Mom for help, but she looked as confused as me.

"No," said Claire. "It's a special place. Daddy promised me there was one here too. He said you'd take me." Claire looked back and forth at us, waiting to be understood. I had no idea what she was talking about.

"Tell us more," said Mom. "Is it a store?"

"NO!" Claire banged her fists on the table. She was getting frustrated. I thought she might cry, but she didn't. Her voice was shaky. "It's a big house where all the old people live. When they have craft day, I go there and make stuff, and help them, and then at the end we have cookies and juice—plus they have a cat."

"Do your grandparents live there?" asked Mom. "Is that why you and your Daddy go?"

Suddenly Claire was laughing. "Daddy doesn't go. He drops me off." Claire held her hands up to her mouth to stop the giggles, but it was no use. Now it was almost impossible to understand what she was saying.

"Daddy can't . . . do crafts—he's allergic . . . to them," spluttered Claire. "And . . . cats too."

Mom and I looked at each other. It sounded unbelievable.

"I like old people," said Claire. "They're supernice and friendly, plus they have good cookies."

I had no idea what Claire was talking about, but Mom knew. I could tell by the way she was smiling.

She clapped her hands together. "That's an amazing idea. I'm sure we could find a nursing home where you and Ash could volunteer, but it's going to take some time. I don't think I can put something like that together for this afternoon. Could you pick something else from your list? Just for today?"

Claire looked disappointed, but she nodded. As she looked over her list, my brain tried to process what Mom had just said. We were going to visit a bunch of old people and do crafts with them? What kind of crafts was she talking about? Friendship bracelets? Potholders? That sounded weird.

Suddenly Claire waved her arm in the air and shouted, "Number two! Are you ready?"

I wasn't ready. I was stunned—too stunned to even shake my head, but I should have. Maybe that would have made a difference.

"Okay," said Mom, smiling. "Let's hear it."

"Buy new outfits at the thrift store!" said Claire.

Mom clapped her hands again. "Oooh! I like it." She looked over at me. "Ash, did you hear that? I don't think you've done that before."

Of course Mom liked it. She loves junk.

Claire jumped up. "I get lots of clothes from there. Daddy does too." She pointed to her scarf, her skirt, and her shirt. "All from the thrift store," she said. She smiled for a second and then twirled.

I looked her over with this new information. She still looked fine, but touching other people's old clothes? That wasn't for me.

"It was only three dollars! Plus I got a hat, but

I didn't bring the hat, because it's for winter." Now Claire was bouncing up and down.

Mom stood up. "Well, that sounds like a bargain. I think I could find fifteen dollars to donate to an excursion like that. You can go a little later. Ash will take you. I can't wait to see what you come back with."

I stood up and walked to the door. "That's awesome, I can't wait." I put my hand in the air like a high five. It was good that Mom couldn't see my face, because I was being one hundred percent sarcastic.

chapter ten

Thriftiness

An hour later, Claire and I were walking to the St. John's church basement thrift store. I'd probably passed it a thousand times but never noticed it—why would I? I like new things, things with printed labels.

Claire wasn't talking much, so for the first time since yesterday, I had a minute to think. Of course, I was thinking about the basement. It must have been a dream. A daydream? A sleeping dream? But why had I fallen asleep so fast? Maybe I had that sleeping sickness thing, where you suddenly fall asleep? What was that called? I couldn't remember. I'd have to look it up. But why would something like that suddenly happen? Brain tumor? Poison? Gas leak? Gas leak! I bet that was it.

"What's a gas leak?" asked Claire.

I stopped and stared down at her. What? Now she was a mind reader?

"You just said gas leak. What's that?" she asked.

"It's nothing." I shook my head. I started walking again, relieved. I wasn't ready for a seven-year-old with a crazy list and supernatural skills. The church was on the next block over. We were almost there.

Claire tugged my arm. "Is it something bad? Is it dangerous?" She wasn't giving up.

I forgot that little kids were like that, always asking the same question over and over again, until you finally gave them an answer they were happy with. There was a word for that, but I couldn't remember what that was either. Maybe there was gas in the basement and it had totally scrambled my brain. Claire followed me to the small building across from the church. I stopped at the door. We'd arrived; the sign on the door said THRIFT STORE OPEN TODAY.

"Can it kill you?" asked Claire.

Wow, she was persistent.

Persistent! Ha! That was the word. It felt good to remember it. I smiled, but Claire's face was screwed up in a frown.

"Sometimes if there's a gas leak, a building can blow up. But it's a really rare thing that hardly ever happens, so you don't need to worry about it. Plus it mostly only happens in basements. Okay?" I gave her my best reassuring grin, opened the door, and walked down the stairs to the basement thrift store. Claire did not follow me.

It took about fifteen minutes to convince Claire that the thrift store wasn't going to blow up. I didn't know it, but she already had a thing about basements—she didn't like them. And now because of me, it was worse. But she loved thrift stores, so for this time only, she agreed to make an exception. Claire was nervous all the way down the stairs, but once she saw the piles of junk in the store, she was back to normal. In two seconds she was gone, lost in the mess.

I was the exact opposite. On the stairs I was fine, but now here on the edge of it all, I felt squirmy. There was junk everywhere; it looked weird and smelled funny, and I didn't want to touch anything.

I shuffled my feet and said, "I'll just wait here by the door." Claire couldn't hear me, but that didn't matter; it was a personal declaration. I felt better with a plan. Claire could have the whole fifteen dollars. I didn't care. I moved to the corner, pushed my back against the wall, and looked around. I caught sight of Claire over to the right. She was trying on some red shoes. I waved, but she didn't see me. Someone else saw me, though—a boy. He waved back. He thought my wave was for him.

I looked away, but he caught my eye and waved again. I recognized that look; it was the look of someone who knew me, but, like usual, I didn't know him back. I needed Lucy. I needed her to say, "That's so-and-so, wave back," or "We don't know him; don't wave." I couldn't do this by myself! Next he'd be over here. I waved back to be polite and looked for an escape. There were only two choices: up the stairs and out, or forward and into the store. I wanted the stairs, but I couldn't leave Claire, so I scooted behind a rack of coats and crouched down.

Who was he? He looked a little familiar, but my brain couldn't find his face or his name. It was always the same. The world knew me, but I never knew them back. Each time it happened, I hoped it would be different, that my brain would work like it was supposed to, and suddenly I'd recognize the person standing in front of me, but it never did. No matter how hard I tried, I couldn't remember faces. The only thing that helped was my ears; I was good with voices.

My hands were busy moving over things on the table in front of me, but I wasn't paying attention. It was just something to do while my eyes looked for Claire, and the boy. If I knew where he was, maybe I could get Claire out of here without him seeing me again? What kind of boy shops in a thrift store anyway? Maybe he was with his mom. That could be embarrassing. Last year Mom said she saw Ben Rutherford, a boy in my class, following his mom around the bra section at Target. That was definitely embarrassing.

There was an open space in the rack of coats in front of me. I used it as my peephole. It took a few minutes, but finally I found him—two aisles over. He was alone; that was too bad. I was hoping to hear him speak. He was bent over, and all I could see was his head and neck. I pushed a blue polka dot coat to the side to get a better view, but suddenly there was Claire, in my face.

"SURPRISE!" she yelled, and threw her arms into the air.

I screamed and fell back but managed to catch myself before I knocked anything over.

Claire pushed the coats to the side and stepped through the rack toward me. She was wearing a floppy hat and an assortment of clothes that were all too big. But I didn't have time to worry about her outfit, because she was full of questions and she was loud—too loud. For sure, everyone in the store could hear her.

"How much stuff did you get? Are we sharing the money even? Can I get more stuff than you?" She pointed to my hands. "Is that what you're getting?"

I looked down—I was holding a wooden tray. When had I even picked it up? I put it on the table next to me and backed away.

"No, I'm not getting it. I don't need anything." I wiped my hands on my pants, but it didn't help—they still felt grimy.

"Why not?" asked Claire.

I held my finger up to my lips and made the shushing sound. I needed her quiet.

She looked around, took a step toward me, and whispered, "Is it a secret?"

I shook my head.

She frowned, and blurted out, "Why?" She pointed to the tray. "How come you don't want that anymore? Why were you holding it if you don't want it?"

Now I knew what was happening—she was going to bug me until I gave her an answer she liked or had something to buy.

I grabbed the tray again. "You're right. I should get this. Let's go."

Maybe now I could get us moving. Get us out the door.

Claire spun around in a circle. "I put it next to a blue pot, but don't worry, I can find it."

I followed her around the store hoping this would be fast.

She disappeared ahead of me, but I found her again as soon as she started singing, "FOUND IT! FOUND IT! FOUND IT!" Why did she have to be so loud? I turned the corner, and there she was, smiling and waving a blue pot in the air. Only it wasn't a pot—it was one of those things kids use for potty training.

I pointed at it. "Don't touch that! It's disgusting."

Claire shook her head. "No it's not!" She looked inside it, swung it around, and plopped it on her head. "See! It's a hat."

I cringed. "Put it down! Let's go!" I tried to use my grown-up voice, but it didn't work. She ignored me.

"Wait," she said. "I want to see it in the mirror." Before I could stop her, she was gone.

I couldn't tell if she was trying to bug me on

purpose or if she was doing it by accident, but either way, I was suddenly feeling very bugged. Fine! If she was going to be like that, I'd just have to force her out of the store. I turned toward the mirror, but then froze; it was the boy. He was in front of me and smiling.

"Hey!" he said.

I was surprised, too surprised to speak; I nodded. It was awkward, him knowing me but me not knowing him back. Plus, if you added him not knowing that I didn't know him, it was even more confusing. What do you do with that? I bent down and started to pick up Claire's stuff. It was something to do, and I couldn't just stand there.

"I'll get it!" said a voice.

It was Claire; she was back, and not wearing the potty hat—at least that was good. She pushed by me and knocked the wooden tray out of my hands. I don't know how, but I caught it before it hit the ground. I held it up in triumph, but only for a second, because suddenly I noticed the picture on the front of it. How had I missed it? I cringed. It was a clown—a large, sad-faced, crying clown—and it was horrible.

The boy was watching me. Suddenly, I felt like I had to explain myself. What if he told people? What if he said, *Hey, guess what. I saw Ash this summer and she was buying this weird clown thing.* Not that he would, but what if he did? But I don't even like clowns! Clowns are creepy! I held out the tray and made myself smile.

"Uh, this is a joke," I said. "For my friend Lucy. I'm sending her weird stuff while she's at camp." I surprised myself—it was a good lie.

"Who's Lucy?" blurted Claire. She had stopped picking up stuff and was looking at me.

"Just a friend, don't worry about it." I turned to her and put my finger up to my lip. Maybe now she'd get it and stop talking.

"Like a secret friend?" she whispered.

"Ha!" said the boy. "Not much of a secret; Ash and Lucy are always together. I was wondering why you were here. Why didn't you go to camp? I saw you at the bus." He was looking at me, waiting for an answer, but my brain was suddenly busy trying to match his voice to a name. I knew that voice, and suddenly it clicked. I had a name—Sam Leavitt.

It was a relief, but only for a second. Sam Leavitt! I was talking to Sam Leavitt? If Lucy had been here, none of this would have happened. She would have told me that I didn't know him. She would have said, “Don’t wave back, it’s Sam Leavitt,” and that would have been that. But she wasn’t here, and now on my own, I’d messed things up. I stole a look. He was still watching me.

I was flustered, but I managed to answer. “Uh . . . I am going to camp. I’m going to meet Lucy later, but I have stuff to do here first.” I glanced down at Claire—she was my stuff. It was hard to see her. The pile was over her head.

Now that I knew who he was, I couldn’t look at him—it was Sam Leavitt! At school he hung out with a completely different crowd. I shouldn’t be talking to him. I had a bad feeling about this, but it was too late. I couldn’t undo it.

Claire’s arm shot out from the pile. “Hi, I’m Claire.” Sam looked confused, but he stepped forward and shook her hand. This shaking hands was definitely a thing with her.

Sam introduced himself to the lump that was Claire, then turned and shot me a grin. There was a space in between his front teeth; I’d never noticed that before. Things like that were good to remember; they were helpful in recognizing people. I grabbed the top of Claire’s pile and pulled it off. Now we could see her head. I nodded toward the front of the store and the cash register. It was time to go.

I put the tray down and grabbed another handful of Claire's stuff. I didn't know what to say to Sam, so I just nodded—kind of like a good-bye. Hopefully he wouldn't follow us to the checkout. I started down the aisle toward the exit, and Claire followed clomping behind me. That's when I noticed the shoes. She was wearing the red shoes again, the ones from before. When we got to the counter, I turned around and spoke to her.

"You can't get those; they're too big, and way too high for you."

It was true. They were pumps, and not at all the kind of thing a seven-year-old is supposed to wear. Claire looked down. For a second I thought she was going to argue, but instead she just nodded and took them off. That was lucky. Plus she was carrying her regular shoes—that was even more lucky. Now we didn't have to go back into the store and look for them.

We piled everything onto the counter. There was no way we were going to get it all for fifteen dollars. We'd probably have to put some back; I was dreading that. But at least we were moving in the right direction—away from Sam Leavitt. The whole not knowing who he was, and finding out who he was, and then having to stand around and talk to him while knowing I shouldn't be talking to him, had given me a headache. Well, at least now I had something to write to Lucy about.

The lady at the checkout, Maureen, was a master. Claire had to introduce herself and shake her hand too. In about four minutes Maureen had us all packed and ready to go. The biggest surprise was the price: only ten dollars and eighty-nine cents. I couldn't believe it. Claire wanted to go back and spend the rest of the money, but I said, "No!" As in *There is NO WAY I'm going back in that store—not even for a million dollars!*

I put the change into my pocket and forced myself to smile. "Let's save it for a special treat on the way home."

Claire wasn't convinced. I tried again, this time with more flair.

"Aren't you hungry? We could get something delicious like ice cream, or fancy cupcakes, or decorated cookies."

"Cupcakes!" shouted Claire. "I love cupcakes!" She turned and ran up the stairs, not a thing in her hands. I guess it was my job to carry everything. We left the store without looking back.

chapter eleven

Gray

Claire and I were walking down the sidewalk. The farther we got from the thrift store, the better I felt.

"Are we getting the cupcakes now?" asked Claire. She was half skipping and half jogging beside me.

I was probably walking too fast. I slowed down. I was wishing I had asked for two bags at the thrift store—one for her and one for me. But all we had was one giant, heavy bag, so it was all me.

"We'll get cupcakes, but first I have to go to the post office to mail Lucy's present." Thinking about it made me smile. I was glad the Sam thing was over.

A block later I was wishing I had done a better job of planning the trip. We should have gone to the post office first, and the thrift store second, because now I had to carry Claire's heavy bag of stuff all the way to the post office, and back past the thrift store again to get home. It was an extra eight or nine blocks of carrying. Claire wasn't happy about the detour either, and she didn't even have anything to carry.

"How much more is it?" she asked. "Is it far? I'm tired."

I grumbled under my breath. What did she have to complain about? "Five blocks," I said. It was a lie; it was really seven.

Claire pointed to some stores up ahead. "Is that it?" she asked.

I didn't answer, but I shook my head. Claire's bag was killing me. Even though I switched sides every half block, my hands looked like claws, stuck in the holding shape even when they weren't holding anything. As we passed one of the stores, VS Depot, I saw a sign in the window: WE SHIP US POST OFFICE AND UPS. It was just what I needed. I made a fast decision.

I opened the door. "We're here," I announced.

"You lied," said Claire. "That wasn't five blocks."

I stepped into the store and looked back at her. "I

wanted to surprise you." Now that was two lies.

Claire frowned and followed me in. The store was small, overcrowded, and plain. There were a bunch of photocopiers up front, and boxes and papers everywhere else; beyond that was the counter. I walked toward it. It wasn't easy to get there carrying Claire's huge bag, but I made it without knocking anything over. A man behind the counter was watching us.

"Good shuffling!" he said.

Claire pushed past me and said, "Thank you."

I knew the compliment was for me, but I didn't say anything. She could have it. I was just happy to put her bag down. I pulled off my backpack and took out Lucy's present. Suddenly I wasn't sure. Normally when you mail something, no one can see what you're mailing, but this was different; my note to Lucy was right there out in the open. Now I was uncomfortable. I didn't want him reading what I'd written. Quickly I turned it over so only the nails were showing.

The man pointed to it. "Do you want a box for that?"

I paused, not sure what to say. I didn't want to sound stupid in case Mom was wrong. Maybe a box would be better.

"I'll show you one and you can decide." The man

smiled, turned, and walked to the back of the store.

Claire noticed it first. I was too busy rereading my note to Lucy. Did it sound weird? Embarrassing? I wasn't watching the man.

Claire tugged on my arm. "He's a little person," she whispered.

"What?" I didn't know what she was talking about.

"Look!" She pointed.

I followed the end of her finger. The man was at the back of the store looking on the shelves, and she was right; he was a little person. How could that be? I peeked over the counter, and there was the answer. A raised platform behind the counter went from the front to the back of the store.

"Pretty clever, right?" asked a voice.

It was the man, and he was walking back toward us. He caught me looking. I felt my face go red. I didn't know what to say.

Claire bounced up and down. "Wow!" She pointed to the other side of the counter. "If I went back there, I'd be supertall."

The man smiled. "You can try it if you want." He looked to the back of the store. "Just hop on back there."

I shook my head. "No, that's okay." I turned to

grab Claire, but she was gone. Ten seconds later she was back, standing across from me on the other side of the counter.

"Hey!" she shouted. "I'm almost as tall as you!"

I hoped she was talking to me, and I was about to answer when the man walked over and stood next to her. She was right; he was only a little taller than she was.

"Look," said the man. He pointed to Claire. "We're twins." He leaned forward and handed me a box. "See if this works."

Claire shook her head. "We're not twins! You're too old, plus I'm a girl."

I motioned for her to come back around the counter and stand with me, but she ignored me and kept talking.

"I'm Claire, and that's Ash." She pointed to me and held out her hand for the man to shake. "We're almost kind of like sisters."

My face turned red again. The sister thing was a surprise, plus normally I didn't give out my name to strangers. I picked up Lucy's present and tried to fit it into the box. If I looked busy, maybe they would ignore me.

"I'm Peter," said the man. He shook Claire's hand

and then offered his hand to me. It wasn't something I wanted to do, but I made myself shake it and say hi. Now I was really wishing we'd walked the extra blocks to the regular post office. The people at the post office were not friendly and chatty; going there was definitely less complicated.

While Claire and Peter talked, I tried to get Lucy's present into the box. Claire was getting Peter's whole life story, asking him all sorts of questions. I couldn't decide if it was interesting or not.

PETER'S STORY

- He was the owner of the store, and he had five other VS Depots.
- The real name of the store was Value Send, but he'd shortened it to make it sound more modern.
- His regular store worker had quit, so he was going to work in the store until he could get someone new.
- Yes, Peter liked working in the store, but he couldn't work there all the time, because he had other things to do.

Finally I couldn't take it anymore, plus Lucy's present wouldn't fit into the box—it was too small.

I put the box on the counter and held up the wood.

"Can I send it like this?" I asked. "Without a box?"

"Sure. Why not?" said Peter. "A lot more fun, and maybe even cheaper, too. Does it have an address on it?"

I turned the piece of wood over and pointed to the address. Peter typed it into the computer and printed out a stamp. I handed him the piece of wood, and he stuck the stamp on.

"Will it stay?" I didn't want it to fall off.

He motioned for me to wait and then wrapped a big piece of tape around the wood—yes, it was going to stay.

He looked it over. "Someone named Lucy's going to love it."

"That's Ash's best friend," whispered Claire. "It's a secret and—"

"No it's not!" I interrupted. "Everyone knows we're best friends; that's why this whole thing is so weird. She's gone away, and I'm stuck here in the gray and grayer."

Peter looked surprised. "What did you say?"

I covered my mouth. I hadn't meant to say gray and grayer. In fact, I hadn't meant to say anything. It had all just come out—like a volcano suddenly erupting. "Gray and grayer" wasn't even my saying; it was from the PJ Walker books. Whenever something was boring or uninteresting, Viola Starr, the detective in the book, called it the gray and grayer.

"That's from a book, isn't it?" asked Peter.

Now it was my turn to be surprised. How did he know that?

Peter nodded. "I read that book. The author is—"

"PJ Walker!" I blurted out. "She's my favorite."

Suddenly Peter smiled. "That's right, and I picked it up because I like a good mystery. I'm surprised you've read it."

I nodded and shrugged. Peter waited an extra second to see if I would say anything, and when I didn't, he continued.

"Anyway, it was called something like *Brave Barry*. Did you read that one? It wasn't half bad. I should dig it out and look at it again."

I smiled; I couldn't help it—he had the title all wrong. "It's *Boris: Bold Beyond Bravery*," I said.

"Right," said Peter. "Did you read it?"

"I've read them all." I smiled. "And now I'm reading the new one, but only a chapter a night so it can last for a while."

I'd given him too much information. He was fiddling with something behind the counter—probably bored.

"Can we get the cupcakes?" asked Claire. She was finally standing next to me. I guess she was bored too. I nodded and walked toward the door.

"Good-bye, girls!" Peter waved. "And don't worry, I'll make sure this goes out tonight." He held up Lucy's present.

Claire waved back and ran ahead of me, beating me to the door.

Something felt weird. It wasn't that he was a little person—for sure that was different. It was something else, but I couldn't figure out what it was.

chapter twelve

Somewhere

After the cupcakes, Claire was a nonstop chatterbox all the way home. It made the time go by faster, which was helpful, because now Claire's bag seemed even heavier than before. As soon as we got inside, Claire tried to grab it.

"Give it! I want to put on a fashion show!"

"No!" I held tight. "We have to wash it first."

I didn't want the thrift store clothes touching all the clean stuff in our house. Mom was mostly on Claire's side, but I made such a big fuss that she finally gave in and took the bag downstairs to the washing machine. At first Claire was mad, but she got over it pretty fast when Mom brought out the chocolate milk she'd bought special for her.

While we waited for the clothes, Claire told Mom about what we'd done. When she got to the part about the boy in the thrift store, Mom looked over at me and raised her eyebrows. It was her tell-me-more look, but I pretended not to notice and went to the kitchen to get a glass of water. When I came back, Claire had moved on to Peter.

"He has a store with a ramp and his name is Peter, and he's only a little bit taller than me and he's a grown-up," said Claire. She took a deep breath.

That was a lot of information in one sentence. Mom did the eyebrow thing again. This time, I helped her.

"He's the guy who owns the VS Depot. You know, the one with the photocopiers at the front of the store. I think you went there once to photocopy something for Dad."

Mom nodded but still looked confused. Peter and the ramp probably weren't there when she'd gone.

When the clothes were dry, Mom sent me down to get them. I hadn't been down to the basement since the dream, and for the first time ever, I was suddenly feeling weird about going down there. Before I left, I asked Mom if we had one of those gas detector things down there. Of course she wanted to know why. You can't ask a question like that and just get a yes or no answer.

When I said "No reason," she told me to quit stalling and get the clothes.

Our washing machine and dryer are on the opposite side of the basement from the workbench and chair—I was glad I didn't have to walk by them. Halfway down the stairs I stopped and took a couple of deep breaths. It was a test for the gas, but I felt fine—not sleepy or strange. Plus Mom had already been down there with the laundry, so it was probably safe.

I emptied the clothes into the basket and walked to the stairs, but something caught my eye, just for a second, over by the workbench. It was probably the wish jar—maybe the light reflecting off the label—but now I was curious. I dropped the laundry basket and walked toward the workbench. I was expecting something—a funny feeling? that same tingling that had happened before?—but there was nothing. Everything looked the same, and nothing felt strange. The jar was on the workbench, and the open wish—the one I'd read—was on the chair. It was a little disappointing. I was hoping for something unusual—proof that what had happened was real. Watching those girls hadn't felt like a dream. Plus my name was on the wish—was that really just a coincidence? I sat down and read it again.

I Wish Ashley Wouldn't Ignore Me

It was the same wish as before, except that when I finished reading it, nothing happened. It was just me sitting in the chair, in the basement, reading a piece of paper. I read it again, and again, and again, but still nothing happened. What a relief. It had been a dream. I hadn't been with those girls. Of course not—that was impossible and unbelievable. Maybe it was stress. Could losing a best friend do that to you? Make you kind of crazy? I picked up the jar; the little paper balls jiggled inside—there were too many to count. I shook it and watched them fall to the bottom. One was stuck, clinging to the side. I unscrewed the lid and poked it with my finger until it fell, joining the others, but now it was misshapen—more of a Frisbee than a ball. I picked it out and rolled it between my thumb and finger to make it round again.

I moved my hand toward the jar to drop it in but then changed my mind. Maybe I should read one more. Just as a test. I pulled the ball back toward me and slowly unwrapped it—nothing was going to happen; it was just paper. I looked down; it was blank, but not completely—there was writing on the other side. My fingers tingled as I turned the paper over, and suddenly I knew. I was wrong—it wasn't impossible, only unbelievable. This paper had power. I read the words, and an instant later I was gone. Only this time I was ready—sort of.

I Wish I Had Brothers

In front of me were the same two girls as before. Dark long hair and short blond hair—they were easy to recognize. They were laughing. And after a few seconds of watching them, I could tell that they knew each other and were friends. We were in a bedroom—a boy's room, messy with boy things. The girls were sitting on the floor in front of an open closet, busy working on something, and then abruptly collapsing in fits of giggles. It reminded me of Claire and the old people craft thing.

I coughed. Could they hear me? They didn't look up. I tried again, louder, but still they ignored me. I gave them one final test, just to be sure.

"Blue elephant!" I shouted out the words and waved my arms in the air. I was a ghost. But it was different from before, because I wasn't scared. I knew

I'd get home again.

I walked closer to the girls. It felt weird to stand right in front of them and have them not see me. They were sitting next to a huge pile of shoes, carefully picking out nonmatching pairs and knotting the laces together. It looked like they were almost done. Suddenly I heard a noise from outside the door—someone was coming. Suddenly two boys burst into the room. For a few seconds everyone was surprised—the girls, the boys, and me. I flattened myself against the wall. What if the boys could see me? The girls backed away from the closet and looked around for an escape. Were they scared too? "So this is your payback prank?" asked the bigger boy.

"It was a joke—don't tell," pleaded the dark-haired girl. She was trying not to smile. That made me feel better.

"I'll get Ashley!" said the bigger boy.

Suddenly the boys grabbed the girls' feet. There was kicking, squealing, and laughter, and a jumble of arms and legs everywhere. And then it was over. The girls were still on the floor and the boys were up standing by the door.

"I told you," said the bigger boy. "You can't prank us!"

"Yeah! Boys win!" said the smaller boy. He looked like he might say something else, but the older boy punched his arm and said, "Come on! We've got to get to practice—Mom's in the car!"

They each grabbed an armful of shoes and ran out the door.

Now it was just me and the girls. They looked at each other and burst out laughing, rolling on the ground, their legs intertwined. As I got closer, I could see why—their shoes, all four of them, were tied together in a big tight knot. The girls sat up and looked at their shoes. It was a mess. There was no way they could untie them. How would they get loose?

"Scissors," said the dark-haired girl—she was the one the bigger boy had gone after. She must be Ashley.

"I guess that's what Spencer and Gavin will do," said the blond girl.

"No they won't." Ashley smiled, pulled out a shoebox, and lifted off the lid. It was filled with scissors. "Every pair in the house!" she screamed. "Plus even the ones from the car! They're going to be so mad!"

"Ashue-mazing!" said the blond girl, and they leaned in and slapped hands. They had done that before—I could tell. I wondered what it meant.

Ashley smiled and clapped her hands again. "Now we're even."

"Serves them right for eating our cookies," said the blond girl.

They burst into giggles, and even though I didn't want to, I felt myself slowly fading away.

Suddenly I was back in our basement. This time there was no welcome home. Mom wasn't calling from the stairs, and the one light above the workbench was gloomy and uninviting. It took me a minute to adjust to the quiet and dark. Mom and Claire were upstairs, only a minute away, but still I felt lonely. I didn't want to be here; I wanted to go back to the girls. The girls had something Mom and Claire didn't, and it was something I needed. For the first time since finding out about Lucy, I was feeling it again—and now I wanted more. It was excitement, adventure—but more than that, watching them made me feel happy.

I stuck my hand in the jar. The balls swirled through my fingers. I smiled. I felt powerful, in control—like suddenly I was the master of a whole new universe. I picked out a ball and studied it. It was just paper, but it had powers; it was a ticket to somewhere else.

A second later I was on my way again.

chapter thirteen

Somewhere Else

I *Hope Ashley Still Likes Me*

The girls were in a bedroom again, but this time it was a girl's room. They were sitting on the floor surrounded by piles of paper and colored pencils—they were drawing. I knew they wouldn't hear me, but I tested them anyway. I picked a color and an animal.

"Pink hippo!" I shouted and waved my arms. It was silly, it made me smile. And just as I expected, there was no response.

Ashley was smiling. "Almost done." She looked over at the other girl and quickly covered her drawing with her arm so the other girl couldn't see it. I moved closer to look, but it was hidden.

"Me too!" said the other girl.

I wished I knew her name. I looked around the room for hints, but there was nothing. Maybe this was Ashley's room.

"We can show each other together, when we're done," said Ashley. She was excited.

The other girl wasn't so sure—maybe she wasn't as good at drawing. I knew how that felt. Sometimes people who were good at stuff liked to show off by tricking you.

There was a girl at school like that, Melissa. She was always asking everyone to draw with her. She'd say, "When we're finished, let's count to three and show each other our drawings." And then on three Melissa would hold up an amazing picture that made yours look like it was drawn by a third-grader. Of course you'd have to say, *Oh, Melissa, yours is so much better. You're such a good artist.* This next part was Melissa's favorite. She'd make her face look all sweet and say, *Oh, really? Thank you,* like she was surprised or something—which she wasn't, because she'd totally planned the whole thing. She'd tricked a lot of people, and once even me—but I learned my lesson. I never drew with her again.

I was lucky. Lucy wasn't like that. Neither of us was a good artist, but still, she was good at other stuff that I wasn't, and she never made me feel bad about it—not once.

Now it was harder to watch the girls. I wanted to keep liking them, but if Ashley was a show-off, that was going to change. Show-offs weren't my kind of people.

Finally the girls were done.

"I'll go first," said Ashley. "On three."

"Okay," said the blond girl. She seemed a little more hopeful; maybe her drawing had turned out. Ashley counted out the numbers, and on three she held out her paper.

"Here." She handed it to the blond girl. "It's for you. It's my phone number. You can keep it in your room, in case you want to call me. And I put kittens and stars on it, because I know that you like those things. And some other stuff too."

I leaned over to look. It was cute, but not a masterpiece. Under her name she had written "Ashley plus Shue equals ASHUE-MAZING!" Shue? Was that the blond girl's name? What a weird name. The blond girl was frozen, just staring at the paper. It made me wish I had more powers than just being invisible—I wanted to know what she was thinking. I wanted to read her mind.

I guess I wasn't the only one, because Ashley finally said, "Well? What do you think? Do you like it?"

"I do! I really do. Thank you," said the blond girl. Her voice was quivery like she was trying not to cry. She got up, found some tape, and taped the paper to the mirror.

Now I knew whose room this was.

The blond girl looked over at Ashley. "It looks good, right?" She forced a smile.

"Sure," said Ashley. "What did you draw?"

The blond girl looked down. Her smile disappeared, and she looked embarrassed.

"Uh, nothing—just a horse for my uncle. It's his birthday on Saturday, and he really likes horses."

"Oh," said Ashley.

Both girls looked at the floor without saying anything.

The silence was painful. A couple of times the blond girl looked like she might be about to say something, but each time, she changed her mind and kept quiet.

Finally Ashley handed her a piece of paper and

said, "Here, write down your number for me."

I was glad about that. It gave the blond girl something to do. She wrote out the name "Shue" and a phone number. Under that she drew a little heart with feet, and a smiling flower. So Shue was her name. She handed the paper back to Ashley, and they both stood up.

"Let's go to Anderson's," said Ashley.

Instantly Shue brightened. "I'll put on my old sweatshirt."

While Shue got ready, Ashley folded up the paper and put it in her pocket.

What's Anderson's? I wondered. *And why change into something old?*

But I never found out, because suddenly I was back home and Mom was calling my name.

"Ash! Ash! Are you okay?" Mom was halfway down the stairs. I shook my head and blinked fast to clear it. It wasn't easy to be suddenly back in normal life. Luckily the basement was kind of dark; I didn't want Mom to see the wish jar, or me just sitting in the chair.

"I'm okay," I answered. "I was going to fold the clothes before I brought them back up." I pointed to the laundry basket halfway across the floor. It was a terrible lie—I never fold clothes, plus the basket wasn't even close to me. Mom took a few more steps down. I jumped up and stood in front of the jar.

Mom shook her head. "Listen Ash, I know this is hard, but you can't hide out here in the basement. I think you're going to be great for Claire, and if you give it a chance, it'll be fun for you too. She needs someone like you."

Mom looked me up and down, to emphasize her point, or to check out if it was true—I couldn't tell which. I didn't say anything. She continued.

"Maybe I pushed too hard for the first day. If you come upstairs and watch her fashion show for ten minutes, you can have the rest of the afternoon off. I'll take her out somewhere."

I nodded. It was a fair deal. Now I just needed Mom to leave first, so I could put everything away. "I'll be right up." I pointed to the workbench. "I knocked a few nails on the ground, and I want to pick them up, so no one steps on them and gets hurt."

Mom started up the stairs, but before she got to the top, she stopped and turned back to look at me.

"Only two more minutes. Okay?"

"Promise." I held up my hand. I had a feeling she

didn't believe me about the nails.

After she left, I picked up the wish jar and stuffed the wishes inside. I pulled a box out from under the workbench and hid the jar behind it. It wasn't the best hiding place, but it was fast, and my two minutes were up. I grabbed the laundry basket and forced myself upstairs. I didn't want to go.

chapter fourteen

Puzzle

Mom and Claire were waiting in the living room. As soon as I put the basket of clothes down, Claire grabbed it and dragged it behind the sofa. I walked over and sat in the chair next to Mom. I wasn't looking forward to this. There was a lot of stuff in that basket; this was going to be a long and painful show. Claire was behind the sofa, singing to herself and getting ready. There was a Grand Canyon of difference between her excitement and my enthusiasm.

Suddenly her head popped up. "Can we have music?"

"Good idea," said Mom. She turned to me. "You pick something."

I didn't complain. My music was definitely going to be better than Mom's. As soon as the music was on, I felt a lot better. Sometimes I forget how music can do that—help change your mood.

Claire's fashion show was a surprise—it was fun and cute. I wasn't going to wear any of her oufits, but on her they looked good. When it was over, Mom and Claire got ready to go out.

Claire was wearing her new old clothes—a dress, a skirt, and a vest. I couldn't quite decide what I thought of it. It was old-fashioned and kind of artsy at the same time. She saw me looking and did a twirl. She was happy.

"Don't you want to come?" she asked.

"No." I shook my head. "I'll stay here."

She frowned. "You're going to miss all the fun. Plus we're going to pick out ice cream for dessert tonight. Don't you want to pick out your own flavor?"

"That's okay." I pointed toward the kitchen, where Mom was. "Mom knows what I like."

As soon as I said it, I knew it was a mistake. Claire didn't have a mom to buy her ice cream. Was she going to feel bad? I tried to fix it. "Hey Claire, why don't you surprise me. You pick a flavor for me. As long as it's not chocolate, I'll like it."

"You don't like chocolate?" asked Claire. "But everyone likes chocolate."

She was right, everyone did like chocolate—everyone except me. I hated it. I couldn't stand the taste. It's not easy to hate something the rest of the world loves. When you do, the world thinks you're strange, but I had a way around it—a way to pretend to be normal.

I sighed, shook my head, and tried to look sad. It was a performance, and it had to look authentic. I glanced at Claire to be sure she was watching me and sighed heavily. I studied my shoes—lies were easier if you weren't looking at someone's face.

"I can't have chocolate," I said. "I'm allergic to it."

That usually did the trick. Once you said "allergy," people nodded their heads and stopped bugging you. But that didn't work with Claire. She kept going. She had questions.

"What happens to you? Will you die?"

Before answering, I checked to be sure that Mom wasn't around. If she heard me, she'd totally bust me on the lie.

I pointed to my arm. "I get giant red itchy lumps all over my arms. It's like getting a hundred mosquito bites all at the same time."

Claire took a step back and covered her mouth. She looked at my arms. There was nothing to see, but I held them out anyway.

"That's not fair. The best thing in the world, and you can't have it."

Claire looked sad, like she might even cry. I started to feel guilty; maybe I'd overdone it.

"It's okay." I smiled. "I'm used to it."

Claire ran over and gave me a giant hug. I wasn't expecting that; now I really felt guilty.

"We're only going for a few hours," said Mom. She was standing by the door, watching us.

I knew what she was thinking; she thought the hug was for good-bye.

I peeled Claire off me and pointed her toward the door. "Have fun!"

Claire took a few steps forward and then looked back. "How about brownies?"

I shook my head. "They're chocolate."

She looked like she couldn't believe it, like this was the craziest thing she'd ever heard. Mom was listening now. I needed to end it before I got into trouble.

"Strawberry and vanilla," I said. "That's my favorite."

"Oh, ice cream," said Mom. "I wondered what you two were talking about. Ash likes strawberry swirl. We'll get her that."

"We can't get her chocolate!" said Claire.

I held my breath and waited for what she'd say next, but she was done—she was quiet. I was safe. At least for now.

"That's right," said Mom. "It's nice how you two already know so much about each other, and it's only the first day." She looked pleased. "Are you ready to go?" She looked down at Clare and frowned. She was probably wondering about the outfit.

They were almost gone. I was almost free. I tried to push them out the door with my thoughts. *Leave! Leave now. Walk to the car. GO!*

"Oh, I put a load in the washer a while ago—can you switch it to the dryer in about twenty minutes?" asked Mom.

I nodded. Claire gave me one last look and followed Mom out the door.

"Don't forget the laundry!" shouted Mom.

I smiled. There was no chance of that. The minute they were gone, I was heading straight to the basement. I couldn't wait to get down there. I watched the car pull away, waited for a second to be sure they hadn't forgotten anything, and then raced down the stairs.

Two minutes later I was in the chair with the jar in my lap. I put my hand in the jar. What was Anderson's? Where was it? Why was Shue so excited? The answer was in here. Could I pick out the right wish? I grabbed a handful of balls and let them slip through my fingers, until only two were left. Which one was it?

I pulled my hand out of the jar, but the top of the jar was narrow, and I dropped one as I struggled to get my hand out. The deciding was done. I forced my eyes to the workbench as I opened the wish and flattened it out against my leg. Nothing would happen until I read it. I knew that now. I liked this power—to read or not to read. Of course I would read, but it felt good to be in control. I alone could press go.

I took a breath and looked down.

I Wish Mom Wasn't So Mean

I was back in Shue's room. That wasn't a surprise—it was always going to be her. These were her wishes. I'd figured that part out.

"And don't even think of coming down here until that room is spotless! This is your own fault. I asked you to take care of this yesterday."

The voice surprised me. Someone was shouting at Shue from the other side of her door. It was a lady, probably her mom. Moms were the only ones who got upset about messy rooms. I looked around; it wasn't that messy. If she wanted to know messy, she should see my room. Shue didn't look up; she just sat on the side of the bed looking miserable.

Suddenly she stuck her head in her pillow and screamed, "I hate you!"

It was muffled, but I heard it. I knew how she felt. Sometimes you just have to get the words out. There was a piece of paper in her hand; she sat up and looked at it.

I stepped forward but then remembered my test words—I hadn't said them yet. Shouting felt wrong, so I spoke in a normal voice, just above a whisper.

"Yellow panda."

I stood for a second watching Shue. I skipped the waving—that seemed wrong too. I sighed and walked toward her; I had a feeling this was bad news. Shue was still staring at the paper. I looked down. It was an invitation to the beach with Ashley's family. I recognized Ashley's handwriting. The invitation said ten thirty. The clock said ten fifty-six. They were gone. No wonder she was upset.

Shue got up and went to her desk. She shuffled the papers until everything was in one giant pile, opened the top drawer, and tried to shove it all in. But the drawer wouldn't close; something was in the way. She pushed harder, but it didn't make a difference; nothing moved. She pulled everything out and bent down and looked inside the drawer. Suddenly she was smiling. She reached in and pulled out something yellow. At first I couldn't tell what it was. But when she held it up to admire it, I recognized its shape. It was a duck, an ugly yellow duck statue.

Why was this making her happy? She studied the statue for a second more and then yanked off its head. I wasn't expecting that. She tossed the head onto her bed; it bounced a few times before landing next to her pillow. I looked back at Shue; she was pulling out a small strip of paper from inside the statue. Now I got it. That's why she'd pulled the head off—she knew the paper was going to be in there. She smoothed out the paper, read it, and laughed.

"So funny, Ashley! I'll get you."

She was talking to herself, just like I did. Maybe that wasn't such a weird thing. That was good to know.

I tried to see the paper but couldn't—Shue's hand was covering it. She walked over to her dresser, opened a little box, and dropped the paper inside. There were other papers in the box, but she closed the lid before I could see any of them. She stuck the head back on the duck and sat on her bed. I wanted to see what Ashley had written. Was it something about Anderson's? I tried to open the box, but my hands drifted through it like clouds. A second later I was home—back in my chair.

I was disappointed. The wish was over too fast. And there had been nothing about Anderson's. I picked out another ball and unwrapped it. I had time for mistakes. Mom and Claire would be gone for hours.

I Wish Pam and Cathy Didn't Exist

A second after I read the words, I was gone again. Shue was standing at the front door of a house, knocking. I shouted out my test words just as the door opened.

"Red fox."

A boy answered. Neither of them looked at me. I didn't bother waving; I knew I was still invisible.

"Hi, Spencer," said Shue. That helped. Of course; it was Ashley's brother. "Is Ashley ready to go?"

Spencer looked confused. "Uh . . . go where?"

"We're having a picnic." Shue held up the bag in her hand. "She's bringing the drinks, and I'm bringing everything else. I even made brownies."

I scrunched up my face. I hated brownies; even the smell of them made me feel sick.

"Are you sure it was today?" asked Spencer.

"Of course!" Shue was getting impatient. "Can't I just go in and get her?"

"Uh . . . you can't," said Spencer. He looked down at the ground and mumbled something.

I didn't catch what he said, but Shue did.

"Gone where?" she asked.

"I don't know." Spencer looked uncomfortable. "She left with Pam and Cathy about twenty minutes ago."

"Is she coming back? Should I wait?" Shue looked like she was about to cry.

Spencer shook his head. "I think she'll be gone awhile."

"But it was a plan," whimpered Shue. "And I made brownies."

They both stood there not saying anything, Spencer looking at the ground and Shue trying not to cry. It was hard to watch. Finally Shue pulled out a tin foil package from her bag and shoved it into Spencer's hands.

"Here!" she sputtered. "You have them."

Before Spencer could say anything, Shue was gone. I felt bad for her, but I was leaving too, slowly fading away—but then suddenly there was a sharp zapping pain and my body was tingling with electricity. It was over quickly, but I froze, scared it would happen again. I waited a minute or two, but there was nothing. I was safe. Why had that happened? It was like the first wish, but worse. I shook my head and carefully moved my arms. I didn't want that feeling again.

I leaned back in the chair, happy to be home. I liked the wishes, but the sad ones were confusing and hard to watch. Ashley and Shue were friends and then they weren't, but why? What had happened? What was the in-between? And who were Pam and Cathy? I shook the jar and watched the balls spin and quickly settle to the bottom and stop. There was a story in there, but I needed a break. I didn't like it when Ashley was mean. I wanted to like her, plus we had the same name. I pulled out the used wishes and hid the jar. I had a new mission. I took the wishes up to my room.

I found a giant piece of cardboard and laid the wishes on top. Where did they fit? Which wish went first? I couldn't pick them out of the jar in the right order, but maybe that didn't matter. Maybe I could still figure out where they went. If I got the order right, the story would make sense. It was Shue's story, and I wanted to know more. I moved the five wishes into place and taped them down. There were spaces for the in-betweens—the wishes I hadn't read yet. The wishes that would fill in the gaps. It wasn't much, but it was a start. It was more like a list, but I called it a map. My wish map of Shue's story. I was going to be like Viola Starr. I was going to be a detective.

chapter fifteen

Gone

After Claire was in bed, Mom came up to see me. I knew she would, and I was ready. I didn't want the talk, but there were things I wanted to know. What had happened to Claire's mom? How had she died? That was a lot to handle. I steeled myself for the sadness.

Mom came in and sat on the side of my bed; she hesitated for a second before starting to talk. I looked down at my hands; it was easier than watching her face.

"Claire's mom and I lost touch a long time ago," said Mom, "but I've always felt close to her. She was . . ."

She tried to continue but couldn't. I looked up;

there were tears in her eyes, and then she was crying. I didn't know what to do. I sat there not saying anything, hoping she would stop. It was a relief when Dad came in and took over. Dad and I don't have big talks very often, so it was still a little strange, but it was better than tears.

Dad started by saying Claire's mom wasn't a bad person. But after what he told me next, I wasn't so sure. One day six months ago, Claire's mom had secretly packed up all her clothes. She was there at breakfast acting perfectly normal, but when Claire got home from school, she was gone. She left her family. How could a mom do that? Without a *good-bye*, a *see you soon*, or even an *I'll miss you*? It was cruel. But that wasn't the end. Three months later she was hit and killed by a train. Dad said it was a tragic accident. I nodded. Dad said the saddest part was that Claire didn't have a mother anymore. I nodded again, but this time I didn't agree. The going was sadder than the gone—especially because the going had been on purpose.

Poor Claire. How would that feel, to have your mom run away from you? Suddenly I was sad; it surprised me. I studied the pattern on my bed—black swirls with bursts of light pink. I forced my eyes to follow the lines, keeping my brain busy, so it couldn't think of other things. So I wouldn't cry. Dad was waiting, saying nothing. Out of the corner of my eye I could see him slowly tapping his three middle fingers against his leg. I counted, one, two, three—four, five, six—seven, eight, nine—how long would he wait? What number could I get to before he finally said something? Fifty? A hundred? He stopped. Had he caught me? I looked up but couldn't tell; his face was blank. And it all came rushing forward, like a tidal wave of Claire, and all I could think of was Claire standing all alone, with no one to love her.

I wiped my eyes. "Claire's dad, he's coming back, isn't he?"

Dad nodded. He patted my shoulder and picked up one of my stuffed toys. It stared back at him, wide-eyed. It was a present from Lucy, an owl—her favorite animal. He put it back on the bed, facedown, so it couldn't watch him. I could tell he was stalling, trying to think of what to say next.

"He's still sad; that's why he called your mother. To see if we could watch Claire for a while. So he could have some time alone—to get better. Does that make sense?"

Dad looked me over to see if I had understood. I nodded. He looked relieved and stood up. The talk was over. He walked to the door. I thought he was leaving, but he turned and stood for a second, leaning on the doorjamb.

"Don't worry, you and Claire will have fun." He smiled and waited for me to agree.

I nodded again.

"So I want a full report when I get back. Promise?"

I looked up, but this time he didn't wait for my nod; he just half waved and walked out.

Dad was leaving tomorrow on a huge business trip—sixteen days. I couldn't believe he would be gone for so long. I was upset about it, but it was just one more thing I couldn't control.

When I came down the next morning, Dad was all packed and ready to go. After we said good-bye and the taxi came to get him, Claire went and got her list. All of a sudden I was nervous. I hated that piece of paper. It was me versus the list, and so far I was always the loser.

Mom and I waited while Claire looked it over. She was taking longer than usual. Was she picking out something especially awful? I couldn't even imagine.

She folded up the list and put it away. She seemed nervous. Maybe this was something huge. I tried to get ready, but how do you get ready for a surprise? It's kind of impossible.

Claire looked back and forth from Mom to me. Finally in a little voice just above a whisper she said, "Can we have a party for Steve?"

I looked at Mom. Who was Steve? Did she know? Claire reached into her backpack and pulled out a stuffed goldfish.

She waved him around. "It's his birthday!" She hugged him tight.

I knew there had to be a twist to this. Something I wouldn't like. A birthday party for a goldfish was too easy.

"Let me guess." I pointed to the goldfish. "He wants to go to the pool." It made sense—goldfish, water, pool. A pool was probably on her list, and I hated the pool, so that seemed about right, but Claire surprised me and shook her head.

She made a face. "I hate the pool, plus Steve can't get wet, because he's got stuffing."

She held him up. I nodded.

I pointed to the backyard. "Can we do the party here?"

Claire nodded. It was unusual, but we weren't going anywhere, and I liked that. Was it safe to relax? Maybe. I breathed out a sigh of relief.

I looked down at Claire. She was waiting, almost patiently, swinging Steve by his fins. I watched her for a second and then switched my brain into party-planner mode. I could do this. Birthday parties were easy—I'd been to a million of them, plus a stuffed goldfish wasn't going to be very picky.

I smiled. "What should we do? Should we—"

But Claire held up her hand to stop me. Before I could ask why, she had taken Steve and was gone, running upstairs. I looked at Mom; she shrugged. Two minutes later Claire was back.

She bounced up and down in front of me. "I want it to be a surprise party. So Steve's resting upstairs where he can't hear us."

A surprise party for a goldfish? Well, that was a first. Mom said we could use anything we wanted and then disappeared upstairs to make an "important" phone call. Mostly it seemed like an excuse to get out of helping.

The first thing I thought of was Goldfish crackers. They were perfect. Or were they? Was it weird to eat goldfish-shaped crackers when the guest of honor was a goldfish? I showed them to Claire and she nodded and smiled, so I was probably over-thinking it. We hung streamers, blew up balloons, drew a HAPPY BIRTHDAY banner, and made goldfish-shaped peanut butter and jelly sandwiches. Those were my favorite—mostly for the shape, not the peanut butter part. I was putting on the raisin eyes when Claire surprised me again, this time with a question.

"Is your dad coming back?" she asked.

I answered without thinking. "Of course. Why wouldn't he?" When I saw the look on Claire's face, I realized my mistake. Now I felt guilty. I'd forgotten about her mom.

"How do you know?" asked Claire.

This time I was more careful; I took a second to think of my answer. *Because he loves us*; that was the right answer, but I couldn't say that to Claire. If I did, she would be sad, so I finally just said, "Because he told me he was." It was simple, nonemotional, and the only other thing I could think of.

Claire thought for a moment and then nodded. I guess her mom hadn't said that.

"Should I blow up more balloons?" I held up the bag of balloons and shook it. I wanted to change the subject and get back to the party stuff—it was safer.

But Claire had more questions.

"Does he have a romance story with your mom?" she asked.

She was still talking about Dad. Mom and Dad and romance?

What did she mean? "You mean how they met?"

Claire nodded and picked a red balloon out of the bag. I stretched it out for her so it would be easy to blow up. Mom and Dad had met each other in high school, but I didn't know much about it. Dad said it was love at first sight, but every time he said that, Mom just rolled her eyes and said he was exaggerating. Claire didn't care about the truth—she just wanted a story—so I gave her Dad's version.

"They were high school sweethearts, and they fell in love the moment they saw each other."

I was right. Claire loved it, and now she wanted more.

"Where were they when they saw each other? Did they both fall in love? Did they talk to each other?"

This was too many questions. I shook my head.

"You should probably ask Mom. It's her story."

Mom wasn't going to be happy about all the

questions. Or with me for starting it. But I had a plan to save myself.

"You should only ask her about it in private. Only if it's the two of you, because it's personal, and kind of like a secret."

I had no idea how this would turn out. There was no telling with Claire, but for now it worked. She didn't ask any more questions.

After we finished setting up the decorations and food, Claire announced that we still had to make games and crafts. I was hoping that we could just eat and be done, but I guess that wasn't happening. I was glad that Mom was back. She helped with the games and said she'd come up with the craft. We ended up with two games: a magnetic fishing game using the end of the broom and some magnets from the fridge, and a sock-throwing game. The sock game wasn't very exciting. I just stacked up some plastic cups and got a few rolled-up socks to throw at them—it wasn't even fish themed. But Claire was a good sport about it. She didn't complain and even made it better by drawing sharks on all the cups.

She held one up and said, "It's the enemy of the goldfish." She didn't have to convince me—sharks were pretty much the enemy of everything, and the number one reason why I was never going to swim in an ocean.

The craft thing was harder, but not for me, because mostly it was just me and Claire waiting for Mom to come up with an idea. Still, it's not exciting to just sit and watch other people think. Mom's big idea ended up being that we should decorate mugs with Sharpies. It seemed a lot like what Claire had already done with the cups, but I didn't argue. I just wanted get on with the party. Of course, the mugs were somewhere in the basement and I was given the job of finding them.

"You're looking for a box with six white mugs," shouted Mom.

She was giving me directions from the top of the stairs. Mom had picked up the mugs on one of her Freecycle trips.

"It could take hours," I complained.

"You can do it. We'll wait for you."

Mom's words of encouragement weren't a lot of help. Looking through all her junk was not going to be fun.

On the way down the stairs I made a plan. If I didn't have one, I knew what could happen.

THE PLAN

1. Put on rubber gloves.
2. Do not go near the wish jar.
3. Find the box of mugs.
4. Take the mugs upstairs.

Before Mom closed the door, I heard Claire ask her about love at first sight; it was another good reason to take my time. I walked straight to the sink and pulled on the rubber gloves. I turned around and scanned the basement. It was filled with boxes—hundreds of them. This was going to take forever. Finally I just made myself walk into the middle of it and get started.

Going through the boxes was faster than I thought it would be. Each one took only a minute or so to examine. Really, the only hard part was moving the boxes around and remembering where I'd already looked. And then I miraculously found them, in box number nine—six white mugs. I couldn't believe it.

I dragged the box over to the workbench and unloaded the mugs. When I was done, I sat in the chair—just for a second, but that was a mistake, because with the sitting came thinking.

I have extra time.

I found those mugs really fast.

Mom and Claire are probably still talking about romance.

I bet Mom won't even be looking for me for another twenty minutes.

I could just do one wish.

I had no choice. I had to do it. I jumped up, grabbed the jar, and picked out a wish.

I Wish Anderson's Was Always Good

Suddenly I was in a Dumpster. Shue and Ashley were rummaging around on the far side, picking through boxes and bags. Maybe they'd lost something. Even though I was only watching, and nothing could touch me, it still grossed me out, being in there with garbage. Floating powers would have been better. I flapped my arms and tried to stretch up, but nothing happened. I was stuck, standing in trash. I took a step forward; at least it wasn't rotting food—most of it was boxes and papers. I was picking my way toward the girls when I suddenly remembered my test words. I hadn't said them. This time I had good ones. I shouted them out.

"ORANGE WHALE!"

It was perfect for where we were—the Dumpster was orange and huge like a whale. I smiled and continued toward the girls. They'd cleared out a tiny corner of the Dumpster and were piling up stationery supplies—pads of paper, pencils, pens, erasers, that sort of stuff. It wasn't what I was expecting. They weren't looking for something. They were being like Mom—collecting junk!

"Look!" Ashley waved something in the air. "Three more pads of paper."

Shue pointed to the ground. "And I found these little bags. We can use them as pencil cases." She looked over the Dumpster, smiled, and spread her arms wide. "I can't believe all this."

Now Ashley was smiling too. "See, I told you. Isn't it great?"

Shue nodded and put her hand over her heart. "From now on, I'm always going to look in Dumpsters."

"And not run on them," said Ashley.

Shue looked embarrassed. For a second I thought she wasn't going to say anything more, but she did.

"Never again," she said. "No running."

I didn't know what they were talking about, but it must have been something bad, because now they both seemed serious.

Ashley got out of the Dumpster, and Shue started handing her the things they'd collected. I ignored them for a few minutes and looked around. We were in the middle of a parking lot, and directly in front of us was the back of a building. I didn't have to wonder what it was, because right on the side of it, in big red letters, were the words ANDERSON'S PRINTING. So this was Anderson's. I'd been hoping for something more exciting. Never in a million years would I have guessed that Anderson's was a Dumpster. There were hardly any cars in the parking lot, but the ones that were there were big and old-fashioned. What did that mean? Was it a clue? Was I going back in time? Suddenly Shue was talking again.

"There, that's it." She handed Ashley the last handful and grabbed the side of the Dumpster and started to climb out. I was glad we were leaving. I stepped forward to follow them, but then things got confusing.

"Ash! Do you hear me?"

Who was talking? Was it one of the girls? How did she know my name?

"Ash! I know what you're doing, and I don't like it!"

Suddenly I knew who it was, and it wasn't one of the girls. It was Mom! I was back in the basement! I panicked and tried to figure out what was going on. She knew about the wish jar! How? Could she see it from the stairs? I shoved the wish I was holding into my pocket. Mom took a few steps down the stairs toward me.

"We're upstairs waiting for you, and you're down

here feeling sorry for yourself. I sent you down here to look for something, not to sit and sulk!"

I relaxed back into the chair; she didn't know what I was really doing. It was a relief, but only for a second, because she was still coming toward me, and if I didn't stop her, she'd see the jar. It was right there, out in the open. I jumped up, stood in front of it, and grabbed a mug off the workbench.

"LOOK! I found them." I waved the mug around.

Mom stopped moving. I scooped up the mugs and walked toward her. The jar wasn't hidden, but if she didn't look behind me, I would be safe. I needed her to look only at me. I clanged the mugs together and kept talking.

Mom leaned forward and held out her hands. "Don't drop them."

As soon as I got to her, she took three. I followed her up the stairs. Halfway up she stopped.

"Thank you for finding these. But this thing with Claire—it's important to me. You have to try harder. Do you understand?"

I nodded and looked down. I knew she thought I was feeling sorry and sad, but she was wrong. I was smiling and relieved, but I kept my head down—she didn't need to see that.

chapter sixteen

Party

Steve's party turned out better than I thought it would. Mom kind of forgot about being upset with me, and I won the sock toss—two good things. Mom wanted me to let Claire win all the games, but I didn't. Seven-year-olds aren't stupid; if she'd won both games, she would have known it was on purpose. She was happy enough about winning the fishing game, and I think that she liked that we were both winners. Plus it was fun to high-five each other and make a big deal about it. Mom didn't win anything, but she didn't care. She was a good loser.

We spent the rest of the afternoon looking for

funny cat videos on YouTube, watching cartoons, and drawing, right up until dinner. Claire is crazy about drawing. Her favorite thing to draw is Steve, her goldfish—only she draws him with legs, so he can do people things instead of goldfish things. It's a little strange, but Mom called it "marvelously creative." I was glad when it was finally time for dinner—Claire takes up a lot of energy.

After dinner I couldn't wait for eight thirty—Claire's bedtime. When Mom took Claire upstairs, I followed them up and went to my room. What I really wanted to do was sneak back down to the basement, but I made myself sit down and write to Lucy instead. The jar could wait until tomorrow.

I had Lucy's letter all planned. I was sending her one of the party hats from Steve's birthday, a shiny red cone with a glittery yellow pompom on top—her favorite colors. Instead of writing on the outside, I was writing on the inside, where no one could see it. It wasn't easy to do; I had to use a very small pencil. I wanted to tell Lucy about Sam Leavitt and the thrift store, but that story was too long for the little space in the hat, so instead I wrote about the birthday party and the VS Depot. I'd tell her about Sam in the next letter. I couldn't believe that Lucy had been gone for two days. It seemed a lot longer, but at the same time nineteen days seemed like forever. That was the countdown number until I was going to meet her. Mom knocked on my door just as I was writing out the address on the back of the hat.

She came in, found an empty spot, and sat on the side of my bed. As soon as she looked at me, I started talking. I hadn't meant to, but suddenly there it was, just coming out of my mouth—an eruption of complaints.

"I don't think it's fair that I have to do everything that's on Claire's list. I don't even know what's on the list. Every day it's a surprise, and I hate surprises. I'm trying to be nice and take care of her, but it's really hard when she's totally in charge of everything we do. I know she doesn't have a mom. But still, it's not fair."

Mom was quiet for a moment, and then she nodded. "You're right."

I was surprised. "I am?"

She nodded again and sighed. "Let me think about how to handle it. And you're right about that list. I don't know what's on there either."

Having Mom say that helped; it was a relief. Suddenly I felt like we were on the same team. Me and Mom versus The List. I just hoped we were going to win.

chapter seventeen

Caught

The next morning when I came downstairs, Claire and Mom were making pancakes again. I guess Claire never got sick of them. I liked pancakes too, but every day was too much for me. The wish jar was downstairs, still out in the open, and I needed to hide it. So before Claire or Mom saw me, I snuck past the kitchen and down to the basement.

It was supposed to be just for a minute, to hide the jar, but once I was holding it, I changed my mind. I sat in the chair, put my hand in the jar, and made my own wish. *I wish I knew which wish was next.* It was a wish trifecta—me making a wish, holding the wish jar, and touching wishes. I waited for an extra second to see if anything special would happen, but it didn't. That was okay; the wishes were enough. I gave the balls a final swirl and pulled one out, hoping it was the wish after Anderson's.

I Wish Spencer Was Around More

We were in Ashley's room. I could tell instantly, because right over the bed was a banner with her name on it. I looked around, but Ashley wasn't in the room; it was only me and Shue. Shue was looking through Ashley's desk, opening and closing the drawers. She was in a rush, but every couple of seconds she stopped, listened, and looked back at the door. What was she worried about? Someone catching her? I didn't want to believe what I was thinking, but I couldn't help it. Was she stealing something?

"Green wolf." I said my test words and walked toward her. I didn't notice it at first, but she was holding something. I looked closer; it was the ugly yellow duck statue, the one with the removable head. After a few more seconds of watching, I knew what she was doing. She was looking for a place to hide it. It must be a game she and Ashley played—hiding the duck in each other's rooms. How fun! Suddenly I felt uneasy, like someone was watching me—but that was impossible. I was invisible. I turned, and there in the doorway was one of Ashley's brothers. I made a guess—Spencer. But he wasn't watching me; he was watching Shue. I wanted to warn her, but I couldn't. All I could do was watch. Shue walked over to Ashley's closet, poked around for a minute or two, and then shoved the duck under a stack of clothes. Suddenly Spencer spoke.

"I could tell on you," he said.

Shue gasped and spun around. As soon as she saw who it was, she smiled and relaxed.

She took a step forward. "Oh, it's you."

It was the first time I'd seen them standing together on even ground. I was surprised. I'd thought Spencer was taller than Shue, but he wasn't, he was shorter.

Shue pulled a brown paper bag out of her pocket and waved it in front of Spencer. "If you don't tell, you can have some."

I didn't know what she was talking about, but Spencer did.

He stepped forward and pointed to the bag. "Let me see. What kind did you get?"

Shue opened the bag so Spencer could see inside.

After about twenty seconds he straightened up,

grinned, and said, "Five Pixy Stix, half the red licorice, and all the orange sours."

Shue nodded. "Okay, but no orange sours."

Spencer wasn't giving up. "What if I tell you a better hiding spot? An amazing one. Is that worth the orange sours?"

Shue thought for a minute. "Maybe." She hesitated. "But it has to be really good."

Spencer walked over to where Shue had hidden the duck and pulled it out.

He turned to make sure she was watching and walked to the other side of the room. "This is where Ashley puts special things."

He stopped in front of the mirror above Ashley's desk and fiddled with it. Suddenly the entire mirror swung open, and behind it was a hidden small shallow cabinet. Shue put her hands up to her mouth. It was obvious she'd never seen it before. The first thing I noticed was a jar filled with small pieces of paper.

Shue pointed to it. "My duck notes!"

There were other things in there too—a few necklaces, a pile of papers, a bunch of Shue's drawings taped to the back of the mirror, a little blue vase, a tiny metal box, and one large sparkly earring.

Spencer motioned to the cabinet. "See! I told you."

Shue was quiet for a moment. She pulled out an orange sour to keep and handed the whole bag of candy over to Spencer.

"You're right, it's amazing. Here."

Spencer looked surprised, but he didn't say no; he took the candy. A second later his mouth was full. Shue put the duck on the shelf and closed the mirror.

She smiled. "I'll meet you downstairs."

Spencer nodded and rushed out of the room, probably scared that Shue would ask for the candy back. He wasn't like me; he wasn't curious. Why was she staying behind? What was she going to do?

The first thing Shue did after Spencer left was check the hallway. He was gone—no one was there. She rushed back to the desk, opened the mirror, and took out the duck. I thought she'd poke around, look at stuff, but she didn't. She glanced at her drawings on the inside of the mirror, smiled, and closed it back up. A minute later the duck was back in its old hiding place, under the stack of clothes. Why had she done that? What did it mean? But I never found out, because seconds later I was back in my chair. This time I moved extra fast. I grabbed a wish, read it, and was gone again in seconds.

I Hope That Man Didn't Really See Us

"White cat!" I said my test words as soon as I saw Shue. Part of me was wishing I'd never started with the test words, but now it was too late to change it. Maybe they were important; I couldn't tell. So now I had to keep doing it, just in case. We were at Anderson's again, only this time the girls weren't happy. They were standing outside the Dumpster, both looking grumpy. Shue stood on her tiptoes and peered inside.

"There's nothing good in there," she complained. "Only food garbage."

Ashley looked over the edge and screwed up her face. "Ewww."

Shue slumped against the side of the Dumpster. "I wore my special sweatshirt for nothing." She pulled it off and wrapped it around her waist. She was definitely grumpier than Ashley.

Ashley walked past Shue and circled the Dumpster. Was she looking for something? I couldn't tell. When she came back around the other side, she was smiling.

Shue was curious. "What? What's so funny?"

Ashley didn't explain but grinned wider. "Come see." She grabbed Shue's arm and pulled her around the Dumpster to the back of Anderson's. She pointed to a pair of men's work boots sitting on the doormat in front of the door and giggled. "We could put stones in them, so when this person puts his boots on, he'll be surprised."

Shue shook her head. She wasn't convinced. "Whose boots are they?"

"I don't know." Ashley shrugged. "Does it matter?"

Shue was still worried. "What if we get caught?"

Ashley frowned and put her hands on her hips. "It's not like it's against the law! It's a joke. Plus it's only a few stones."

Shue thought for a moment and then slowly bent down. She picked up a pebble. Ashley was more enthusiastic—she grabbed a handful. Quickly a few stones turned into hundreds, and soon the boots were completely full to the top. The man wasn't going to be surprised when he put his shoes on—he was going to be surprised the minute he saw them.

Shue stood back and admired the boots. "I bet—"

Both girls looked up, startled; the handle on the door next to the boots was moving.

"RUN!" yelled Ashley. They raced off down the street. I followed them, panting to keep up. Even in this fantasy world I was still a bad runner.

The girls turned right at the end of the block and ran toward Ashley's house. I followed them through the front door and up to Ashley's bedroom. Ashley ran straight to the window, dropped to the floor, and peeked out from behind the curtain.

"It's a man," she whispered. "He's there!"

Shue crept forward to look. Funny, I hadn't noticed it before, but from Ashley's window there was a perfect view of the Dumpster and the back of Anderson's. While the girls hid on the sides, I stood in the middle of the window and looked out. That was the benefit of being invisible.

A man was standing at the edge of the road, looking in the direction of where the girls had run. He was holding one boot and wearing socks.

Shue seemed nervous. "Do you think he saw us?"

Ashley looked up. "Probably just our backs. And you can't recognize someone from their back."

Shue looked down at her shirt and shook her head. "I probably shouldn't wear these clothes again."

Suddenly Ashley grabbed her arm. "Look!" She pointed.

The man was shaking the stones out of his boot.

"I think that one was mine," said Shue.

How could she tell? Weren't both boots the same? The man gave the boot a final shake and shoved it on his foot. Suddenly he was shouting and hopping around on one leg. He yelled, lost his balance, and fell to the ground. We burst out laughing. It was ridiculous. The man yanked off the boot and turned it upside down. I couldn't be sure, but I think something fell out.

"My squished stone!" laughed Shue.

"Stop!" gasped Ashley. She waved at Shue. "I can't breathe. I'll pee my . . ."

Suddenly they were gone, and the next voice I heard was Mom's.

". . . BELIEVE IT! THAT'S IT! NO MORE BASEMENT! For a week! Do you hear me? We've been looking all over for you. And you're hiding out again!"

Mom was halfway down the steps, and she was glaring at me. I couldn't see her eyes, but sometimes you can tell about glaring from a voice, and her tone definitely said glaring. I jumped up and ran to the bottom of the stairs. I was busted. There was no way around it.

"Upstairs now!" barked Mom. I followed her up. She lectured me the whole way, and I let her. The only way to defend myself was to tell her about the wishes, and I couldn't do that. What if telling someone ruined everything? What if it stopped the magic? I had to stay quiet. I couldn't take that chance.

chapter eighteen

Patience

Claire was pretty much the only one talking during breakfast. Mom said a few things, but I could tell she was distracted. She was probably feeling guilty; she always got that way after she yelled at me. When we were done with breakfast, Mom stopped Claire from getting out the list. Instead she made an announcement.

"Today we're going to skip the list; let's do something else." She paused for a second to make sure we were paying attention. "How about we go to one of those tree-top adventure parks. Do you know what that is?"

Claire shook her head and I nodded. Mom's surprise made me instantly feel better. I'd been wanting to go to one of those places forever. Mom is big on the philosophy of going outdoors and moving around if you are in a rut. I knew why this was happening—it was for me. Because I was sad about Lucy being gone, and being forced to take care of Claire. But Mom had it wrong; I didn't have a problem with Claire. So really it was only a half rut, but it didn't matter; I was glad we were going. I listened while she explained everything to Claire.

I already knew about the rope bridges, the zip lines, and the different challenges in the trees, but the part I was not expecting was when Mom said, "I'm going to do it too!" I couldn't imagine her walking across a tightrope in the trees. She didn't seem like that kind of person. It was the kind of thing I was going to have to see to believe.

It didn't take long to get ready. The hardest part was getting Claire to wear the right kind of clothes—you can't wear skirts and dresses to go on a zip line. Mom finally had to pick out a T-shirt and shorts and stand there while Claire put them on. When we got in the car, Mom let me pick out the radio station. I took that as a good sign—I was probably forgiven.

Sometimes when a good song comes on, you can almost feel like things are perfect. I was having that exact feeling, when all of a sudden I saw Peter walking down the street.

"Hey Claire!" I pointed out the window. "Look, it's Peter."

Claire squealed and waved, but he was too far away to see us. Mom gasped and swerved the car. I thought it was because of Claire, but it wasn't. It was because of me.

Mom pulled the car over and stopped. "Ash! Did you just recognize someone? I can't believe it. That's amazing."

I sat up; she was right. Of course I knew why it had happened—Peter was pretty distinctive, smaller than other people—but still, that kind of thing never happened to me! I smiled and leaned back against the headrest.

"Why is that so amazing?" asked Claire. "I do it all the time."

I leaned farther into the seat and closed my eyes. I didn't want to explain this. Mom waited for a minute to see if I would answer. I kept quiet.

Mom pulled out into traffic, and then, when we were going again, she answered Claire.

"Ash has face blindness. It was something she was born with. It means she has trouble recognizing people." I knew this wasn't going to be a fast explanation. Regular people usually had lots of questions, so with Claire it was going to be even worse. I kept my eyes closed. I was right, Claire had a million questions, but Mom was patient and answered most of them. My favorite was "If I grew a mustache, would she still recognize me?" It was hard not to laugh when she asked that.

When we got to the adventure park, the first thing we had to do was put on special safety harnesses and gloves. They weren't very comfortable, but when you're wearing something that can save your life, you can't be picky about a little discomfort. Even Claire seemed okay with it.

The adventure park was just like I was expecting it to be except for one thing—Mom. Claire wasn't scared, I was slightly scared, and Mom was totally not scared at all. I couldn't believe it. She was like a mountain goat, good at everything. I was shocked. I'd lived with her my whole life. How could I have not known this before? When I asked her about it, she just shrugged and said, "Oh, I've always had good balance."

We got home early, which was good, because there was a postcard from Lucy in the mail, and seeing it reminded me about sending hers off. So far I was on schedule—one every other day, just like I'd promised. I took a few minutes and read her message. She was having fun canoeing and swimming, and the food was good. She said she missed me, but the big news was that she had slept outside for a whole night with only a sleeping bag—not even a tent. That didn't make me jealous. I liked sleeping in things, things like tents, which kept bugs out. I put the postcard down and got myself ready to go to the VS Depot. I invited Claire, but she said she didn't want to go, even when I suggested bike riding.

She frowned and shook her head. "I don't like bike riding!"

This was bad news. I loved bike riding, and Dad had even fixed up my old bike for Claire. I pulled her over to the window and pointed to it. It was leaning against the garage. I was hoping she'd be excited about the supercute kitty helmet, the new bell, and the fun pink flag on the back—we'd bought all those things special for her. But she just looked at it and shook her head. It was too bad we hadn't known about her goldfish thing. A goldfish helmet might have changed her mind. I left Claire with Mom and Steve—she was drawing him again—and went to get my bike.

My favorite thing about my bike is that Lucy and I have the exact same one—color, size, everything. We got them together last year. The only difference is that she has a silver basket and I have a black one. We called them our twikes—twins plus bikes. Pulling my bike out of the garage made me sad—you shouldn't separate twikes, and Lucy's was now in Portland.

Riding to the store was ten times faster than walking. I was there in minutes. Peter was at the counter just like I was expecting, and I waved to him as I walked in.

"Hi, how's the book?" he asked.

The question surprised me, so I didn't answer right away. This new book was different from the other PJ Walker books. Viola was great as always, but I wasn't so sure about some of the other characters. Mainly it was a character named Percy who I was having trouble with. He spent a lot of time telling stories that had nothing to do with the mystery. If you are trying to solve a mystery, it's kind of annoying to have to listen to a story about the time someone caught a squirrel in his bathroom—even if it's kind of funny.

"It's okay," I answered. "But Percy's stories are kind of long."

Peter looked surprised. "Really? What chapter are you on?"

"Just finished four." I put the party hat on the counter and glanced up—he was staring at me. I looked around—suddenly I was feeling uncomfortable. There was a huge banner with a giant picture of a goldfish on it hanging over the photocopiers. It was advertising posters—I hadn't seen it before. I didn't want to talk about the book anymore.

I pointed to the banner. "Is that new?"

Peter nodded. "Yes. We're having a special. Do you need a poster?"

"No." I shook my head. "But why a goldfish?"

Peter shrugged. "You don't like goldfish?"

"No, I do. They're okay." Now I was feeling awkward again. I should have made Claire come with me. People liked her. I pushed the party hat forward. "I need to mail this."

Peter shook his head. "I bet you'll like it better if you give it time." For a second nothing happened, and then we both reached for the hat—me to take it back, and him to weigh it.

Peter laughed. "I'm sorry, I meant give the book time, not the hat. The hat is fabulous. Did you have a party?"

I sighed. "Sort of, for Claire's goldfish."

He pointed to the poster and smiled.

I nodded.

After that everything went smoothly. He stamped the hat, I paid, and we both said good-bye. As I was stepping out the door, Peter called out to me.

"Remember!" he shouted. "If it's in the story, it has meaning. Just keep reading."

I nodded. Next time I was definitely bringing Claire, whether she wanted to come or not.

When I got home from mailing the hat, I reread Lucy's postcard. It was hard to really know what was going on from only eight sentences. I hoped she was okay.

When Claire went upstairs to bed, I went up too, to read my book. This wasn't like in the beginning—it wasn't the best part of my day, but Peter was right, the book was getting better. It took all my energy to get to the last word of the chapter without falling asleep—it had been a long day.

chapter nineteen

Old-Fashioned

When I woke up the sun was shining and the air was warm, but that was only the weather. My personal forecast was anxiety and dread. Today was crafts at the old people's home, and I kept imagining a sea of old faces, and me having to shake everyone's hand. It felt like a nightmare, only I wasn't going to wake up and have it be gone—it was real and it was going to happen. I forced myself out of bed. Maybe there'd be some kind of minor disaster and we wouldn't have to go. Nothing with injuries, but enough to keep us at home. It was unlikely, but I was hopeful, and that helped me get dressed and down the stairs. As soon as I walked into the kitchen, Claire ran over and jumped in front of me, blocking my way. I tried to push past her, but she wouldn't move.

"Claire!" I grabbed her shoulders and moved her to the side. What was she doing?

She grinned and followed me over to the cupboard. "You recognized me! I knew you would."

I pulled out the cereal box and smiled. Now it made sense. I grabbed a handful of cereal and walked to the table. Claire followed, waiting for me to be as excited as she was. She still didn't get it, how it all worked. It was complicated, strange, and hard to understand, but I tried to explain it.

"Of course I know you. I'm expecting you here. But if I saw you next to some other kids in a store or something, and I wasn't expecting to see you, then maybe I might not recognize you."

Claire thought about it and shook her head.

"No. You'd know me. I know you would."

I popped some cereal into my mouth and nodded. I wished it were true—everyone likes to be recognized.

Claire was the only one who had pancakes that morning. Mom was finally sick of them too. Was it even healthy to eat pancakes every day? Mom made Claire eat a couple of slices of pear, so she was maybe thinking about that too. Claire talked nonstop about the craft thing all morning. She had enough enthusiasm for a hundred people, which was good, because I didn't have any. It was a nice thing to do, help old people, but that didn't mean I wanted to do it. It was a hard morning—her wanting me to be as excited as she was, and me forcing myself to ignore the basement. I knew if I went down there and got caught, I'd be dead. I couldn't risk it, so I worried about it instead. The wish jar was out in the open. What if Mom went down there and saw it? Would it all be over? I spent the morning hovering close to the basement door, ready to run interference in case she did laundry. It wasn't easy—pretending to be normal on the outside, while being a wreck on the inside.

The craft thing was at two o'clock, but by one o'clock Claire was dressed and ready to go. We left fifteen minutes early, because Mom was tired of Claire asking, *Is it time yet?* every twenty seconds. I was nervous about giving up my post by the basement door, but Mom said she was going grocery shopping while we were at the craft event, so that made it easier. The wish jar would be safe until we got back.

The old people's home was close by, only ten

minutes away. Mom came in with us to check it out. I was still hoping we'd get to turn around and go home, but the minute we walked inside, I knew that wasn't going to happen. The entrance was nice, the lady at the front office was friendly, and the craft room was perfectly fine. Claire was bouncing up and down; she could hardly contain herself.

Marjorie was the lady in charge of the crafts. She seemed kind of like a grown-up version of Claire. She was superhappy to meet us. When we got to the craft room, I could see why—she needed our help. It was almost two o'clock, and everything was still in boxes, waiting to be set up. Of course Marjorie fell in love with Claire—why wouldn't she? The hand-shaking thing was a real icebreaker, and not something you'd expect from a seven-year-old. After we all shook hands, Marjorie showed us what to do. Mostly it was just setting out the supplies on the tables. The craft for today was painting ceramic tiles, so we put out markers, stamps, paints, brushes, cleaning supplies, and, of course, tiles. The door to the craft room was closed, but it had a window, and I could see people lining up outside. That made me a little nervous.

When it was time to start, Claire and I stood to the side, and Marjorie opened the door. It was hard to keep Claire still, but I did my best.

Suddenly Claire was shouting, "Look! Look!" She wriggled past everyone coming into the room and disappeared into the hall.

I called after her, but it was too late—she was gone. I had no choice but to chase her. I was furious. I stomped out the door. She was standing just outside the door.

As soon as she saw me, she pointed to a room down the hall. "It's him! The boy Sam, from the thrift store. He's here."

I froze.

She grabbed my arm and pulled me down the hall. "Let's say hi."

Normally I would have said no and pulled back, but I was confused—still transitioning from furious to surprised—and not feeling anywhere near normal. Suddenly we were in front of the door, looking into the room.

"SEE! I told you, it's Sam." Claire pointed.

I wasn't so sure. There were four people in the room: a boy, an old man, an old lady, and another man—probably not as old as the other two. They were standing around a table full of boxes, talking. Why would Sam be here? It made no sense. It couldn't be him. It was just someone who kind of looked like Sam. The old man pushed by us and walked down the hall without saying a word. He seemed grumpy.

"HI, SAM!" Claire yelled and waved wildly. I froze. Claire really needed some kind of warning light or a buzzer, so I could be ready for her embarrassing outbursts. Everyone in the room looked over. The boy smiled.

"Hey," he said. "What are you guys doing here?"

I recognized the voice. It was Sam! "We're doing crafts down there." Claire pointed to the craft room. She was bouncing up and down, excited. "You have to come see. We're making things."

I knew I should say something, but I was too shocked to speak. I nodded and tried to smile. A second later I was standing alone in the hall, and Claire was in the room shaking hands with everyone. I wanted to leave, but my feet wouldn't move. Finally I got it together, leaned in, and grabbed her arm.

"We need to go back." I pulled her into the hallway. My teeth were clamped down so hard, my jaw was hurting.

Claire shouted and waved to everyone.

"Bye Sam, bye Miss Sato, bye Mr. Fred." She skipped down the hall beside me.

"That was lucky I saw Sam. You wouldn't have recognized him without me." She looked up for confirmation.

I nodded, but it wasn't a yes-I'm-so-happy-you-helped-me nod, it was a you're-making-my-life-miserable nod. On the outside they maybe looked the same, but their meanings were completely different.

Considering how everything had started, the craft event turned out pretty well. Except for the whole Sam thing. I had a good time. We didn't have to do much. Mostly it was cleaning brushes, providing encouragement, and opening the paint containers when the lids were hard to get off. Near the end we even got to paint a tile ourselves. Claire painted a picture of Steve, and I wrote Lucy's name in fancy script. We each had our favorites.

Once everything was cleaned up, we walked outside and helped Marjorie load the boxes into her car. Claire wanted to go back inside, but I made her stay with me by the front door. Mom would be by any second, and as soon as she pulled up, we were out of there. I wasn't hanging around any longer than we had to. Claire leaned against the side of the building fidgeting.

"Why can't I just go in and see if they have cookies?" she complained.

I shook my head. "They don't have cookies."

"But what if Marjorie's wrong," she said. "Maybe they normally don't have cookies, but today as a surprise they have them."

I ignored her, but she kept talking.

"I wish they had a cat. Why don't they have a cat? This isn't as good as the one by my house. They have cookies and a cat."

I smiled; suddenly I had a feeling we weren't going to be coming back.

"What are you so happy about?" said a voice.

I froze and spun around. It was Sam. Mr. Fred was with him; he nodded at me and walked over to talk to Claire. Sam stood in front of me, waiting for an answer. He didn't need to know my private thoughts, so I answered his question with a question.

"What are you doing here?"

"It's kind of a summer job," said Sam. "I'm helping Miss Sato put some of her slides in the computer, so we can make a slide show for her anniversary party."

I had no idea what he was talking about. He could tell—I probably had a blank stare on my face. I'd forgotten to fake understanding with a smile or a head nod.

He frowned. "Do you know what a slide is?"

I shook my head.

Suddenly he was animated and excited. "It's an old-fashioned way of showing a photograph. Instead of the photo being printed on paper, it's printed on a small piece of plastic that has a cardboard frame around it. And when you want to see the photo, you put the slide into a projector, and that projects the image so you can see it big on a screen."

This time I nodded, even though I was still completely confused. Sam grinned and continued talking.

"I come here Mondays and Fridays to set up the projector, fill it with slides, and show them to Miss Sato. I'm transferring all the photos she likes onto my computer, so I can make a slide show with titles and captions."

I probably should have said, *Wow! That's amazing*, but enthusiasm is hard to fake when you have no idea what someone is talking about. So instead, I just said, "Oh." I looked toward the driveway, but it was empty—no Mom. I wanted her to come save me.

Sam held up his hand. "Wait, I can show you." He took off his backpack and pulled out a long skinny box. He opened it and held up what looked like a two-inch-square piece of cardboard. It was a big white frame with a smaller, dark square in the middle. He took a step forward and held it in front of my face. "Look in the middle, at the dark square. Can you see the picture?"

I didn't want to step closer to him, so I just strained my eyes. It wasn't easy to see, but he was right, there was some kind of picture there. Sam handed me the slide so I could take a closer look.

"Hold it up to the sky," he said. "Just don't touch the middle part. If it gets scratches on it, it ruins the picture. That's a picture of Miss Sato's special bag. It's from Japan."

I held the slide up to the light, squinted, and then covered my mouth. I couldn't believe it. The bag was in the shape of a goldfish. It was a goldfish bag. What was the chance of that? Another goldfish thing.

"What's wrong?" asked Sam.

I handed back the slide.

"Goldfish." I shook my head. "Ever since Claire came, it's been goldfish everywhere. Like it's a sign or something."

Sam put the slide away. "Why goldfish?"

I shrugged. "I don't know. It's her favorite animal."

Finally Mom pulled into the driveway. Claire ran to the car and opened the door.

She yelled and waved. "BYE, MR. FRED! BYE, SAM!"

I started to get in but stopped and gave Sam a half wave. He was okay, different than I thought he'd be—maybe even kind of nice.

"See you Monday!" shouted Claire.

I snapped on my seat belt, and Mom pulled out into the street.

"It's Friday," I said. "The craft thing is just once a week."

"I know." Claire bounced up and down. Even a seat belt couldn't hold her still. "But now we can come on Monday! Mr. Fred invited us to a concert, and it's on Monday."

"Wow." Mom looked back at us and smiled. "That sounds fun. I'm glad you had such a good time."

"We did." Claire beamed.

I ignored her and looked out the window.

She didn't care. She kept talking. "And Mr. Fred taught me a new word. Nifty! It's old-fashioned. I'm going to use it a lot. Mr. Fred said that's the best way to remember a new word."

Monday? Really? We had to come back on Monday! I slumped back against my seat. There was no winning with Claire; just when you got a handle on things—bang! Suddenly there it was, a new surprise staring you in the face.

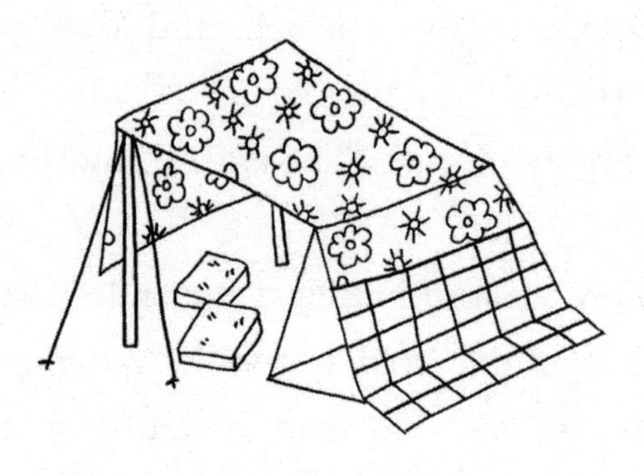

chapter twenty

Cheat

I usually sleep in on Saturdays, but today I got up extra early. It was the only way I could think of to sneak down to the basement without getting caught. Mom and Claire were still asleep, and if I was lucky, they'd stay that way for at least thirty more minutes. It was a relief to see the wish jar right where I'd left it—nothing had been moved. I twisted the lid back on. What I really wanted to do was sit in the chair and pull out a wish, but I resisted—it wasn't worth what could happen if Mom caught me.

I grabbed the two wishes I'd already read, shoved them into my pocket, and crept back toward my room with the jar. My heart was racing, and my fingers were crossed the whole time up the stairs. As soon as I got to my room, I closed the door and leaned back against it. I'd made it. I got out the wish map, put it on my desk, and threw the two used wishes on top. I'd stick them on the map later, but first I had something important to do: try a new wish.

I sat on the side of the bed and studied the jar. It was the first time I had seen it in real light, outside the basement. Now it seemed less mysterious, just like an ordinary jar with a pretty label. Maybe the light in my room was wrong—too bright. The basement was probably better for magic—dark and gloomy. I stuck my hand in the jar and spun the balls around. *Please find a happy one.* I was getting tired of the sad wishes. I picked one out and rolled it between my finger and thumb. Was it a good one? There was no way to tell. I closed my eyes, smoothed out the paper, took a deep breath, and looked down and read it.

I Hope Spencer Doesn't Tell on Us

I should have been on my way to a new adventure, but I wasn't. Instead, I was still sitting on my bed. I wrapped up the ball, put it in the jar, and pulled it out again and unwrapped it. Maybe I'd done something wrong. I read it again.

I Hope Spencer Doesn't Tell on Us

Still nothing. There wasn't any magic. Now I was nervous. My hands were sweaty and shaky. I picked out a new ball; maybe that last wish was broken. Could that even happen? I didn't waste time thinking. I opened the new wish and read it.

I Wish Ashley Wouldn't Ignore Me

But it was the same—nothing happened. But wait—I'd already seen this wish. I jumped up and pulled out the map. Yes, there it was at the top of the board, the exact same wish. What was going on? Why were there two wishes exactly the same? And why weren't they working? I had an answer, but I ignored it—instead I tried everything I could think of to make them work. I put them in the jar, took them out, wrapped them up, unwrapped them, sat on the floor, sat in the chair, stood up, and even twirled around, but nothing made them work. The magic was gone. I didn't want to believe it. I wouldn't believe it. And suddenly I knew why there were two wishes for the same thing—if you really wanted something to come true, it was impossible to stop wishing.

It was still early. Mom and Claire weren't up yet, so I grabbed everything and snuck down to the basement. I was desperate. It was the only thing I could think of. Maybe I had to be in the basement. Maybe I had to sit in the chair. Maybe it wasn't broken.

On the way down the stairs I rolled the Spencer wish into a ball. I dropped it into the jar, sat down in the chair, and then pulled it out again. I had my own wish too; it wasn't on paper, but it filled my head. *Please work. Please work.* I opened the wish and looked down. I knew it by heart, but I made myself slowly and carefully read each word on the paper.

I Hope Spencer Doesn't Tell on Us

Ashley and Shue were at the Dumpster again, and as soon as I saw them, I screamed—it was a scream of joy. I felt like I could run up and hug them, but of course I couldn't. I stayed back.

Ashley was looking into the Dumpster. "There's usually good stuff inside."

I walked over and looked inside—it was empty.

Shue took a step back and shrugged. "That's okay." She didn't seem disappointed. She looked around for a second and climbed up onto the edge of the Dumpster.

Ashley looked surprised. "What are you doing?"

Suddenly I remembered the test words; I hadn't said them yet. It took me a minute to think of something, but it was worth the effort.

"Brown owl." It was a dedication to Lucy.

Shue was now standing on the edge of the Dumpster, her arms reaching out on either side for balance. It wasn't like the adventure park; she didn't have a harness to keep her safe.

"Maybe you should come down," said Ashley. She seemed nervous.

Shue smiled. "I'm okay—I'm good at balancing. What do you think? I bet I can make it all the way around in less than two minutes. Time me."

Ashley shook her head, but that didn't change Shue's mind. Finally Ashley gave in; she looked at her watch and said, "Go."

Shue started. She was good at balancing. We watched her make her way around the lip of the Dumpster. There wasn't much room to walk—it was only five inches wide—but she didn't have any trouble.

"Five more seconds," shouted Ashley.

Shue was about ten steps from the end; she wasn't going to make it. She tried to run, but that was a mistake—I saw her wobble.

"STOP!" Ashley screamed, but it was too late. Shue was going to fall. Suddenly Ashley was there, next to the Dumpster. A second later they were both on the ground. They cried out, moaned, and slowly rolled apart.

"Should I get Mom?" said a voice. I recognized it; it was Spencer. Where had he come from?

"I'm okay," whimpered Ashley.

Shue was quiet, but a few seconds later she mumbled a weak "Me too."

Both girls groaned and slowly forced their bodies to sit up. There was a check of arms and legs—luckily nothing was broken.

Shue looked at Ashley. "You saved my life. Why?"

Ashley shrugged. "I'm a good pillow." She rubbed her arm; a bruise was starting to show. "You almost made it."

Shue nodded. "I'll pay you back one day, I promise."

"Okay." Ashley groaned and tried to smile, but her smile turned into a creepy grin—probably because of the pain. She stood up but then immediately leaned over again, bracing herself against her legs. "But it has to be something big, because I'm probably going to be sore for a week."

Shue rubbed her shoulder. "It'll be huge—you'll see." She struggled to her feet.

Suddenly Ashley straightened up and turned her attention to Spencer. "You won't tell on us, right?"

Spencer took a few steps forward. "You know that Mom said no Dumpster diving." He looked over at

Shue, waited an extra second for effect, and nodded his head. "Okay, I won't tell."

I wanted to know what would happen next, but for me it was over. I was back in the basement. My head was spinning. There were too many feelings all at once. I was relieved that the wish had worked, happy that it was a good one, but filled with dread when I heard footsteps upstairs. I grabbed the jar and the wishes and sprinted to the top of the stairs. I carefully turned the knob and slowly opened the door, but it didn't matter. Claire was standing right in front of me. We stared at each other, me not knowing what to say, and her knowing that I was cheating.

"You aren't supposed to go down there," she whispered.

I nodded. She was looking at the wish jar.

I hugged it close to my body and tried to cover it up. "I had to get this. It's for a project. It's special and private." This wasn't going to work. There was no way Claire wasn't going to ask me a million questions. I felt sick.

Claire was quiet for what seemed like forever. She looked down the hall left and right and then nodded her head. "Okay, I won't tell."

It was a miracle, and exactly what I needed to

hear. I whispered, "Thank you," and sprinted up to my room. I closed my door, leaned against it, and slowly dropped to the floor. I let myself stay there for a minute or two, but I couldn't rest for long. I hid the jar and the map and ran back downstairs. I had to make sure Claire didn't say anything to Mom.

After breakfast—pancakes for Claire—she surprised us by finally letting us see her whole list. It was impressive and way too long. It took a while, but Mom finally convinced her that it would be better to make her list shorter. Some of the stuff on there was impossible, like drive a tractor, ride on an elephant, and see the end of a rainbow—she obviously had some real big expectations for this summer. Mom worked with her, and together they got the list down to ten things. I was a little disappointed that the elephant was gone. I was curious to see how Mom was going to make that happen—plus secretly I'd have liked to ride on an elephant too.

CLAIRE'S NEW LIST

1. Do crafts with old people.
2. Buy new outfits at the thrift store.
3. Have a yard sale.
4. Go to Hawaii.

5. Have a birthday party for Steve.
6. Make cookies.
7. Carve a pumpkin.
8. Bounce on a trampoline.
9. Go on a treasure hunt.
10. Make a fort.

When the list was done, the first thing Mom said was "I'm sorry we can't really go to Hawaii. But we can try and make a pretend Hawaii; would that be okay?"

I was still hoping for the elephant, but Claire didn't want to make any more changes to her list.

She smiled at Mom and said, "Pretend Hawaii is okay with me. It's nifty." I had a feeling that we were going to be hearing a lot more of that new word. Thank you, Mr. Fred.

We spent the rest of the morning talking about the list. Claire did a lot of looking at me and smiling, but she was good; not once did she say anything about the basement. It was a huge relief. It made me want to pay her back. I had two ideas. When Claire went to the bathroom, I asked Mom about them.

"Do you think I could make a fort for Claire today, and then tomorrow maybe we could do the Hawaii thing?"

Mom loved the fort idea but was pretty skeptical about Hawaii. Pulling off a tropical island paradise in one day seemed kind of impossible to her, but I said I could do it. I just needed some special supplies from the store. I didn't say, *Plus I really want a coconut so I can send it to Lucy in the mail.* That thought was up there, but she didn't need to know about it. Finally Mom agreed, and I put a list together of stuff she should buy. I was excited; pretend Hawaii was going to be fun.

It took all afternoon to make the fort, and when we were done, most of the backyard was covered. We pretty much used every single blanket in the whole entire house, except for the ones on our beds—we weren't allowed to use those. I attached a rope that went from the house to the garage and over to the big tree in our side yard. These were the main supports for the blankets, but we used other stuff too—boxes, big buckets, and even a shelf that we emptied and dragged out from the garage. When it was done, it looked more like a hobo village than a fort, but Claire liked it. Her favorite thing to do was to go in and out of it and scramble through the passageways. She must have done it a hundred times. It was a testament to my building skill that the whole thing held together and didn't just collapse right on top of her. I was proud of that.

Claire, Mom, and I were all supposed to have dinner in the fort, but at dinnertime Claire announced, "It's a kids-only fort!"

Mom said that was okay, and she could eat in the house, but I didn't want that. I wanted her in there, in the tent, helping with Claire. We'd already spent all afternoon together, and I needed a break. At first Claire complained, but finally she agreed that Mom could come in for dinner if she left right after eating. That wasn't really good enough for me, but Mom said not to worry, that things would work out. I wasn't convinced, but dinner went well, and Mom ended up being right. For dessert she brought out banana bread, strawberries and ice cream, a book, and a postcard for me from Lucy. I was surprised about the postcard.

While we ate dessert, Mom read Claire a story, and I read my postcard. Lucy had gotten the name sign, and she loved it—and she especially loved how it hadn't come in a box. Mom's idea had been great. I looked over at her; she was reading to Claire. If she had looked up, I would have given her a smile, but she didn't. She was too busy reading. I went back to the postcard. It was mostly a giant thank-you. I think Lucy felt bad that she couldn't send me cool things too. She tried to make her postcard look fun by drawing little pictures on it, but there is only so much you can do with a piece of paper. I smiled. She was going to flip out when she got the coconut. After the story, Claire didn't want Mom to leave, and I could tell that Mom was happy to stay.

When the food was cleaned up, I got out some flashlights and made spooky shadows on the outside of the tent. Claire loved that, and Mom being in there with her made it not scary. I felt a little sad that Lucy wasn't here; she would have liked making shadows. The only bad part of the night was that we had to take the fort down superfast, and it was right when I had almost figured out my most impressive shadow yet, the giant squid. Raindrops can really ruin your fun.

Before I went to bed, I pulled out the wish map and added the new wishes. Now I had nine wishes, all in order, but they were only pieces, just snippets of the story. It was going to be hard to wait for more, but I'd have to. Mom was not going to let up on the basement ban. I was pretty sure about that.

chapter twenty-one

Aloha

I woke up in the morning and made a list of things to not think about, and then I promised myself I wouldn't think about them for the whole rest of the day. It wasn't going to be easy.

THINGS TO NOT THINK ABOUT

1. The wish jar and how I can't use it
2. The book I'm reading and how I'm not loving it
3. Lucy being gone

Today was Hawaii day, and Hawaii is fun!

I'd never been to Hawaii, but I'd seen it on TV,

and I'd seen that Elvis movie *Blue Hawaii* about twenty times, so I felt pretty confident about being able to pull it off. Basically Hawaii is about relaxing. You lie around in the sun, you float in the water, and you eat lots of tropical fruit and listen to fun beach music. Mom had bought me everything I needed, the sun was shining, and I was in the mood for lounging. It was going to be a good day. The first thing I had planned for us was a pedicure. Sand, bare feet, nice toenails—they went together.

Claire was excited about the pedicure.

"I know how to do it," she squealed. "You can do me, and I'll do you, but I get to do you first! It'll be nifty."

I wasn't so sure I wanted Claire painting my toenails, but I made myself be positive. Plus we were in the backyard; if it turned out horrible, no one would see it. I handed her the color I'd picked out.

I was right to be nervous; she was terrible at it. There was polish everywhere. My toes looked like they'd been in some kind of nuclear meltdown—it had been a mistake to pick blue. They were definitely not nifty, but I lied and told her I loved it. After the nails were done, Mom called me upstairs. The ladder was pulled down from the attic, and I could hear her up there rummaging around. I wasn't crazy about the attic. It was even more disorganized than the basement, plus it smelled funny. Mom said it was just a little musty, but I didn't believe her—it was probably a dead squirrel. I waited at the bottom of the ladder until she finally poked her head through the door.

Mom waved her hand at me and said, "Catch this."

I put my hands up and caught some kind of large, tangled, flowery ball. I untangled it as she climbed down the ladder. Suddenly I knew what it was. It was perfect—it was the one thing I hadn't thought of. It was two Hawaiian leis.

"Where did you get these?"

She was next to me now and smiling. "Your father and I got them from a birthday party. It was ages ago."

Mom tried to push the ladder back up into the ceiling but fumbled with it. I looked over; she had something in her left hand. I couldn't tell what it was, because it was small.

I pointed to it. "What's that?"

She hid it behind her back. "I might show you later. I'm not sure."

"Is it for today?"

She shook her head. "No, don't worry about it. Let's go downstairs."

As soon as I got downstairs, Claire and I put on our leis and went outside. We had towels to lie on, Hawaiian music playing, a Slip 'n Slide, a kiddie pool with water and colored plastic fish, a medium-sized pile of sand, supplies for making grass skirts, and two coconuts—one for each of us. Claire was most excited about the coconuts.

She cradled hers like a baby. "I'm going to keep it forever." She swung it around and danced with it.

I'd never opened a coconut before. I wanted to see the inside.

I pointed to her coconut. "Let's break it open and eat it."

Claire looked horrified. She shook her head, took a step back, and held on to it extra tight. "NO! You can do that to yours!"

Now I was the one shaking my head. I was saving mine for Lucy. In the end we left the coconuts just like they were, and we ate pineapple and mango instead.

I should have known, but Claire was not good at relaxing. Instead of a relaxing day in Hawaii, we had a busy day in Hawaii. We pretend-surfed on the Slip 'n Slide, made a mini sand castle with the sand, hid things in the sand, buried half of Claire under the sand, made grass skirts and hula danced, collected rocks and pretended they were seashells, snorkeled in the kiddie pool, fished in the kiddie pool, had a water fight in the kiddie pool, painted Lucy's address on my coconut, made a bed for Claire's coconut, and finally, near the end, lay on our towels. I was exhausted.

"This is the best pretend Hawaii day I've ever had," said Claire. "Can I tell you about my favorite parts?"

I nodded. Even lying down she didn't stop talking, but I didn't mind. At least we were being still.

We ended Hawaii day before dinner, so there was time to mail Lucy's coconut. This time Claire definitely wanted to come—she was excited about surprising Peter with it.

She bounced up and down. "I bet he's never mailed a coconut before."

I brought out the bikes so we could ride, but as soon as Claire saw them, she changed her mind and said she didn't want to go. At first I was mad—it wasn't fair of her to be so wishy-washy—but then I had a new thought, and it changed everything. *Maybe Claire didn't know how to ride a bike.*

I pointed to the bikes and asked her, "Claire, can you ride a bike like that?"

She looked at the ground. I didn't need any more of an answer. Riding a bike is not something you can teach someone in thirty minutes, and that's how long we had until the VS Depot was closing. I was tired, and I didn't want to walk, but what other choice was there? Suddenly I had another idea. I went to the garage and pulled out Dad's old trailer bike. It wasn't easy. It was long, and the extra half bike on the back kept getting caught on everything. Mom's boxes of junk were like an impossible obstacle course. It was a miracle I got it out, but it was worth it, because as soon as Claire saw it, she brightened.

"I can ride that kind of bike!" She ran over and jumped on the seat at the back.

Suddenly the whole thing tipped to the right. I pushed but could hardly keep it up. Now I wasn't so sure; I'd never ridden this bike before. What if I couldn't do it? I made Claire get off, so I could practice riding it by myself. I rode up and down the block. Without anyone on the back it was easy, but as soon as Claire hopped on, everything changed. Now the bike was wiggly like crazy. What if I fell, crashed, killed us both?

"Let's go!" shouted Claire; she was excited.

I was scared, but I tried. The first trip down the street was terrifying, but after a few more times of up and down, I started to feel better. And after two complete times around our block, I knew we were going to be okay.

The trip to the VS Depot was fast and easy. As soon as we got there, Claire hopped off the bike and ran in. By the time I'd parked the bike and walked in, Peter already knew about the coconut and Hawaii day. Claire was fast at sharing news.

He waved at me and said, "Sounds like you girls have been having fun."

Claire nodded and looked at me.

I smiled. "We have."

It took a while for Peter to figure out how to get the stamps to stick to the coconut. While he did that, Claire drew pictures of Steve on scrap paper. I was glad she was doing that instead of running up and down the ramp. I guess she was tired from our day too. Everything went smoothly until Claire saw the goldfish poster. It was good that there weren't any other customers in the store. Not everyone thinks screams of joy are pleasant to listen to. Peter was supernice about it, though, and said Claire could have the poster when the sale was over. She was so happy, you'd have thought he'd promised her a golden pony.

I was glad that Peter didn't bring up the Percy

book. I'd been having trouble with it lately. Last night I hadn't even read it—I'd been too tired. Next time I'd come prepared. Not that he probably cared, but I'd said I was a huge PJ Walker fan, and that'd look like a lie if I didn't even finish the book. And so far he was right—it was getting better.

Before we left, Peter gave Claire a little pad of paper for her Steve drawings. He said it was left over from a job he'd printed. Claire is good with manners—she said thank you just like she was supposed to. She put the pad of paper in my backpack, and we waved good-bye. The ride home was a lot harder—it was more uphill—but Claire pedaled too, and that helped. The second we got home, Claire jumped off the bike, grabbed my backpack, and disappeared. This was no surprise, because for the whole ride home, all she'd been talking about was what she was going to draw on her new pad of paper. I could have really used her help with the bike, but I was stuck on my own. It was impossible to get it back into the garage. After scraping my leg on the pedal three times, I gave up and just leaned it against the fence. We were probably going to be using it again anyway.

The minute I walked in the door, Claire attacked me.

"Look," she squealed. "It's the best Steve I've ever drawn." She waved the paper in front of my face. I couldn't see a thing.

"Wait." I grabbed her arm and held it still so I could look. It was a picture of Steve standing on a boat, and if you bought into the whole goldfish-with-legs thing, he was perfectly proportioned.

"Nice job." I was about to hand the pad back when something at the top of the page caught my eye. It was a drawing of two little palm trees on an island. I looked closer; had Claire drawn them too?

"Did you draw those?" I asked.

Claire shook her head. "That's on all the pages. Can I have it back now? I want to color Steve."

Claire pulled the paper away and went back to the table. The palm trees on the island were a weirdly perfect ending for our Hawaii day. Sometimes when things are so perfect, it can make you feel a little uneasy, and that was the exact kind of feeling I was having. I felt that way the whole rest of the night right up until I crossed another day off the calendar. Knowing it was only two more weeks until I would see Lucy at camp made me instantly feel a whole lot better.

chapter twenty-two

Fishy

All Claire could talk about all morning was the concert at the old people's home, and how great it was going to be. I was glad when it was finally time to go. At least sitting in the concert would be better than just talking about it. But I was wrong—the concert was awful. And it wasn't just me; Claire thought so too. A lot of the old people seemed to like it, but that was probably only because they had hearing problems. We saw Mr. Fred and the grumpy man who had walked past us the other day. It turned out that he was Mr. Fred's father and was married to Miss Sato—we were surprised about that. The grumpy man's name was Horace Gripes, which is kind of a perfect name for a grumpy person. He was nicer today, and he seemed to like talking to Claire. Claire is like the golden retriever of people—everyone loves her.

After the concert Claire and I went outside to get on our bike. Turns out the trailer bike is a great way to get around. As I was bent down unlocking the bike, Claire pulled on my arm. When I looked up, she pointed.

"It's Sam. He's coming over here."

She was good at pointing him out, but I was getting better at recognizing him too. That usually happened once I got to know someone. I made a mental list of physical traits for everyone I knew. So far Sam's list was that his hair was always messy, his ears stuck out, he was an inch taller than me, he was slim, he liked plain T-shirts, there was a space in between his two front teeth, and he always wore black Converse sneakers. The T-shirt and the sneaker thing were the most helpful, because they were easy to see from far away.

"Hi," said Sam. He had his arms full of stuff. It took me a few seconds, but then I realized that the bike next to ours was probably his. Not many old people were riding around on mountain bikes.

Claire was excited to share her news. "Did you know that Mr. Gripes is Mr. Fred's dad, and that he's married to Miss Sato?"

Sam nodded. Of course he knew; he worked with Miss Sato.

Sam looked uncomfortable. "It's kind of weird," he said.

"What?" asked Claire.

I pulled the chain out from between the wheels of my bike and stood up.

"Mr. Gripes doesn't want the anniversary party, and Miss Sato does."

I snapped the bike lock shut and put everything into my backpack. "Who's the party for?" asked Claire.

Sam was quiet for so long that I wasn't sure he was going to answer Claire. But then he leaned forward and whispered, "It's for both of them, for their fortieth wedding anniversary. And I don't think they like each other very much anymore."

"Yikes!" I made a face.

"Exactly," said Sam. He put his pile of stuff down next to his bike and grabbed his lock.

Claire was standing next to us. All of a sudden she looked sad.

"They don't love each other?"

Sam shrugged. Claire didn't say anything, but I could see it coming. She was getting agitated.

"We have to make them fall in love!" cried Claire. She moved next to Sam to convince him, but she accidentally bumped into his pile of stuff, knocking everything to the ground. The worst part was the slides—they were everywhere.

She covered her mouth. "Sorry!"

Sam bent down. "It's okay." That was nice of him, but it wasn't really true; if the slides got scratched, he could get into trouble.

I bent down to help him. I felt guilty; it was kind of my fault. I was in charge of Claire. Though really it was kind of an impossible job. All you could do was follow behind and pick up the pieces.

"Can you help them?" Claire was almost crying. She looked back and forth from me to Sam and me again. "Can you make them fall in love again? Can you do it, Ash?"

She was still talking about Miss Sato and Mr. Gripes, but I knew why she was so upset. Sam didn't, but I couldn't explain it to him, not with her being right here. I couldn't say, *She's kind of sensitive about love, because her parents fell out of love, and her mom ran off to be alone and was killed by a train.* Sam had no idea what was going on, why she was acting so strange, but that didn't matter. Claire was more important. I had to calm her down. I held her hands and pulled her gently down next to me.

"Okay." I nodded. "I'll try. But right now let's just help Sam pick up his stuff."

Claire nodded. She wiped her hand over her eyes. "Do you promise?"

I promised, but I crossed my fingers behind my back. I could lie to her, but not to the universe. I knew I could always get Claire to forgive me, but the universe was different. I didn't want to mess with that. Claire picked up a slide and held it out for me. I took it and picked up a few more. Soon I had a little pile in my hand.

I handed them to Sam. "They're out of order now, aren't they?"

Sam nodded, but he didn't seem mad. I told Claire to help with the other things, but to leave the slides for me and Sam. I knew she wouldn't be careful, and I didn't want her putting her fingers on the photos. I held a few up to the sky and looked at them before handing them over to Sam. They all had people in them, posing, smiling—captured in moments of happiness.

Claire had recovered, and now she and Sam were talking.

I wasn't listening until Claire said, "Do you have a trampoline?"

Sam didn't answer. I crossed my fingers and hoped that the answer would be no.

"Do you?" Claire asked him again. She was persistent. If you looked up the definition of "persistent," a giant grinning photo of Claire would probably pop right off your computer screen.

Sam smiled. I didn't know him well enough to say for sure, but it looked like a sneaky smile. He looked right at me and said, "No, but my neighbors do, and I can use it whenever I want."

I knew what was going to happen next. "Bounce on a trampoline" was number eight on Claire's list. In two seconds she was going to invite us over to Sam's neighbors' house. I had to stop her before that happened. I opened my mouth to say something, but no words came out. Instead I stared at the slide in my hand. I couldn't believe what I was seeing. Claire and Sam were still talking, but I stopped paying attention; what I was looking at was more important. It was a photograph of the back of Anderson's. I was sure of it. It was the same building, the same Dumpster, and the same door where the boots had been. It was the exact place where I'd been with Ashley and Shue. I didn't have building blindness. I knew I was right. The name on the building was too small to read, but I knew what it said. It had to be Anderson's.

I looked over at Sam and held out the slide. He took it from me and kept talking.

"So just have Ash call me when you want to come over."

Claire clapped her hands and jumped up and down. I ignored her.

"What's that picture?" I pointed to the slide in Sam's hand.

Sam held it up and squinted. "Oh, that's the weird one. I was surprised that Miss Sato picked it, but she said it was important. I don't know why—there's not even anyone in it. Most of the other pictures have people in them."

"Do you know what the building says?" I tried to sound casual, like it didn't matter.

Sam looked again and shook his head. "It's too small to read. Why?"

I didn't want to seem desperate, but I was. It wasn't easy to sound normal. "It just looks familiar.

Can you find out about it? Can you ask Miss Sato tomorrow?"

He shook his head again. "I only come here on Mondays and Fridays, but I can blow it up on the computer tonight and look. I'm at the pool tomorrow and Wednesday, so if you come by, I can tell you what I found out." He put the slide in the box with the others. It was a special box with a slot in it for each slide. He looked back at me. "These pictures are from a long time ago. So it's probably not what you think it is."

I nodded. "I know, but I'm a little curious."

This was a big lie. I wasn't a little curious, I was hugely curious. I tried to look relaxed, but it wasn't easy; my mind was racing.

I was glad Claire wanted to leave; it was hard being an actress, and my head felt like it might explode.

We pedaled home in record time—even Claire said it was fast.

When we got home, there was a postcard from Lucy waiting for me on the kitchen table. I took it up to my room to read. I had told her about Peter and the VS Depot. Mostly she thought it was strange that he was a PJ Walker fan. She was kind of right, because in my whole life, I'd never met anyone else who even knew about PJ Walker's books.

In the middle of the postcard was a little picture of someone sitting inside a canoe, waving. Lucy is good at drawing, so I could tell that it was supposed to be her. It was cute. Under the picture was a whole list of questions about Claire for me to answer; it was nice that she was interested, but answering them all was going to take a while. It would have been easier, and more fun, just to talk about everything on the phone. Sometimes writing a letter, even to a friend, can feel kind of like homework. At the very bottom of the postcard was a sentence about how Lucy had made a new friend. It was hard to believe, but her new friend's name was Claire, just like my new friend—only my Claire was more of a job than a friend. I put down the postcard. I couldn't write back. Not right away. I had too many other things to think about. I stood up and walked around the room, trying to clear my head.

Finally I just sat on the bed. Walking around wasn't working. The only person who could help me was Sam. When he blew up the picture and read the sign on the back of the building, then I'd know. Was it really Anderson's, or was it just some other place that looked exactly the same as Anderson's? Just thinking about it made me shiver. It was going to be hard to wait, but maybe it would only be until tomorrow. All I had to do was get Claire to the pool and find Sam.

I took out the wish map and studied the wishes. I wanted to go back to the Dumpster ones—look around, pay more attention. Could I do that? Would they work twice? It was too dangerous to try. Mom was sitting in the kitchen, and there was no way to get down to the basement without her seeing me. I was just going to have to wait. I put the map away and pulled out the PJ Walker book. I was not excited about the story, but I opened it and forced myself to read.

chapter twenty-three

Face

I spent a good part of the morning trying to get Claire to agree to go to the pool. If Lucy had been here, she would have been shocked. I usually avoid the pool as much as I can. I hate it. For me, going to the pool is like being plopped down with a bunch of penguins and then being asked to tell them apart. It's impossible. At the pool, no one is wearing their regular clothes or looking like they normally do—I can't recognize anyone. But still, I wanted to go. I wanted to find Sam and ask about the photo, and I needed Claire's help. I'd never find Sam on my own.

It was a battle, and no matter how hard I tried, Claire wouldn't give in.

I stood in front of her, furrowed my brow, and tried to sound like Mom. "You have to go!"

"No I don't!" she said. She crossed her arms and stared me down.

I tried again, this time with a threat. "Well, if you don't go, we're going to stay here, and you're going to learn to ride that bike." I pointed toward the garage. I felt good about this one. I could see that she was hesitating.

"What if we go tomorrow? Do I still have to ride the bike?" She seemed nervous.

I could feel victory. I didn't back down. I looked her in the eye and said, "Yes!"

Claire thought for a minute, then ran off and reappeared with the kitty helmet on. It was over; I'd lost.

We spent the rest of the morning going up and down the road, me holding the back of her seat, and her wobbling and almost hitting every parked car. It was stressful. By lunchtime she was getting better, but my back was killing me. After lunch we tried again, and then suddenly, she could do it. She wasn't great at stopping, but she could ride. I stood in the driveway and watched her go back and forth. I'd never taught anyone anything before. Watching her made me feel proud—for both of us.

Mom had bought us a watermelon, so I made Claire stop practicing so we could slice it up and eat it.

"But I don't like watermelon," complained Claire.

I wasn't sure I believed her. How could she not like watermelon? Watermelons were delicious.

"Have you ever tried it?" I asked.

She nodded and made a gagging sound. I put the watermelon on the table. Claire played with it and spun it around while I went to get a knife.

When I came back, she said, "Look—it has a face."

I looked, but I couldn't see it. She pointed to two dark green blotches—the eyes—and a longish squiggly line of brown—the mouth. I took a step back. Now I saw it. She was right—it was a face. And seeing it suddenly gave me an idea—a great idea! An idea that could make a watermelon-hating person into a watermelon-loving person.

I stabbed the top of the watermelon with my knife. "Let's carve it."

Claire was confused.

I pointed the knife to the eyes she had shown me.

"Like a pumpkin—we can make a face."

Suddenly, she got it.

"That's on my list!" she shouted. Now she was excited. She wanted the knife, but I told her she had to wait.

"There's an order to carving. Clean first, carve second." I cut the top off the watermelon.

If there was ever a carve-off between pumpkins and watermelons, pumpkins would be in trouble. Watermelons had lots of pluses. One of the best pluses was the cleaning-it-out part. I hate cleaning out pumpkins—they're slimy and stringy—but the watermelon was completely different. It was easy to scoop, and the insides were delicious. I'd tasted raw pumpkin before—it's disgusting.

Claire drew on the face, and I cut it out. I thought she might be upset that I wasn't letting her use the knife, but she didn't seem to care. When we were done, I put a fake candle in the watermelon and we took it into the garage to see it glow. It was kind of disappointing, because it really wasn't dark enough yet—it would be better at night. But still, Claire was excited, and she ran off to get Mom. It was good that Mom came, because she knew stuff about watermelons that we didn't. She said watermelons rotted faster than pumpkins, and that we needed to put it in the fridge, or it would shrivel up and go mushy. I guess that's why pumpkins are better than watermelons after all—too bad. We put the watermelon in the fridge and got ready to go down to the VS Depot.

I had another letter for Lucy. I'd finished it before the bike lesson. Mom had finally used up the last of the pancake mix, so I took the empty box for my letter. I'd taken it apart, written on the inside, put some candy in it, and glued it all back together. At first I wasn't sure if I was going to like it as much as the other stuff I'd sent her, but now that it was finished, I did. I painted some extra things on the box to make it look better. I changed MIDLAND PANCAKES into LUCY'S PANCAKES and painted Lucy's address in fancy script. The other plus was that the pancake box, when it was all opened up, had lots of room for writing. I didn't write about Sam—I still wasn't sure what I thought of him, and even a pancake box wasn't big enough to explain everything that had happened so far—so mostly I wrote about what I was doing with Claire, and Peter. I didn't really have any answers to the questions she'd asked, but I'd try to get some today.

Even though Claire could now ride her own bike,

she wanted to take the trailer bike. In a way that was good. It was less for me to worry about—she couldn't crash into anything when she was sitting right behind me. When we got to the store, Peter wasn't behind the desk, so Claire ran to the back to find him. They both walked up to the counter together—two small people suddenly getting bigger. By now Peter was used to me giving him strange things to mail. He'd probably have been shocked if I had handed him a normal letter. I took the pancake box out of my backpack and set it on the counter.

Peter picked up the box. "Who's been eating all the pancakes?"

Claire bounced up and down. "It was me! I ate the whole box."

I nodded. "Well, most of it."

Peter put the box on the scale and pulled out some stamps.

"Does your friend send you odd things too?" he asked.

I shook my head. "She's only allowed to send postcards and letters."

"Speaking of letters"—Peter stuck the stamp on the box—"have you gotten to the part in the book where Percy sends Viola a letter?"

I shook my head again.

Peter nodded. "Well, I think you'll like it."

Now I was curious.

Peter shook his head. "I won't give it away, but it's kind of a twist in the story."

I wanted to know more, but he changed the subject and told Claire that he had another pad of paper for her. They walked to the back of the store to get it. A minute later Claire reappeared carrying a large pad of paper. Across the top of the page were the words "Woodman & Sons." It was a relief that it was something normal.

I'd been hoping to ask Peter some of Lucy's questions, but Peter was working on something behind the counter, and Claire was by the door, ready to go. It was too late. Lucy would have to wait. Plus, there probably wasn't anything unusual to discover anyway.

On the ride home I brought up the pool again, but that only reminded Claire of Sam, which made her remember my impossible promise to make Mr. Gripes and Miss Sato fall in love. There was no way I could make that happen. That had been a dumb thing to promise. It ended up being a silent ride. And even though I didn't want to, I couldn't stop thinking about Sam. Was he part of this whole wish thing?

Maybe it was just another coincidence. Could I make myself believe that?

Claire finally got another call from her dad that night. It was only the third one. At first I thought they'd talk every night, but I guess he was busy with work. Claire said he had to travel a lot, all over the country. I'd been meaning to ask Mom what he did, but I kept forgetting. I guess I had more important stuff to think about. Claire and her dad only talked for a few minutes, but I could tell that it made a difference. When she got off the phone, she was superhappy. While we were setting the table for dinner, she told me a little bit about it.

"Daddy's been busy. He had to go on a scuba diving thing to help some people."

Scuba diving. I didn't know he was a scuba diver. That was kind of cool; maybe that's why Claire loved goldfish.

I couldn't believe we hadn't talked about this before. I wanted to know more. "Is that his job? Is he a marine scientist?"

Claire shook her head. "No, he fixes things, so sometimes it's other stuff, but this time it was scuba diving stuff. He had to go really far away, and he saw a shark, a real live one, but he wasn't scared."

I handed Claire the forks and put the knives and spoons out around the table.

"Has your dad been to Hawaii? Or other places where there are sharks?"

I waited for an answer, but Claire ignored me. There was no way she hadn't heard me. I was standing right next to her.

She fumbled with the forks and looked down. "I don't know."

Something about this was weird. Claire put the forks on the table and went to the kitchen to be with Mom. I waited for a few minutes, but she didn't come back. I guess our conversation was over.

After dinner we took the watermelon out of the fridge and put it out on a little table in the backyard. I put the candle in it. Mom served us ice cream, and we ate and watched the face flicker in the darkness. Claire's drawing was kind of uneven—one eye was bigger than the other, and the mouth turned up on the left and drooped down on the right—but still, I liked it. Plus, I could say something about it that I couldn't say about a human—*I'd recognize that face anywhere.*

chapter twenty-four

Love

I woke up thinking about Anderson's. It was too late to sneak into the basement, because I could hear the faint voices of Mom and Claire in the kitchen. I pulled on my bathing suit, shorts, and a shirt. I had a mission—we were going to the pool no matter what! I needed to know what that sign said. Part of me was hoping I was wrong, that it was somewhere else, that it didn't say Anderson's. The wishes by themselves were enough. I didn't want it to get bigger. I wasn't sure I could handle bigger.

I sat on the side of the bed and pulled on a sock. The PJ Walker book was next to me. I picked it up, flipped through the pages, and found Percy's letter. Peter had been right; it was a twist in the story, and it explained a lot. Now I liked Percy more, even felt sorry for him. The letter explained Percy's childhood—how he'd lived in an orphanage and had never been adopted. Mostly it was because he was different—he had one short leg and his foot turned in the wrong way; and then there were the three moles on his nose, and his crossed left eye. The kids at the orphanage had liked him once they got to know him, but no parents ever did. That explained why he'd told Viola those crazy stories about his childhood. The truth was boring—and maybe too painful.

It was hard to imagine Percy as a funny-looking kid. Now that he was a grown-up, he seemed handsome, confident, and outgoing, but that was the new him—after all the operations. Now he was perfect, and no one would ever be able to tell what he used to look like. It made me wonder: Which was harder—having something different about you that everyone could see, or having something different about you that was hidden? I didn't have time to decide, because five seconds later Claire charged into my room. When she'd first arrived, I'd made a rule about knocking first, but now it didn't seem as important.

"Do you know how to make Miss Sato and Mr. Gripes fall in love?" asked Claire.

I shook my head.

"Well, I do." She sat on the side of my bed. "All you have to do is find out what Miss Sato's handwriting looks like, copy it, and write a love letter to Mr. Gripes. It's perfect, because when Mr. Gripes gets the letter, he'll think it's from Miss Sato and he'll fall in love with her again."

Claire was extra pleased with herself. I could tell she couldn't wait for me to get started, but her plan had flaws—lots and lots of flaws. Mostly I was stuck on the "write a love letter to Mr. Gripes" part—there was no way I would ever be able to do that. Part of me even felt sorry for Miss Sato—Mr. Gripes didn't seem very lovable.

I shook my head. "I can't write a love letter."

Claire was surprised. "But it's perfect!"

Her plan was nothing close to perfect. But I knew Claire—if I didn't have another plan to offer her, or a really good reason not to do it, she wouldn't give up.

I wanted her to believe me, so I looked her in the eyes and said it again: "I can't write a love letter." There were about a hundred reasons why I didn't want to do it, but I told Claire the one I thought would make the most sense to her. First I explained that it was against the law to write a letter and pretend to be someone else. I wasn't sure if it was really against the law, but it seemed like it should be.

We sat there for a few minutes, both silently thinking our own thoughts. I studied the swirls and splotches on my bedspread—I seemed to be doing that a lot lately.

Finally I spoke. "Plus I've never been in love."

Claire stared at me, shocked.

"You haven't?"

I nodded, shrugged, and stood up.

"So I don't even know how to write a love letter."

Claire looked at her hands. I had won.

But I wasn't done. I had a plan—a plan to get us to the pool and satisfy Claire, both at the same time. We were going to be love detectives. On the way down to the kitchen, I described it to Claire. At first she said no, but I was ready for that.

"If we don't go to the pool and talk to Sam, I won't find out any more information about Miss Sato and Mr. Gripes. We need to be good love detectives."

Claire was quiet. I took that as a win. I had a good feeling about everything working out.

But suddenly Claire changed the subject. "Do we have to go into the water?"

Why would you go to the pool and not go into the water? The swimming was the only good part. In the water, you did your own thing. Nobody bothered you, and you didn't have to meet or talk to anyone.

"I'll go, but only if we don't go in the water!" Claire turned her back to me.

Now I was annoyed. "What's the matter? Can't you swim?"

Suddenly Claire burst into tears and ran out of the room.

I found her in the living room. She was lying on the sofa, her head buried in the cushion, but she wasn't crying.

I sat down next to her. "I'm sorry. I didn't know, but guess what. Learning to swim is a lot easier than learning to ride a bike."

Claire looked up. "Is that true?"

"Yes, and I can teach you." I smiled, and she sat up.

Now I felt even better about going. It would be good to have something to do at the pool. I liked having a plan—a plan was good.

chapter twenty-five

Discovery

The pool was crowded like I knew it would be. I purposely talked to Claire the whole time, hoping that no one would notice or see me. The worst is when you catch someone's eye and they say hi. I wasn't going to let that happen—my eyes were glued to Claire. And she had her mission—find Sam. There was no way I could find him in this sea of people. I needed her to do it. Someone behind me laughed; I resisted the urge to turn around and look. We did two quick tours around the perimeter of the pool, but there was no Sam.

I pointed to the pool. "Maybe he's in the water."

Claire pulled back.

"We'll only go in the shallow end, where you can stand." I nudged her forward. "I promise."

It took Claire forever to get into the water. I could tell that she didn't trust that the bottom wouldn't suddenly drop out from below her feet, even though I was standing there waiting for her and nothing was happening to me. It wasn't easy to be patient, but after another five minutes she was in. I thought she would cling to me in terror, but she didn't, and once she felt more confident, she even showed me how she could float. I was surprised—floating is the hardest part. All I had to do was teach her how to move her arms and legs. In no time she'd be swimming.

When I was little my favorite stroke was the dog paddle, so I started with that. Claire picked it up quickly, but once she figured it out, the swimming lesson was over. She didn't want to learn any other strokes. We dog-paddled for a while in the shallow end, until Claire decided she was hungry. There was a concession stand next to the pool, near the deep end, so I made her a deal. She could get whatever she wanted as long as she stood in line and paid for it herself. I didn't want to stand in line. Lines were a nightmare. It was the exact kind of place where I'd run into someone I couldn't recognize. I was safer in the water.

I glanced over at it—nobody looked familiar, but that didn't mean anything. Maybe I knew them all. Maybe they were all from my school. I looked again. It was at times like these that I needed Lucy. I couldn't believe she was leaving me! For a second I was gone—inside my head—feeling sorry for myself, but Claire tugged at my arm and pulled me back to the now.

"Can we get the money?" She pointed to the food.

I nodded. I was hungry too.

We got out of the pool and walked to our locker. Maybe Sam was sick; maybe that's why we couldn't find him. I pointed to the slide—a couple of boys were waiting in line—but Claire shook her head; he wasn't one of them.

I gave Claire the money and had her walk back to the pool with me, so she could see where I would be watching her from. I was going to be in the pool, in the deep end, but I could see the concession stand without any problem. After I gave her my order—a hot dog with ketchup, water, and potato chips—I let her get in line. It was long, but it seemed to be moving quickly. The pool was warm, and it was pleasant treading water and watching her. After about five minutes Claire was at the front. I scanned around for a place for us to eat—somewhere away from the crowds. There was a small tree by the fence—it was secluded; we'd sit there. It was near the parking lot, but I didn't mind. I got out of the pool, grabbed my towel, and walked toward Claire. If I timed it just right, our food would be ready to scoop up as soon as I got there—it was perfect. But perfect didn't happen. What happened next can only be described by one word: disaster.

As soon as Claire saw me walking toward her, she screamed out my name and yelled, "I FOUND HIM! HE'S HERE! IT'S SAM! HE'S RIGHT HERE!"

I froze. Everyone in line looked at Claire and then at me. Now what?

"LOOK!" yelled Claire. "He's making our hot dogs!" She bounced up and down and pointed to the other side of the counter. My throat felt dry, my ears burned, my stomach felt sick, and more than anything I wished I was invisible. I forced my feet forward, but it wasn't easy. What I really wanted to do was turn, run in the opposite direction, and jump back into the pool. How long could a person hide under water? I made myself move forward, until I was finally standing there—next to Claire.

"Hi, Ash!" said a voice.

It was a girl's voice, someone behind me. I turned and looked. The girl was taller than me—blue shorts, white top, and short wet hair. I had no idea who she was, but she knew me. I knew I should say more, chat with her, be friendly, but I couldn't. I fake-smiled, mumbled hello, and then turned back to Claire. Great, now I had her to worry about too. I grabbed Claire's shoulders and held them—for support, and so she'd stop bouncing. Her energy was making me crazy, but mostly I needed her to be quiet, so I could have a moment to think. But quiet was impossible.

"SEE, I FOUND SAM JUST LIKE YOU WANTED ME TO!" shouted Claire. She looked up at me proudly and pointed across the counter. I cringed. Now everyone knew I was looking for him. And worse—he did too! But she was right, it was Sam. He was standing behind the counter, putting hot dogs into buns. Why was he here? I looked down at my feet, but that only made me feel worse. I'd forgotten about Claire's painting job; my toenails were embarrassing—a nuclear disaster. I should have fixed them. When I looked up again, Sam was standing in front of us, grinning.

"Two hot dogs, two potato chips, one water, one

lemonade, and an ice cream sandwich. Is that right?" he asked.

Claire leaned forward on the counter. "Why are you working here?"

I picked up the hot dogs and chips as fast as I could. I didn't want to chitchat, plus now the line behind us was huge.

"Keep it moving! Stop talking to your girlfriend!" shouted a boy from the kitchen.

"I'm not his girlfriend!" answered Claire.

Sam shook his head. "Ignore him. It's my brother."

I didn't know Sam had a brother. I stole a look. He was older than Sam, definitely a teenager.

"Ash," said Sam.

That surprised me. Him saying my name like that. I blushed.

"I'm finished at one; that's in ten minutes. Do you guys have a plan? Where are you eating?"

For a second my brain went blank, but then I remembered, yes! There was a plan. We had one. Claire held the drinks, and I picked up the ice cream sandwich. We had everything; we could leave. I motioned toward the parking lot with my head.

"We're going to be over there by the small tree."

Sam nodded and turned back toward the kitchen.

And then my feet were moving, without me even thinking of where we were going, and so fast that Claire had to run to keep up. I was in shock.

We got to our spot and sat down. Right away Claire started eating, but I couldn't. My emotions were catching up with my body. I felt dizzy, queasy, embarrassed, and tired all at once.

Claire pointed to my hot dog. "Are you going to eat that? Can I have it?"

I nodded. A few chips and water—that was all I was going to be able to manage. I closed my eyes and lay back on the ground. We were in the shade, but the air was warm and still, and if Claire had stopped talking, I could have almost fallen asleep.

"HI, SAM!"

I bolted up. Sam was standing beside us. How had he done that? I hadn't even heard him coming. He was like a ninja. He plopped down between us—not so ninja-like anymore.

"I brought nachos and fries." He held them up. "I get them for free."

Claire leaned over and grabbed a handful of french fries. For a little kid she could really eat a lot of food. I took a chip—mostly to be polite. But it's hard to eat just one of those things. Once your tongue has tasted the deliciousness of nacho, it always wants more. I ended up eating half of them, but Sam didn't seem to mind. He had a lot of other stuff to eat—a burger, a pretzel, a milkshake, and a doughnut.

Claire had a lot of questions for Sam. I thought that might get annoying, but he didn't seem to care. He was good with little kids, and he answered them all. I was happy to listen; you can learn a lot by listening.

Claire asked about the concession stand.

"Normally they don't let kids like me do it, but Gary's working there, so they're letting me try it out. And if I do a good job, then next year I can work more hours."

Claire asked about Gary.

"He's my brother. He's sixteen. He's okay, but sometimes he's not."

Claire asked about working.

"I'm saving up for a car. As soon as I turn sixteen, I'm going to get one."

That surprised me. I'd never met anyone who was saving up for something that far in advance—something they couldn't even use yet.

After that Claire switched to detective mode and started asking about Miss Sato and Mr. Gripes.

Claire asked about why they didn't like each other.

"I don't know."

Claire asked about how they met.

"I think Miss Sato used to live next door to Mr. Gripes."

Claire asked about what they liked to do. But before Sam could answer, I asked my own question. I couldn't wait anymore—I had to know.

"Did you find out about the building name on the slide?"

Sam held up his hand for me to wait. He reached into his pocket, pulled out a small slip of paper, and waved it in the air. "I wrote it down so I wouldn't forget."

I held my breath.

He looked at the paper, squinted, and then said, "Anderson's."

I gasped and covered my mouth. Both Sam and Claire were staring at me.

Sam looked confused. "Is that what you thought it was?"

I nodded but couldn't explain. I couldn't say, *I saw it on one of my trips, while I was time traveling to somewhere that is REAL and that MISS SATO KNOWS ABOUT.* That's the kind of thing a crazy person would say. I knew what was coming next; I got ready.

Sam put down his milkshake and studied me. "How did you know?"

I took a deep breath, looked right at his face, and answered him. It was a big fat lie, and I told it perfectly. "I think they filmed a movie there. I saw that building in a movie, but I can't remember what the movie was called."

I crossed my fingers, hoping he'd believe me.

He nodded and picked up his milkshake again. "Too bad. I bet Miss Sato would like to see that movie."

I nodded, agreeing with him. It was scary and impressive, how good I was getting at lying. Feeling confident, I continued.

"If I remember the name of the movie, I'll tell you." I paused for a second, uncertain whether to ask or not, but I had to. I cleared my throat and tried to sound calm. It was the opposite of how I was feeling. "Do you think you could ask Miss Sato why she has that slide?"

Sam nodded. He took a long sip of his milkshake. "I'll do it on Friday; she loves talking about the pictures. Plus I need to ask her what the title of that slide is; they're all out of order."

I looked over at Claire. Did she understand that she was to blame? She smiled back. Nope. She'd forgotten about it already.

For the rest of the afternoon Sam hung around with us in the pool. We tried to teach Claire to swim, but she was resistant to everything except the dog paddle. I kind of didn't blame her—the dog paddle is efficient and easy. It was fun having an extra person there with Claire, and it made time go by much faster than normal. As we were getting ready to leave, Claire brought up the trampoline again. This time Sam invited us to come over.

"Why don't you come over tomorrow, before my neighbors get back? That way we can have it all to ourselves." He smiled.

I nodded like that was a good idea, but it didn't really matter. I wasn't planning on hanging out and jumping. I'd let Claire bounce around for a few minutes, and then we'd leave.

I picked up our towels and stuffed them into my backpack. "What time should we meet you? And where?"

Sam pulled out the small piece of paper with the "Anderson's" name on it. He wrote an address on the back, handed it to me, and tapped his watch. "Seven o'clock."

I looked at the address: 412 Melborne Lane. That was close to my house, only two blocks away. I wasn't expecting that.

"I'm close to you," said Sam.

I smiled like I'd known that all along. But it was another surprise—how did he know where I lived?

It was easy to get Claire to leave the pool. I thought she'd make a fuss, but she didn't. She said she was tired. I knew this was the truth, because usually she's pretty good at helping me pedal, but this time I had to do it all by myself.

I forced myself not to think about the Anderson's thing, but the minute I walked into my room, it consumed me. It was all I could think about. Was it a coincidence? And if it wasn't, what did that mean? Looking at the wish map didn't help. Nothing had changed from four days ago. I took out the wish jar and shook it up. The answer was in there—somewhere! Tomorrow was the last day of my basement ban—I was so close. Should I risk it? Try to sneak down now? I was tempted. I opened my door and right away heard voices in the kitchen—Mom and Claire talking. Decision made—I'd wait.

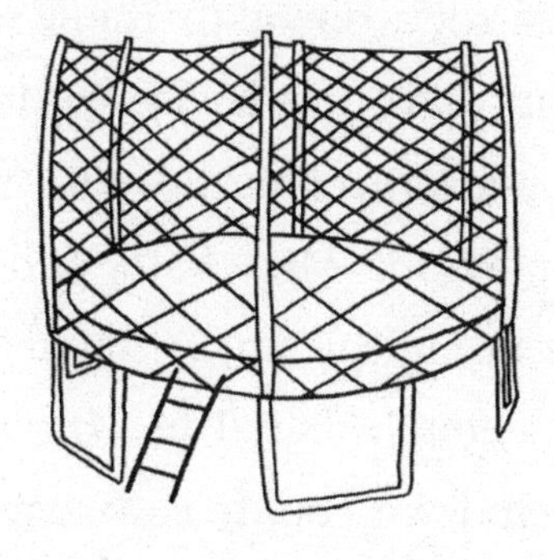

chapter twenty-six

Bounce

The first thing I did the next morning was write to Lucy. I'd saved one of the empty french fry wrappers from the pool. It was distinctive, and as soon as Lucy saw it, she'd recognize it. It had a little drawing of a pool surrounded by palm trees. Our pool didn't look anything like that—I guess it was false advertising, or hopeful dreaming. Lucy was going to be surprised when she saw the wrapper. I'd never been to the pool without her. The french fry wrapper wasn't very big, so there wasn't much room to write, but I fit in a few sentences about teaching Claire to swim.

Claire and I rode down to the VS Depot after lunch. We didn't have much else to do. Claire was still waiting for me to come up with some kind of brilliant love plan for Miss Sato and Mr. Gripes. Every time she brought it up, I changed the subject. I wasn't brave enough to tell her the truth—that it was hopeless, and we couldn't do anything. When we got to the store, Claire disappeared inside ahead of me. There wasn't anything unusual about that, but when I went inside, I couldn't find her. Peter was at the counter, but there was no Claire. He shook his head when I asked him if he'd seen her. That was strange—I'd seen her go in. Peter and I both called her name, but she didn't answer. Now I was nervous.

Peter started toward the back of the store. "I'll check the back, and you look out front again."

I ran to look. Claire was definitely not out front—I felt sick. When I rushed back inside to tell Peter, she was there, standing next to him.

"She was outside the back door." Peter patted her on the arm. "She must have passed through the store without me seeing her." Claire seemed fine and even smiled at me. But I was furious, and I couldn't keep my feelings inside. I shouted at her.

"DON'T EVER RUN OFF AGAIN!"

She looked surprised. "I didn't run off. I was just outside. Looking for Peter."

It was a big misunderstanding, I could see that, but somehow I was still mad. I knew I should stop, take deep breaths, hold my words in, but I couldn't. They spilled out, loud and strong.

"You have to stay with me! And not run away! EVER! Do you understand?"

Claire looked like she might cry. I instantly felt bad.

"I wouldn't run away," she whimpered. "I'd never do that. I'm not like . . ." She stopped and was quiet.

I froze. I knew who she was thinking about. Peter was bent down behind the counter, maybe looking for something, or maybe hiding. It's not fun to watch people fight. I walked over to Claire to apologize.

"I'm sorry for yelling. Are you okay?"

She nodded and sniffed. I put the french fry wrapper on the counter. Peter was standing up again. I guess he could tell that the worst was over. I was embarrassed. I couldn't look at him, but I forced myself to chitchat for Claire's sake—to distract her, so she'd stop thinking about her mom.

"Claire did a great job learning to swim yesterday! You should have seen her. She was amazing." I looked at Claire, but I couldn't tell if it was working.

Peter walked over, stood in front of her, and put both of his hands on the counter. "So Claire, tell me. Did you swim like a goldfish?"

He was trying to help. Claire shrugged and said, "My mom ran away once, but it was for a reason. It was a love reason. She was in love with . . ." She paused for a moment, looked around, and said, "Roman Helvetica. He was from Paris. They were in love. Real love."

Peter looked sad for a moment but then smiled.

"That's a beautiful love story, but are you trying to avoid my swimming question? Because if you swam like a goldfish, I have a surprise for you."

Claire perked up a little and gave me a quick glance. I forced a smile, but I was thinking about what she had said. Who was Roman Helvetica? Was it true? Mom hadn't said anything about a romance.

"I swam like a goldfish," said Claire. She shot me another glance, and I nodded. I wasn't going to disagree with her.

"I thought so," said Peter. He slapped his hand against the counter and turned around. "I'll be right back."

He walked to the back of the store and disappeared. Claire and I waited in silence—it seemed like forever. Finally he was back. He handed Claire a large envelope. She opened it and squealed.

"LOOK, ASH! LOOK! IT'S STEVE!" She was bouncing up and down. It was Claire being back to normal. I smiled and looked at the pad of paper. It was similar to the other pads Peter had given her, only at the top of this one was a drawing of Steve. How had he done that? Peter answered my question before I even asked it.

"I used some of the drawings you left here the other day. It's not hard to do."

Claire was bouncing up and down and singing. "I love it! I love it! I love it!" She squealed and ran around the counter to give Peter a hug.

I was confused. How had he done this so fast? It was almost like magic. I had to ask.

"How did you have it ready, special for today?"

Peter shook his head. "It wasn't for today. It was just for sometime—and today seemed like the right sometime."

I nodded. He was right about that.

I looked down at the ground, embarrassed. It's not always easy to look people in the face, but Peter deserved it—he'd saved me. I forced my eyes up and said, "Thank you."

Peter nodded and winked.

Claire was happy all the way home, and as soon as we parked the bike, she ran in to show Mom her new pad of paper. I wanted to ask Mom about Claire's story, but I couldn't get her alone without Claire around.

After dinner I got some things together for the trampoline excursion. I wanted to make it special, to make up for this afternoon. I was lucky; Claire hadn't told Mom about me yelling at her. I would have gotten in trouble for that. Mom is not a fan of yelling.

While I was waiting for six thirty to turn into seven o'clock, I read my new postcard from Lucy. She'd gotten the party hat, but not the coconut. I didn't like how postcards took so long. The party hat was ages ago. I wanted to hear about the coconut. She asked about Peter again, but I had done a bad job at getting more information. I hadn't even thought about it while we were there today. Lucy said she and her friend Claire were practicing some kind of dance for the talent show. I was going to miss it, because it was the Saturday before I got there. It was a nice postcard, but it didn't make me feel excited about camp. It was strange, but it made me sad. It was like we were living on two different islands, and the postcards were a crummy bridge. Mostly that was my fault; I wasn't telling Lucy about everything that was happening. But it was too hard; I just couldn't write, *Oh, yeah, and I've been time traveling* on a postcard.

Mom wasn't too crazy about the trampoline outing, but when I told her it was only a few blocks away, she relaxed. It helped that she thought Sam and I knew each other better than we did. She didn't need to know the truth—that we'd only met recently. That kind of thing would make her nervous and maybe make her change her mind.

Claire and I walked to Sam's house, because Mom didn't want us riding the bike home in the dark. We passed Lucy's house on the way. Claire asked if it made me sad, just looking at the house. I nodded. I didn't want to talk about it.

Sam's house was bigger than I was expecting. I don't know why, but I always expect friends' houses to be the same as mine. I was hoping that Sam's older brother didn't answer the door, because he hadn't seemed that friendly at the concession stand, but I didn't have to worry—it was Sam. He didn't invite us in; instead he grabbed his backpack, and we walked around his house to the backyard. There was something strange about it—like we were being sneaky.

“This way,” whispered Sam, and we followed him through the bushes to the yard next door.

As soon as Claire saw the trampoline, she was off and running. Sam was fast too. He caught up with her before she stepped on the ladder. I was glad to see that it had a net; I'd promised Mom that it would.

“There are a couple of rules.” Sam was standing in front of the ladder, forcing Claire to listen. “You have to take your shoes off, and you can't scream.”

It took Claire about two seconds to take off her shoes and promise not to scream, and then she was up and bouncing.

“Come on.” Sam pulled off his shoes. “Let's get on too. It's better with more people.”

I was about to say no but changed my mind—maybe I'd try it, just for a few minutes. Once I got up there, I was surprised; it was a lot more fun than I thought it would be. The bouncing was fun, but superbouncing was the best. To give someone a superbounce, you bounced right next to them just as they were landing. If you did it right, your bounce sent them up in the air extra high. We had to be careful with Claire, because she was smaller than us. I didn't want to superbounce her right over the net and into the bushes. Plus when she went superhigh, she screamed, and Sam didn't want that. That was the hardest part, to be quiet while we were having fun.

Sam knew a ton of trampoline games, and we pretty much tried them all. When it started to get dark, I brought out the light sticks. Originally I was just going to give them to Claire, but since we were all jumping, we shared them. It was a full moon, so the light sticks didn't look as cool as I'd thought they would, but no one seemed to mind.

After the jumping, I brought out the snacks and we sat on the trampoline and had Goldfish crackers and apple juice. It wasn't anything special, but it was nice to have snacks. I looked over at Sam; he tossed a Goldfish at Claire, and she tried to catch it in her mouth but missed.

I had a question for him. Something I'd been thinking about since we'd arrived. I picked up a Goldfish and studied it until I was brave enough to ask.

I popped the Goldfish into my mouth. "Are we allowed to be here?" I glanced at Sam.

He turned and grinned. His teeth were like mini light sticks in the moonlight—supershiny—and the dark space in between the front two was even more noticeable. I wondered if mine looked the same. I held my lips together. Sam stretched his arms out and lay back on the trampoline. He was quiet, but I didn't need the words—I had my answer. We were trespassing. I wondered who the neighbors were. I almost asked, but it didn't matter. I grabbed a handful of Goldfish. Why ruin it? It was more fun this way. The secret was kind of exciting, plus we weren't hurting anything. Claire was lying down too, so I joined them and stretched myself out. I stared up into the sky. If you looked long enough, you could see new stars—tiny rewards for your patience. I sighed; the saltiness of the Goldfish, the coolness of the air, the moon, the stars—it was all perfect.

Sam had lied to me, or at least tricked me. I should have been mad, but I wasn't. The truth would have kept me away, and that would have been sad. I would have missed this. And right now, with the universe open in front of me, I was happy.

"Look," said Claire. "It's a whole moon." She pointed.

I smiled. "It's called a full moon."

"Strange things happen on full moons," said Sam.

I shot him a glance. I didn't like spooky stories, plus I didn't want Claire to get scared.

Claire sat up. "Like what? Like secret things?"

"Sure," said Sam. "Or secrets. Do you have one?"

Claire was quiet for a minute. It made me nervous. I didn't want her to talk about her mom. That was probably more than any of us could handle. I touched her arm. "The secret doesn't have to be about you." I smiled, hoping she understood.

"Oh, okay." She smiled back at me, leaned over toward Sam, and whispered, "My secret is that Ash has face blindness."

"Wait! NO!" It was too late. Now it was there—out in the open—impossible to ignore.

Sam sat up. "What's face blindness?"

He was studying me. Probably looking for it, this thing he'd missed, this thing that was there but he couldn't see. I hated this part, the explaining it. It was embarrassing and dumb. Face blindness—it sounded like something I was making up. At least it had a medical name—prosopagnosia. I liked using that better; it sounded more tragic and impressive.

Claire jumped in and gave Sam a quick explanation. "She can't recognize faces, but if you're staying at her house, she can, and she'll probably know you."

It wasn't bad if you already knew what face blindness was, but for Sam it was totally not helpful. He was still confused.

He looked over at me. "So it's a real thing?"

I nodded, and even though I didn't want to, I gave him the whole explanation. When I was done talking, he shook his head. That wasn't unusual; my problem was hard to believe.

"Is that why you ignored Megan Webber yesterday?" He asked.

Now I was confused.

"At the pool, in the line. She was standing behind you. She said you totally ignored her."

I thought back to the pool and dropped my head in my hands. Of course, that's who it was. The girl behind me with the wet hair was Megan. Now I felt bad. Megan was always nice and friendly; well, that was finished. She'd probably never talk to me again.

"I told her you were stressed out. I think she bought it." Sam grabbed a few Goldfish, threw them up, and caught them in his mouth. "You seemed pretty stressed."

I nodded. Why was he being so nice?

"That stinks!" Sam shook his head again. "Instead of a superpower, you have an invisible nonpower."

He thought for a minute, smiled, and said, "I bet you love Halloween."

"Why?" I asked.

Sam pointed at me. "It's the one day where everyone

is exactly like you. Nobody knows who anybody is."

He was right. I'd never thought of that before.

Claire was excited to have a new topic. "Last year I was an evil cat. But I don't know what I'm going to be this year." She looked at us and shrugged.

Sam and I both said it, at the exact same time, like we'd practiced, but of course we hadn't.

"Goldfish!"

Sam walked us home. I was surprised about that but didn't say no when he offered. He wasn't any different from before—even though now he knew my secret.

When we got to my house, he turned and said, "See you tomorrow."

It took me a second to remember that tomorrow was craft day again. A whole week had gone by already—that was hard to believe.

Claire wanted to wave at Sam until she couldn't see him anymore, so I waited with her, standing on the sidewalk, until he turned the corner.

She looked up at me. "I like full moons. They're fun."

I nodded. Claire reached up and held my hand. It was the first time she'd ever done that, and she held it tight until we were all the way into the house. It was nice, but nice really wasn't the right word to describe it. It was more important than just nice; it was a gift.

That night, after Claire went to bed, I asked Mom about Roman Helvetica. She said the name sounded familiar, but she was pretty sure it had nothing to do with Claire's mom.

I shook my head. "Do you think she made him up? Why would she do that?"

Mom thought for a minute. "Maybe it's easier for her if she has a story."

Mom said I could come to her room to talk more, but I was too tired to even try. It must have been the bouncing on the trampoline. It was probably more exercise than I thought it was.

I didn't want to think about Claire's mom. But now she was there, floating around in my brain. Who does that? Just leaves their family. No wonder Claire had a story. I pulled out my book, glad to be distracted, but after a few minutes of reading I had a feeling I was just trading one storyteller for another. I hadn't noticed it before, but Claire was a little bit like Percy.

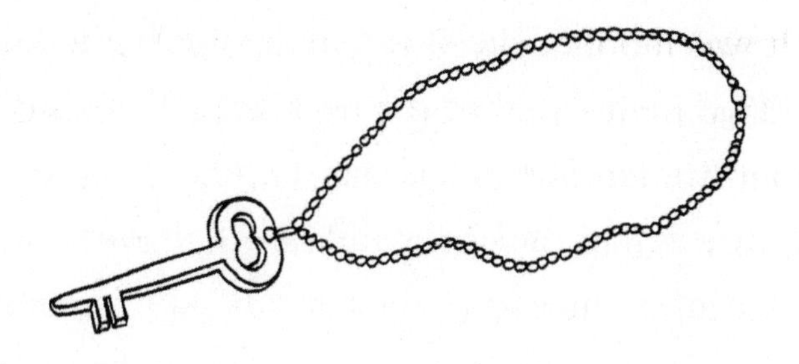

chapter twenty-seven

Like

When I came down for breakfast, Mom was waiting for me.

"Here." She took my hand and pressed something into it. It was an old-fashioned key on a pretty silver chain.

I was surprised. "What's this for?"

"It's symbolic," she said. "Because your week is up for the basement. I don't understand why you want to go down there, but if it's important to you, I'm . . ." She paused for a minute and then added, "Fine with it."

I didn't know what to say.

Suddenly Mom seemed uncomfortable, like she was worried that she was making too big a deal out of this. She pointed to the necklace. "You don't have to wear it, but you can if you want."

I untangled the chain and pulled it over my head. It was long; the end of the key landed just above my belly button. I straightened up and looked down. I liked it. Mom started again.

"It's mostly a thank-you, for this week. For everything you've done with Claire. She's having a great time. Younger girls really look up to older girls. When I was young I . . ."

I shifted my weight and looked down. Mom stopped talking.

I looked up and smiled. "I like it. It's nice."

She looked relieved. "I'm taking Claire out later. So you'll have some free time, on your own, to do . . ."

I nodded. I knew exactly what I was going to do. Mom waited a few seconds to see if I had anything to say, but when I was quiet, she continued.

"We'll be back for lunch, because you have the craft thing this afternoon."

I hadn't forgotten about it. In fact, I was kind of looking forward to it. Mom would have been surprised about that. We stood there for a few seconds, kind of awkwardly, and then I stepped forward and gave her a hug. Suddenly two more arms were around us.

"GROUP HUG!" shouted Claire.

It was exactly what we needed—seven-year-old joy.

Mom and Claire left about two hours later. I worried all morning that something would happen to stop them from going—a stomachache, a flat tire, a freak windstorm—but nothing did. I tried to act calm and normal, but I couldn't wait for them to leave. The second the car pulled out of the driveway, I ran up to my room, pulled one of the Anderson's wishes off the wish map, and grabbed the wish jar. It had been a while since I'd held it—my hands trembled. I tried not to think of the negatives, but they followed me down to the basement. *What if the jar was broken? What if the wishes didn't work? What if asking Sam about Anderson's had ruined everything?*

I had to find out. I couldn't wait. I sat on the chair, reached into the jar, and pulled out a wish. There was no swirling of balls, no meditating on the choice, and no closing of eyes. I held my breath and unfurled the paper, and as each word appeared, I read it out loud.

I Wish Summer Wasn't So Boring

Suddenly I was gone, and instead of being in the

basement, I was with Shue, in her room. She was sitting on her bed, looking down at her hands. But in this first minute of being there, I didn't care about her. It was all about me.

"PURPLE PLATYPUS!" I shouted and jumped in the air. It was a celebration. The wish jar had worked!

If I was ecstatic, Shue was the exact opposite. She looked sad and droopy. I missed it at first, but her lips were moving. She was singing. It started out quietly, but as the seconds ticked by, she got louder and louder. I didn't recognize the song. The lyrics were unusual—a mix-up of sad, happy, and silly. What kind of song talks about eating muffins? And then I got it—she was making it up. The more she sang, the more animated she became. She wasn't sitting on the side of the bed anymore—now she was dancing around the room.

She swung her arms and leaped into the air, but she misjudged the landing part and crashed into her dresser. I laughed—she was the opposite of graceful. But she didn't care; she continued without stopping. She pulled a dress from her closet. Now she was singing about love, and the dress was her prince. He spun above her head, wiped out a row of stuffed animals from the top of the desk, and knocked over the chair, and landed in a heap on the floor. The romance was over. Shue bounced on the bed, still singing, but now I couldn't understand the words. It was hard to believe that this was the same Shue as before. She was so crazy and funny. Finally she collapsed on the bed, lay still, and stared up at the ceiling. What was she thinking? I walked forward, but it was over. I was fading away.

I was back in my chair. I rubbed the chair's arms. I liked this chair. What a strange time machine. I smiled; that had been a good wish, one of the best, but where was Ash? Shue's song had been about everything—her parents, her boring summer, her room, her pretend prince, and even what she'd had for breakfast—but there'd been nothing about Ash. Why hadn't she mentioned her? I tried to remember if I'd seen Ash's drawing taped to the mirror. I hadn't. The mirror had been clean. I smiled—I was a good detective.

Now I wanted to try something new. It was risky, but I needed to know. Could a wish work twice? I wanted to go back to Anderson's. See if I'd missed anything—pay more attention. I pulled the used wish out of my pocket and rolled it into a ball. It was my favorite Anderson's wish. I placed it in the jar, careful to keep my eye on it, and then pulled it back out. I opened it and read the words.

I Wish Anderson's Was Always Good

I was ready to go, but nothing happened. I was still in my chair. It hadn't worked. I panicked and quickly picked out a new wish, hoping I hadn't broken anything. As soon as I read the words, I was gone.

I Never Want School to Start

When I arrived in Ashley's bedroom, I was smiling. Shue and Ashley were sitting on Ashley's bed; they were talking. I tuned them out to think of a test word. It was getting harder to think of new colors—I'd have to research that, so I'd be ready for next time. It took me a few seconds, but finally I had one.

"Gold monkey." I said it and walked toward the girls. They were still talking.

"Once school starts, things will be different," said Ashley. She was smoothing out a little piece of paper against her leg.

Shue fiddled with her shoelaces. "No it won't." She tied a double knot.

Ashley shook her head. "I'll be in high school, and you'll still be in middle school."

I could tell that Ashley thought this was enough

of an explanation, but Shue was still confused. Ashley glanced around the room like she was looking for help, but there was no one else—just them and me, and I didn't count.

Ashley folded up the paper. "I'll be busy with school. Plus our schools are in different places."

Shue thought for a moment and then brightened. "But you live only two houses away, so I'll still see you all the time."

"Maybe, but it won't be the same. You'll be with your middle school friends, and I'll have friends too."

Shue wasn't giving up. "But it's only a year. Next year I'll be in high school too. We can walk to school together."

"Okay." Ashley sighed. I could tell she wasn't agreeing with Shue, but she was giving up.

Shue held up the little charm on the end of her necklace and looked at Ashley. "Friends forever."

I hadn't noticed it before, but both girls were wearing the exact same necklace—a silver half circle on a silver chain.

Ashley tapped her half circle against Shue's charm. "Friends." She frowned and picked something up off the bed. It was the yellow duck. She held it up and made a quacking sound. "I found it really fast this time."

I looked over at her closet. There was a pile of clothes on the floor, and the shelf where I'd seen Shue hide the duck was empty. Shue nodded. She seemed sad. Was she upset about the duck? And then I realized it wasn't the duck—it was the promise. Ashley hadn't said "forever." A moment later I was gone. This time it wasn't a slow fade back to reality; it was more like a lightning strike—fast, electric, and slightly painful. I hated the painful comebacks, but now I had a feeling about them. It wasn't something I wanted to test, but if I kept reading wishes, I'd find out. I hoped I was wrong, because I knew they were in there—the bad wishes, the ones where Ashley and Shue were fighting—and so far those were the ones that hurt.

I gripped the arms of the chair and shuddered. Suddenly I heard noises upstairs. Mom and Claire were home. Maybe that's why I'd come back so fast. I put the used wishes in my pocket and hid the jar. As an afterthought I grabbed a notebook off the bench and carried it upstairs with me. It was blank and missing a page, but that didn't matter—it was a perfect prop.

Mom didn't say anything when I came up from the basement, but I knew that look—she was curious.

I motioned toward the notebook.

"I'm writing a story, and I like that chair down there. It's perfect for thinking."

She was surprised.

"A story? That's great." And then she nodded as if suddenly everything made sense. "Well, let's make sure you get some time to work on it."

I smiled. The notebook had worked even better than I'd thought it would. Instead of a one-time ticket, I had a lifetime pass.

"The light down there is terrible." Mom shook her head. "I should get you a better light."

"NO!" I panicked. She couldn't touch anything. Everything had to stay the same. "The light's good. I like it. Don't touch anything, please!"

Mom nodded, but I could tell it was only temporary. She liked makeovers. Great, now there was something new to worry about.

Claire couldn't wait to get to the old people's home. She had a big plan: she was going to interview both Miss Sato and Mr. Gripes.

"I'm going to find out how to make them fall in love again."

It was brave of her to want to interview Mr. Gripes. I told her she could have fifteen extra minutes after the craft event. It was good to put a time limit on it—an interview with Claire had the potential to go on for hours.

We rode the trailer bike to the old people's home. Sam's bike was already there; it was strange, but just seeing it made me happy. The minute we walked into the craft room, I could tell that something was wrong. Sam was standing there waiting for us, and as soon as he saw me, he grabbed my arm and pulled me into the hall. Claire wanted to follow, but I made her stay with Marjorie and help set up the supplies for frame painting.

As soon as we stepped out of the craft room, Sam said, "Miss Sato had a stroke on Wednesday, and she's in the hospital."

There was no warning, he just blurted it out. I didn't know what to say. He rubbed his hands together and looked at the floor. I followed his gaze; he was shuffling his feet. I knew how that felt—I hated that nervous energy. I didn't know anything about strokes, only that they were bad. Could people die from a stroke? Yes, I thought so.

"Is it bad?"

Sam nodded. I thought that would be it, but he let out a sigh and said, "She can't talk, or move, and Mr.

Gripes is with her at the hospital."

Sam looked lost. I wanted to help, but what could I do? Should I say something? What if I made things worse? Was it better to say nothing? It was making me nervous, both of us standing there together, being quiet. I had to break the silence.

I didn't know if it was the wrong thing to do, but I asked him anyway. "Do you want to paint frames with us?"

After a moment Sam nodded and followed me back into the craft room. As soon as I saw Claire, I froze. We couldn't tell her the truth. She'd be devastated. I turned to Sam.

"We can't tell Claire the truth. It will scare her."

Sam nodded. This wasn't going to be easy.

Painting the frames turned out to be okay. Sam wasn't as talkative as usual, but I think I was the only one who noticed. Claire was, of course, disappointed, sad, and full of questions when she found out about Miss Sato. The story ended up being that Miss Sato had to go to the hospital for a stomachache. I couldn't decide if that was a good lie, a bad lie, or even the right thing to do. But I didn't get away with it—the universe punished me. My frame was a disaster. I couldn't concentrate with Sam sitting next to me. I tried to paint a cat but ended up with a blob with pointy ears. At least it was something to joke about, and by the end, Sam seemed more like his regular self.

We left before Sam did. He had to wait around for Mr. Fred to get back from the hospital. I thought his job might be canceled, but he said Mr. Fred was going to help him finish the slide show.

Claire and I rode home in record time. I was riding away from the sadness, and she just wanted to go fast. For the first time since he'd left, I started missing Dad. It wasn't like I hadn't missed him all along, but now for some reason it was worse. He called every night, and usually I didn't talk to him—mostly Mom just gave me an update—but tonight was different; I wanted to hear his voice.

After dinner, and after talking to Dad—for only one minute, because he had to rush off to a meeting—I went upstairs. I still had the morning's wishes in my pocket. I pulled them out, found where they went on the wish map, and taped them down. After everything was cleaned up, I flopped down on my bed. Poor Shue; Ashley was up to something. I was watching the girls, but did I really know them? If I met them in real life, would I like them? Would they like me? Would we be friends? I pulled out my book but didn't open it. I tapped the cover, making myself decide. Shue was easy. She was nice, funny, and trustworthy. We'd be friends. But Ashley was a toss-up. I wasn't so sure. I'd have to wait and see. I opened the book; it had gotten a lot better. I was liking it again. In fact, I was liking a lot of things lately.

chapter twenty-eight

I didn't get up early like I wanted to—that meant no basement. When I came downstairs, Mom was already in the kitchen making pancakes. I was getting sick of the smell of them. I looked around but didn't see Claire. "Where's Claire?"

Mom pointed upstairs. "Still sleeping."

"Are you having pancakes?" She had a stack of three or four already made, and there was another one cooking in the pan. I hoped they weren't for me. I'd had enough pancakes for a year.

Mom shook her head. "No, they're for Claire, when she wakes up." She pointed to the stack on the counter. "All you have to do is heat them up for her in the microwave. I'll be gone for most of the day. Sonia and I have a few flea markets to go to, and I'm helping her move around some furniture."

Sonia was Mom's junk-shopping friend. I was glad she had Sonia; it meant she didn't try to drag me along with her.

I put my notebook down on the table, walked to the fridge, and grabbed a yogurt. "When are you coming back?"

Mom looked at her watch and counted in her head. I knew what that meant—she'd be gone for a while.

She looked up. "Definitely for dinner, but probably sooner."

I nodded. It didn't matter much. Apart from going to the basement and mailing Lucy's frame, I didn't have any plans. The cat painting from yesterday still looked bad, but I'd written the words BLOB WITH POINTY EARS underneath it, and somehow that made it better. Now it looked like it was bad on purpose. Too bad you couldn't fix all mistakes with captions. Mom dropped the pan into the sink, interrupting my thinking. I looked up.

"If you want to go downstairs and work for an

hour or so, I can be here in case Claire wakes up. I'll just call Sonia."

It didn't make sense. Why was she changing her plans? I was going to say something but caught myself. Mom was looking at my notebook. She was changing her plans for me.

I grabbed a pen out of the drawer and walked toward the basement door. "Thanks," I said. "It'll be good to write some notes."

Mom nodded, looking pleased. I opened the door and started down to the basement; halfway there I remembered the notebook—I'd left it on the table. I rushed back upstairs to get it. Mom was at the sink—too busy to notice me. I grabbed it and snuck back out the door. If I had time, who knows, maybe I'd even write something.

It felt good to be back in the basement, and for the first time ever it was worry free. I had an hour to myself, and no one was going to stop me. It felt like a gift. I grabbed the wish jar and pulled out a wish. If I was fast, maybe I could get through three. I opened it and read it.

Please Make Spencer Be Wrong

Shue was standing at Ashley's front door—I recognized it. She was knocking. The door opened and it was Spencer; I recognized him, too. I was getting good at this. I moved toward them and said my test words.

"Bronze pig." I had a feeling about this wish—it didn't seem like a good one. It was going to hurt to go home. I shivered just thinking about it. I forced the thought out of my head and turned my attention back to Spencer and Shue.

Spencer looked unhappy. Shue sensed it—she took a step back.

He shook his head. "Ashley's not here. She's out with Pam and Cathy."

Shue looked down and turned to go. Spencer called after her. "You should forget about her—she's a bad friend."

Shue took a few more steps away, but then turned and looked back at Spencer.

"She's just busy. It's school." She waved awkwardly, and was gone.

And so was I—back in my chair, but not before passing through what felt like an electrical fence. It was fast, but not fast enough to be painless. I shook my hands, like the pain was water, trying to get rid of every last drop.

It was the shortest wish ever, but two important

things had happened, and they were both bad. The first was good to know but bad to experience. I had been right about the pain. When something bad happened to Ashley and Shue, I felt it too—it was like we were connected. The wishes weren't free; they had a price.

The second thing was worse. It was more of a forever thing, and it made me sad. I was starting to not like Ashley. I pulled a paper ball from the jar and held it in the air. This had better be a happy one! I was threatening the universe. I just hoped the universe was listening.

I Wish We Could Always Make Surprise Pies

"Silver tiger." I said my test words as soon as I saw the girls. I glared at Ashley. Why was she so mean? We were all standing in a kitchen. The girls were at the counter laughing—at least that was a good start.

Shue looked over at Ashley; she seemed a little nervous. "I've never made these before."

Ashley laughed. "That's because I invented them. You'll like it—it's fun."

On the counter in front of the girls were rolling pins, metal baking sheets, a bowl full of dough, and a bag of flour. They were making something—probably surprise pies like it said on the wish.

Shue looked around. "What do we put inside?"

Ashley smiled. "That's the good part. It can be anything we like, except for disgusting things that no one will eat. My mom will get mad if we waste the dough." She moved toward the cupboard. "Let's get things out."

Soon there was a large pile on the kitchen table. I couldn't see everything, but there was chocolate sauce, butterscotch sauce, marshmallows, chocolates, a bunch of different jams, applesauce, and lots of candy.

The idea was pretty easy. Roll out the dough, cut out a small circle, put something in the middle of the circle, fold the circle in half, and then crimp the edges of the half circle with a fork. Now I understood the surprise part—it was impossible to know what was in the middle of the pie until you ate it. What a fun idea. I was glad Ashley was being nice to Shue. When Shue had trouble with the rolling pin, Ashley was patient and showed her exactly what to do. Why couldn't she always be nice like this?

Suddenly Shue was laughing. I looked over; she had put a lollipop in the center of one of the dough circles and was folding it up.

Ashley clapped her hands. "I love it! Let's make

three more, so we can all have one."

"It's a pie-cycle," said Shue, and she laughed again.

Pie-cycle! I liked it too.

I wanted to stay, watch more, but it wasn't my choice. Slowly I faded away, and then I was home.

I grabbed another wish from the jar. I was power wishing—cramming as many wishes into an hour as I could.

I opened it, read it, and was gone again.

Please Be True Forever

I was in Shue's room. She was sitting on her bed holding something. Why was she always sitting on her bed? I looked around the room—there was a chair, but it was piled high with clothes. I guess that was the answer.

"Amber otter." I whispered my test words and walked over to her. The ugly duck head and body were on the bed beside her, detached. She was holding a piece of paper, probably the note from inside. She smoothed the paper out and held it up. It was almost like she was doing it for me—so I could read it. Of course she wasn't, but it was nice to pretend. It made it seem like less of a one-way relationship. I thought about the girls constantly and they didn't even know I existed. The handwriting on the note was Ashley's. It said, "I'm glad we are friends." No wonder Shue was smiling. She folded the paper into a square, stood up, and walked toward her desk. But I didn't see her get there; I had faded away.

I smiled; there was no pain. Sometimes when I came back, it was like waking from a deep sleep. My brain worked, but my arms and legs felt fuzzy, and it took a few extra seconds before everything felt like it was attached. I felt groggy. Maybe it was all the back-and-forth in such a short span of time. I reached for another wish but stopped myself. I could hear Claire's voice upstairs. I was torn. To wish, or not to wish. My eyes felt heavy. Why was I so tired? I closed the jar, hid it, and put the used wishes in my pocket. Claire was singing now; I recognized the song. I dragged myself up the stairs—one step for each beat. I opened the door, and suddenly I was me again.

Walking into the kitchen was like walking out of a fog.

chapter twenty-nine

Surprise

Mom left just minutes after I came back upstairs. Claire was done with breakfast and was sitting at the table singing and drawing. As soon as she saw me, she jumped up.

"Do you think Miss Sato is better?"

I shook my head. I was hoping that that would be enough, but I was talking to Claire, so of course it wasn't. She wasn't one to give up.

"Can we call the hospital and find out?"

I pointed to her colored pencils.

"Why don't you draw her a card? Everyone likes cards. And when you're done, we'll go to the VS

Depot, and when we get home, we can make cookies."

I hadn't planned on making cookies—that had just slipped out. But now that I'd said it, I liked the idea. Maybe we could even try something different, like surprise cookies. It probably wasn't as good as surprise pies, but I couldn't make pastry. I wasn't that much of a cook.

Claire made two cards for Miss Sato. One had a big heart on the front, and the other had a picture of Steve, with a word bubble that said GET WELL SOON. They were cute, and if Miss Sato had been able to see them, I'm sure she would have liked them. It was weird to think about her lying in bed, totally unaware of everything around her. I shook my head to get rid of the thought.

Like usual, we rode to the VS Depot, and when we got there, Claire ran in ahead of me. This time I had a plan: find out more about Peter and the PJ Walker books. Maybe Lucy was right—maybe it was suspicious that he knew who PJ Walker was. But mostly it was just going to be something to talk about so I could get my head away from thinking about Miss Sato and the wishes.

Peter was behind the counter, and by the time I got up to it, Claire was too. Peter gave her some colored paper, and she ignored us, disappearing into her drawings. Peter smiled and waited patiently for what I was going to give him. What was he imagining? Something amazing? After the coconut, the frame was kind of a letdown, but it was all I had. I pulled it out and put it on the counter. He frowned and then smiled. I knew why—the frown was for the drawing, and the smile was for the caption. It was nice how the caption made the picture suddenly good.

I gave myself a countdown—three, two, one—and I started: "So, I'm liking the book now."

Peter nodded and put the frame on the scale. I continued.

"PJ Walker is such a good author, but not many people know her. How did you find out about her?"

Peter turned toward me.

"Really?" he asked. "I thought PJ Walker was quite popular."

I didn't know what to say; I nodded. This was harder than I thought it would be. I tried again.

"Have you read all her books?"

Now Peter was smiling. Why? He pushed a button, printed out the stamp, and stuck it on the frame. "What makes you think PJ Walker is a her?"

For a second I was confused. What did he mean?

Of course PJ Walker was a her—but then a second later I wasn't so sure. Did I have proof? I'd never seen an author photo, and the bios on the backs of the books never used the words *her* or *him*—they only said "author." But PJ Walker had to be a her; Viola Starr, the main character, was a girl. I shook my head, but it didn't help; the pieces didn't fall into place.

"I'm sorry," said Peter. He'd stopped smiling. "I didn't mean to confuse you."

I nodded. He held up the frame to show me where he'd put the stamp, and I nodded again.

"Maybe you're right, maybe PJ Walker is a she. But does it matter? You like the books—that's the most important thing, isn't it?"

What he was saying made sense, but it did make a difference. I didn't want PJ Walker to be a man. I liked her being a she, and I wanted it to stay that way. Claire looked up, and I motioned toward the door. It was time to go. I left without waving or looking back. I was upset. Just because something is true, it doesn't mean you want to know about it.

Claire helped pedal home, which was good, because I wasn't feeling very energetic. As we got closer, she got more and more excited about the cookies. Sometimes Claire's energy was contagious, and it filled you up like a balloon. When we got home, we parked the bike and went inside. We had a mission—cookies!

Before we started, I checked the mail. Just as I was hoping, there was a postcard from Lucy. It made me happy that we were both keeping our promise. No matter what, we sent one every second day. I was in a better mood this time, and reading about all the cool stuff she was doing made me feel excited about camp. There were only eight days left. It was hard to believe. In eight days I'd be zip-lining with Lucy.

"What kind of cookies are we going to make?" asked Claire.

I put the postcard down and smiled. I had an answer for her. "Surprise cookies!"

After we made the cookie dough, Claire and I picked out a bunch of stuff to use for the surprises. I even found some lollipops. Now we could do exactly what Shue and Ashley had done, only ours would be cookie-cycles. At first, making the surprise part was kind of hard—there's not much room in a cookie to hide anything. But after a few tries we figured out how to make it work. We made the cookies larger, and put two together with the surprise part in the middle—like a filling. Most of Claire's surprises had to do with chocolate. I was going to have to be careful when it was time to eat. Chocolate was not a surprise I wanted to bite into.

We made a lot of cookies, but my favorite was the one I made for Lucy. Even though she'd only mentioned one new friend in her letters, I knew she must have more. Why wouldn't she? Everyone loved her. She was a little like Claire—superfriendly, without the unpredictable and crazy part.

Lucy's cookie was a lot bigger than any of the other cookies. I started with a big circle of dough and then put all of Lucy's favorite stuff on top—peanut butter chips, marshmallows, M&M's, and chocolate chips. After that I took six lollipops, unwrapped them, and arranged them around the edge of the circle with their handles sticking out, and covered it all with another circle of dough. When it came out of the oven, I wasn't so sure what I thought of it, but after decorating it with icing, I was happy. The lollipop handles sticking out made it look like some kind of strange, exotic flower.

When Mom got home, she came straight into the kitchen. She was probably following her nose—the house smelled delicious.

Claire pointed to the cookies. "They're surprise cookies!"

Mom stopped moving and gasped. "How did you think of that?"

She looked at me, but I shrugged; I couldn't tell her. Mom's favorites were the ones with the lollipops in them—the cookie-cycles. What's not to like about a cookie on a stick? Claire was too excited to keep any secrets, so before Mom even had a chance to pick out a cookie to eat, Claire told her what all the fillings were. So much for the surprise part. When Mom saw Lucy's cookie she went and got her camera. I took that as a good sign.

Before I went upstairs for the night, I looked up some new color names on the computer. I didn't want to give up on my can-you-hear-me? tests, but it was getting harder and harder to think of words. Plus it was wasting wish time—me trying to think of a color, when I should have been paying attention to what was happening. It didn't take long; after only a few minutes, I had a list. I wrote them down in my notebook, and because I wanted to be extra prepared, I picked out a test word for the next wish—fuchsia cow.

It was nice to be excited about the *Have Mercy, Percy* book. I'd never had so many different feelings with a book—loving it, being annoyed by it, almost hating it, and finally loving it again. Was it on purpose? Did everyone who read it feel this way? Or was it just me? I was going to have to ask Peter about it. It would be something good to talk about, after the way we'd walked out of there today.

chapter thirty

Lucky

I brought my notebook down to breakfast with me again. I felt a little guilty about tricking Mom, but having it work was worth it.

As soon as I put the notebook on the table, Mom said, "Claire, after breakfast you and I are going to run some errands."

Claire put her head down and looked mopey. She'd been with us for only a little while, but already she knew the truth—running errands with Mom was not fun. Mom tried to make it sound exciting, but the only thing that helped was when she threw a thrift store into the mix as a reward—Claire couldn't resist a thrift store.

While Claire and Mom were getting ready to go, I went down to the basement. I still wasn't used to it—me being downstairs alone, and Mom being okay with it. Claire was doing some kind of dance routine, and it seemed like it was purposely right over my head—*thump, thump, thump.* There was no way I could do the wishes until they were gone—it was too distracting. I grabbed the notebook and wrote down some fake notes. It was probably good to have a few pages filled, just in case—even stupid-sounding notes were better than nothing. A blank book would be hard to explain. Finally the thumping stopped, and I heard the back door slam. They were gone. And then a minute later I was too.

I Wish Every Summer Would Be Like This

Ashley and Shue were lying on a roof. They were just outside a window. I peeked in—it was Ashley's room. The moon was full and the stars were out, just like it'd been for me on the trampoline. I smiled. I knew how they felt. The girls were quiet, not talking, looking up at the sky. I started to say my test word but stopped myself. Fuchsia cow was wrong; even whispered it seemed loud and garish. I ran through my list of colors for something better. It seemed silly, but it mattered; I would remember it. My memories of this wish would last forever.

The minute I thought of it, I knew it was perfect: *lavender seal*. It was beautiful and mysterious. I whispered the words and moved toward the girls.

Shue sat up and turned toward Ashley. "I got us something."

Ashley sat up. "I hope it's food—I'm starving."

Shue shook her head. "Sorry, no food. This is better." She held her hands out in front of Ashley, each one a closed fist. "Pick one."

Ashley thought for a moment and pointed to the left one. Shue opened them both. Each hand was holding the exact same thing—a silver necklace with a silver half-circle pendant.

Ashley gasped. "Really? For me? I can have it?"

Shue handed Ashley the necklace, and they put them on. I was waiting for Shue to say something cheesy about the half circles being like halves of the full moon, but she didn't. And Ashley didn't either. They just sat in silence, looking up at the stars, smiling.

When I got home, I was smiling too. I picked out another wish and read it, happy to be going back.

I Wish I Was Going to High School

Ashley and Shue were walking on the sidewalk. It

was a busy street, much busier than the other streets we'd been on. It caught me by surprise, so instead of shouting my test word, I said it quietly.

"Amber crow."

Just like before, the cars were big and old-fashioned. The girls crossed the street, walked down the block, and stopped in front of a small grocery store.

"How much do you have?" asked Ashley.

Shue put her hand into her pocket and pulled out a handful of coins. She counted them and said, "Thirty-six cents."

Ashley dumped her coins into Shue's hand. "Twenty-four cents."

Shue counted up the coins. "That's sixty cents total. So we get thirty cents each."

Ashley motioned toward the store. She looked nervous. "We should figure out what we're getting before we go in."

Shue nodded. She looked around to make sure no one else could hear her and then whispered, "They're kind of mean in there."

From the outside the store looked like a regular market, but when we got inside, I could see that I'd been wrong. The whole front of the store was filled with candy. As soon as the girls walked in, a woman rushed forward from the back of the store.

"What do you want?" she barked.

Shue was right—she was mean.

Shue pointed to some orange candy in a jar. "Four of those, please." The woman dropped the candy into a little brown paper bag; she neither smiled nor frowned—she was expressionless. Shue gave the lady the rest of her order, and when she was done, the woman shook the little bag and said, "Thirty cents!" Shue handed her the money. As soon as Ashley's order was done, the girls left the store.

They walked about halfway down the block and stopped. Shue reached into her bag, found an orange sour, and popped it into her mouth. She shook her head. "That lady makes me nervous."

Ashley nodded. She took a bite of red licorice. "Do you know what else I'm nervous about?" She didn't wait for Shue to answer. "High school." It was a nice segue.

Shue sucked loudly on her candy.

"What part?" she asked.

Ashley thought for a minute, twirling the licorice around her fingers. "Well, the friends part I guess. What if there's no one there I like?" She paused and then added, "I wish you were going too."

Shue was probably wishing the exact same thing.

When the fade-out happened, I was ready for it. The zap was short and fast, but being ready made a difference. The surprise zaps were totally different; they were bad.

I squeezed the arms of the chair and winced. It was over quickly, and the mild tingling in my arms and legs only lasted for a moment. I shook out my limbs.

Everything was quiet upstairs—Mom and Claire were still out. I sat down and picked up the jar. Should I do another wish? What if I picked out a really bad one? Would the pain be worse? I picked out a wish. I could put it down—not open it. But that was only in theory, because the truth was, once it was in my hands, there was no going back. I looked down and read it.

I Hope We Never Get Caught

As soon as I saw the Dumpster, I smiled. This was exactly what I'd wanted and been hoping for—another Anderson's wish. The girls were over by the Dumpster, but for now I ignored them. Instead I looked around, taking in the scenery, in case there was something here that I'd need later. We were in the parking lot next to the Dumpster; Anderson's was in front of us. There were buildings to the left, and a row of apartments to the right—everything looked the same as before. After one final scan, I shouted out my test words, *olive snake*, and walked toward Shue.

She looked especially grumpy.

"It's empty again," she complained.

She was wearing her special sweatshirt—the one for Dumpster diving. She pulled it off and tied it around her waist.

"We could do the rocks again," said Ashley. She pointed to the back of the building. The man's boots were there, like last time.

Shue shook her head. "That's boring. We already did that."

Ashley nodded. They shuffled their feet in the gravel and wandered off in opposite directions around the Dumpster. I followed Shue. She looped wide and walked by the apartment buildings. Suddenly she stopped. She was staring at something. I followed her gaze over the gravel parking lot and up three small steps, to the back door of one of the apartments. There were shoes in a row on each side of the door. I knew what was next—lots and lots of rocks. She turned and ran quickly back toward Ashley.

"There's a bunch of shoes over there," she whispered. She pointed to the apartments.

Ashley bent down and picked up a handful of stones.

Shue shook her head. "No, let's do something different."

I followed the girls back toward the apartments. Now that we were closer, I could see the shoes; they were mostly men's shoes except for one bright red pair of women's pumps. Shue motioned for Ashley to wait. I followed Shue as she crept up to the door. I didn't like this idea. What if someone suddenly opened the door and caught her? Shue picked up the two red shoes and waved them at Ashley, and then she was gone, sprinting toward Anderson's. I raced to keep up with her. I was right behind her. A few seconds of work and then she was done. She'd stuffed the red shoes inside the man's boots. I had only one thought—the man was going to be mad.

Ashley must have been thinking the same thing, because she said, "Let's get out of here. We can watch from my window."

Moments later we were running, and we didn't stop until we were safely in Ashley's room.

We watched for fifteen minutes before anything happened. Ashley was the first to notice something. She squealed; it reminded me of Claire. I'd never heard her do that before.

"Outside the apartment," cried Ashley. "Look! It's the lady. She's looking for her shoes."

Shue shook her head. "She's never going to find them. We should have made an arrow, or left a clue."

She looked disappointed.

Suddenly the door to Anderson's opened, and a man stepped out.

"It's him!" whispered Ashley. She ducked behind the curtain. It was the same man as before.

He looked around the parking lot, leaned forward, and tossed a box into the Dumpster. A minute later he was yelling and waving one of the red shoes around. I was glad we were watching from far away: he was kind of scary. Suddenly he threw the shoe into the Dumpster. We all gasped. I looked over at the lady; she was watching him. He grabbed his boot, turned it over to make sure there weren't any stones in it, and pulled it on. The other red shoe was in his hand; he pulled his arm back to throw it in the Dumpster but suddenly noticed the lady. She was waving and yelling at him.

Shue leaned back and turned to Ashley. "This is amazing."

Ashley nodded and smiled. "I know. Do you think he thinks she did it?"

Shue shook her head. "No, I'm pretty sure he knows it was us."

The man pulled on his other boot, and he and the lady walked toward each other across the parking lot—the lady more slowly since she had bare feet. When they met, the man handed her the shoe. Now they were talking.

"I wish we could hear them," complained Shue. She leaned forward, but it wasn't going to help; the window was closed, and the man and the lady were speaking quietly.

Suddenly they were laughing. The man ran back to the Dumpster and climbed in. He came out with the shoe and walked it back to the lady. They laughed some more.

Ashley smiled. "I think she likes him. Maybe they'll fall in love and live happily ever after." She moved away from the window and twirled in a circle.

Shue was watching her. "Does happily ever after really happen?"

Ashley shrugged. "I don't know, maybe, but probably only if you're lucky."

I wanted to stay longer, but I was fading away. It was time to go back. I braced for a shock, just to be safe, but I wasn't expecting one. This was a good wish. A second later I was back in the chair with only a dull tingle in my arms and legs. I'd been right. I should have been smiling, but I was too tired. My brain felt foggy. I closed my eyes and sat back in the chair, and only woke up when I heard the door slam. Mom and Claire were home.

Mom opened the basement door and called down to me.

"Ash, are you down there?"

I heard footsteps on the stairs. I jumped up, quickly hid the jar, and ran to the bottom of the stairs.

Mom was halfway down. She was holding up a small plastic bag. "Can you put these in the laundry?"

I held up my hands, and caught the bag.

"Claire picked some things out at the thrift store. There's something in there for you, too. So just dump it all in the washer and don't look. She wants it to be a surprise."

I walked over to the washing machine, put in the soap, emptied the bag, and closed the lid. Mom didn't have to worry about me peeking; I wasn't even tempted. I could wait. I was happy to wait. Whatever it was, I probably wasn't going to like it. I'd have to fake being excited and happy. I just hoped it wasn't something with a crying clown on it; I was pretty sure I couldn't fake being happy about that.

chapter thirty-one

Missing

While we waited for the laundry to be done, I stood outside and watched Claire practice riding her bike. Just watching her made me smile. I liked that I had helped her learn something, and now she could do it all by herself. Maybe that was how teachers felt? Though it was hard to imagine they got the same feeling from helping some kid learn the six-times tables.

She was getting better at riding and now only wobbled when she stopped. I would have liked to stay outside all afternoon and avoid the thrift store gift, but Claire had a good sense of time. I don't know how she did it, but she stopped practicing right when the laundry was done. When we walked into the house, Mom was just coming up the stairs from the basement. She smiled and handed Claire a brown paper bag. I didn't even have time to wonder about it, because Claire squealed, shook it in front of my face, and shoved it into my hands.

"Open it!" She bounced up and down. "You're going to love it. It's great!" And then she got serious— "We washed it, so don't worry about it being dirty."

I had no idea what to expect. I wasn't good at stuff like this—surprises, being put on the spot, the unexpected. But there was no avoiding it or stalling. I opened the bag and pulled out a T-shirt and a pen.

Claire pointed to the shirt. "Read the front!" She could hardly contain herself.

I turned the shirt over and read what was printed on the front: BE CASH LUCKY. I didn't get it. What was great about that? I looked again; maybe I'd missed something. The word "Be" was on top of a white oval starburst shape. CASH LUCKY was inside the starburst, and colored red, so that it stood out. Under all that, in smaller letters, was a swirly logo that said LOTTO 98. I got it, the shirt was advertising the lottery of 1998—but what I didn't get was why Claire thought I'd like it. It was an old shirt, and she was wrong, I didn't love it. Claire was staring at me, waiting for a reaction. Why would I want this? I tried to smile, but it was harder than I thought it would be—the best I could do was a sneer.

Claire laughed. "You don't get it, do you." She leaned forward and grabbed the pen off the table.

I watched as she crossed out two letters on the shirt—the *C* in cash, and the *K* in lucky. Suddenly I got it. It was amazing! Now I was smiling for real. With the *C* and the *K* crossed off, the shirt said ASH LUCY. I loved it! How had she found this?

I held up the shirt. "How did you notice this?"

She shrugged. "I don't know—as soon as I saw it, I figured it out."

I shook my head. It was hard to believe. It was so cool. Suddenly I knew exactly when I was going to wear it—it was perfect for my first day of camp, and Lucy was going to love it. Thinking about Lucy made me miss her, but I counted out the days in my head—only seven left. It was exactly one week from today. I walked over to Claire and hugged her. It was a thank-you for the shirt, but also for making the weeks go by fast. I'd be seeing Lucy in no time.

After lunch Mom drove Claire and me down to the

VS Depot. I thought she'd complain, but she didn't; she said she was happy to help. It was good that she felt that way, because there was no way I was getting Lucy's cookie down there by bicycle. Even though she didn't say anything, I knew there was another reason why she was being so nice—she was curious. She wanted to meet Peter. I told her she could wait in the car out front, but she insisted on parking and coming in with us. Claire was gone and in the store way before me. I was used to that. What I wasn't used to was her coming back out again. She looked disappointed.

"Peter's not here. There's a lady in there instead, and her name's Wendy."

Mom sighed. "Well, that's a shame. I was looking forward to meeting your friend."

I was disappointed too, and suddenly I was feeling something else. What if it was my fault that he was gone? Maybe it was because I left without saying goodbye. Should we stay, leave? And who was Wendy?

Mom gave me a nudge forward. "I'm sure Wendy knows how to mail things." She brushed past me and held the door open.

Mom walked over to a rack of greeting cards, and I followed her in. Claire was at the counter talking to a girl. It had to be Wendy. She looked nice enough. She was young and had her hair tied up in a scarf. I walked to the counter and put down the tray. Lucy's cookie took up most of the space, but on the side were two smaller cookies—special treats for Peter.

The girl stopped talking to Claire and looked at the tray. "Wow, that's some cookie!" She looked over at me. "You must be Ash; I'm Wendy. Claire's been telling me all about you." I waited for a handshake, but it didn't come. Maybe she was like me—not a hand shaker. That was a relief. I nodded hello.

"I need to mail this." I pointed to the big cookie. "And in a box." This wasn't like the other times—we couldn't just stick a stamp on it.

"Okay." Wendy nodded. "Let me get you one." She turned and walked to the back of the store.

Suddenly Claire was nonstop tugging on my arm. I pulled my arm away, but she grabbed it again, and pointed to the counter.

She was close to tears. "The ramp! Peter's ramp! It's gone!"

I peered over the edge. She was right. The ramp was gone. So Peter was gone. Was it forever? When Wendy got back, Claire asked about a hundred Peter questions.

"Where's Peter? Where's his ramp? Is he coming back? How can we give him his cookies?"

That was a lot of questions. Wendy shook her head.

"I don't know Peter. I work at one of the other stores with Laurie. She just sent me here for the day."

Claire was getting worked up; tears weren't very far away.

"So you're only here for today?" I asked.

Wendy nodded. I looked down at Claire and patted her shoulder.

"See, that probably means Peter will be back tomorrow."

Claire pointed to the tray. "What about his cookies?"

Wendy smiled. "Oh, I can eat those."

Claire looked up, startled. She wasn't in the mood for jokes.

"I'm sorry. I was just kidding," said Wendy. "I'll get another box and you can put them inside with a note." She put her hand over her heart. "And I promise I won't touch them."

Claire didn't react. For a second Wendy seemed disappointed, but she didn't say anything, she just turned and walked to the back of the store to get the box.

Mom was right about Wendy's packing skills. She

did a great job of wrapping up the cookie, and Mom paid a little extra to get it there faster since it was food. Before we left, we put Peter's cookies in a box, and Claire wrote him a note.

As soon as we got home, Claire made four more cards for Miss Sato.

She handed them to me and said, "We have to send these to the hospital."

I looked over the cards, but didn't say anything. We couldn't send them. I had no idea where Miss Sato was. I didn't even know where the nearest hospital was. I was trying to think of a nice way to say, *No, I can't do that* when Mom came up with a better idea.

"Why don't you take them to the nursing home? I'm sure they can get them to Miss Sato."

Claire thought about Mom's idea for a minute.

"I can give them to Sam, and he can give them to Mr. Fred, and he can give them to Mr. Gripes, and then he can show them to Miss Sato." She paused and ran back to the kitchen table. She made three new cards—a thank-you for each person in her chain to Miss Sato.

chapter thirty-two

Because

When I came downstairs the next morning, Mom wasn't in the kitchen, but Claire was. She was sitting at the table, drawing.

"I'm making a 'welcome back' picture for Peter," she said.

I nodded. He'd only been gone a day, but I was hoping he was back too. The PJ Walker book was good again, and I wanted to talk about it. It's more fun to be excited when someone is excited along with you. Excited alone just isn't the same.

I put my notebook on the table and grabbed a poppy-seed muffin off the counter.

"Do you want one?" I asked.

It was kind of a test, to see if Claire would eat something other than pancakes. It didn't look like she'd had any yet; her plate was still clean.

She shook her head but didn't look up.

I sat down with the muffin. "It's really good." I took a bite.

Claire made a face. "What's the black stuff?"

I picked one out and put it on my finger. "Poppy seeds." I held it out for her. "They're the special part that makes it taste good."

She leaned forward and looked. "Seeds?" She shook her head. "That's bird food."

I finished the muffin. "Have you seen Mom?"

Claire nodded. "She had to go to the store for more maple syrup." She looked up and then suddenly noticed my notebook on the table. She made a grab for it, but I was faster. I pulled it away before she got to it.

She sat back in her chair. "What's inside? Drawings?"

"No, it's . . ." I stopped myself before I went any further. Here I was about to lie again, but what choice did I have? I had to keep the lie going. "It's for my writing. I'm writing a story."

Now Claire was interested. She pushed her pencils to the side, like she was hearing some kind of fabulous secret that needed all her attention. "What kind of story?"

I hesitated.

"Is it a love story? Does it have to do with that jar thing you were holding?"

I thought for a second. Sure. Why not? If she wanted a love story, I could tell her a love story. In fact, it could be anything, because it was a story within a story—fiction on top of fiction—and I wasn't really writing anything. This time the lying felt worse. But it was too late to turn back, so I moved ahead—colorfully. I had Claire's full attention, so I tried to make it good.

"Well, it's a love story. But it's more than that. The girl in the love story has amazing adventures, because she's got a magical jar that is filled with tickets to all sorts of wonderful and strange places." I was surprised; it felt good to be talking about the wishes, even if it was in code. It was a release.

Claire leaned in closer. Now we were almost face-to-face. "Is the girl like me?"

I nodded. Why not? Claire would be a great character. Fun, energetic, brave, daring—but kind of sad too. "But she's older than you, and pretty wise."

"Like an owl?" asked Claire.

I looked down and flicked a few stray poppy seeds off the table. "No, like a person who knows and understands things." Talking about the story almost made me want to write it. It was unlikely I'd follow through, but sitting there with Claire, I felt creative.

I stayed with Claire until Mom got back, and then I went downstairs to the basement.

I was liking this routine—time traveling after breakfast. I pulled out the jar and picked a wish. There were a lot left in the jar—maybe thirty or forty. I was glad about that; I didn't want to be near the end. I didn't like ends, or beginnings even—I was more about middles. Middles were comfortable. I opened the wish and looked down.

I Hope the Lady Finds Her Shoes

Ashley and Shue were in Ashley's room. They were looking out the window. I walked toward them and said my test words, "*Beige llama.*"

"Nothing's happening," complained Shue. She twirled the edge of the curtain around her finger, released it, and then started again.

Ashley shrugged. "We had to do it. You know that. Sometimes people need a push to fall in love."

She glanced out the window for a second and turned back to Shue. "Can we do something else instead of just sitting here watching? What if they don't come out for hours?"

Shue ignored the question. "What if the lady comes out first?" She pointed to the back of Anderson's. "Will she know where we put them?"

Ashley looked back out the window. "Of course! Last time, he was like Prince Charming fighting the Dumpster dragon to get her shoe. She wouldn't forget that."

Shue wasn't sure. "Not much of a prince; he was the one who threw it in there."

"Ugh!" Ashley threw her hands up. "Can't you be just a little romantic?"

For a second I wasn't sure what would happen next. Was Shue going to be upset? Were they going to argue?

Shue was quiet for a minute or two, and then she spun around to face Ashley. "How about this: The princess has lost her magic shoes. She's sad, distraught, but she's not alone—a prince has seen her. He will help her. He carries her across a rocky desert in search of the shoes. He is tired and thirsty, but he doesn't give up. He gets his energy not from food or water, but only from her beauty. Finally he sees the shoes, but oh, no, they are being guarded by two evil boot dragons. The prince must battle them. The fight is dangerous, and the dragons are strong, but the prince is victorious. He holds the shoes up and smiles at the princess. She jumps into his arms and they live happily ever after." Shue twirled and looked up.

Ashley was smiling. "Not bad; I didn't know you had it in you."

Shue looked out the window, lingered for a second, and then turned back to Ashley. "Okay, we can do something else."

Suddenly I was back in my chair. It was fast and without pain. I smiled. Suddenly the basement door opened. The light from the kitchen shone down on the top half of the stairs.

"Can we go give Miss Sato her letters now?" It was Claire. She was leaning through the door.

She'd never come down, I knew that. "Can you hear me?" she shouted. "Are you writing?"

I put the wish jar down and groaned. The pain couldn't stop me, but Claire could. I didn't want to go upstairs yet. I heard Claire talking to Mom. Maybe Mom could pull her away so I could have more time.

"Am I bugging you?" shouted Claire.

Yes, she was. I waited a second, but didn't hear Mom. I guess I had to go upstairs.

"I'm coming," I shouted.

Now Mom was talking to Claire. I didn't hear what Mom was saying, but I heard Claire's response.

"See, I wasn't bugging her."

I rolled my eyes and put everything away. I took a deep breath and ran up the stairs. Sometimes when you are forcing yourself to do something you don't want to do, faster is better than slower. Like pulling a Band-Aid off your arm—it hurts less.

It didn't take me long to get ready, but Claire still complained that she'd been waiting forever. I didn't say anything, but her forever was probably only five minutes long.

The first thing I noticed when we got to the old people's home was Sam's bike. Now I felt better about coming. I made Claire wait for me while I locked up our bike, and we walked in together. I didn't want anyone telling her a different Miss Sato story than the one she already knew. All we had to do was find Sam and we'd be safe. We found Sam in the room where we'd seen him on that first day. He waved when he saw us. He was sitting with Mr. Fred, and they were looking at slides with the projector. There was a picture up on the wall, a man and woman.

Claire pointed to the woman. "Is that Miss Sato?"

The woman in the picture was much younger than the Miss Sato we knew. She was smiling, and the man she was standing next to was tall and handsome.

"Yes, those are my parents," said Mr. Fred.

Claire looked confused.

"It's Miss Sato and Mr. Gripes," he explained.

"But they look so different." Suddenly Claire seemed sad. "And so beautiful. It's not fair that they had to get old."

Mr. Fred nodded. Looking at the pictures probably made him feel like that too.

"I like this picture." He smiled. "It was taken before I was born. They had their whole lives ahead of them." He was quiet for a minute and then told Sam he could have a twenty-minute break. Sam grabbed a snack from his backpack and walked outside with us. I let Claire go first. Even though she could have given her cards to Mr. Fred, she'd held on to them. She had to do it her way.

When we got outside, she handed Sam the big pile of cards.

"Can you give these to Mr. Fred, to give to Mr.

Gripes, to show to Miss Sato?"

Sam started to flip through the cards, but she stopped him. "The one on the top with your name on it is for you. But don't open it until after you give the cards to Mr. Fred, because it's a thank-you card."

I could almost see Sam's brain at work, trying to make sense of what Claire was talking about. Finally he looked up and smiled. I guess he got it.

Sam and I sat under the big tree near the front driveway. Claire ran around the other side of the tree to chase a squirrel. When she was far enough away so that she couldn't hear us, I asked about Miss Sato.

Sam took a bite of his cheese stick, swallowed, and answered me.

"She's getting better. She still can't move very much, but she can kind of talk, and Mr. Fred said they're expecting her to get a lot better."

I nodded but was confused. What did "kind of talk" mean?

"What can she say?"

Sam put his cheese stick down and leaned forward.

"It's kind of weird."

I looked around for Claire. I didn't want her to hear this. She was fine, over by the steps, digging a hole with a stick. I looked back at Sam. He continued.

"She can only say one word. It's a Japanese word, *raishuu*. Mr. Fred says it means 'yesterday.'"

Why a Japanese word? Was Miss Sato Japanese? She didn't look Japanese. Maybe she was part Japanese. I asked about the word.

"Why is she saying 'yesterday'?"

Sam shrugged. He said no one could figure that out, but they were trying. Miss Sato could blink once for yes and twice for no, but so far that hadn't helped very much. It was still a mystery.

Now was definitely not the right time to ask about Anderson's, but that didn't mean I wasn't thinking about it. I fiddled with the chain and key around my neck—too bad it didn't unlock something useful, like the mystery of Anderson's. Claire and I followed Sam back inside. It wasn't part of the original plan, but Claire decided she had to personally give Mr. Fred his thank-you card. She said it was more polite to do it in person, but I think she just liked all the attention. I stood in the doorway while Sam got the projector running again. Mr. Fred was making a big deal of the card, and Claire was loving it. Suddenly Sam was standing next to me. I hadn't noticed him move from the projector. I jumped.

He touched my shoulder. I jumped again. I hoped he didn't notice.

"Can you get me something?" he asked.

"Sure." I nodded.

He explained what he needed, and then I was off—on my little mission. All I had to do was go to Miss Sato's room and pick up a slide tray he'd forgotten on the table.

I'm not great with directions, so I was a little bit nervous, but I got there without any trouble. I unlocked the door and went in. I was in a living room; off to the side was the small table Sam had described, and on it was the slide tray. I picked it up and turned to go, and there right in front of me on the wall was Miss Sato's goldfish purse. It was the one I'd seen in the photo, but in person it was much more beautiful. Claire would have loved it. It gave me an idea: maybe Mom and I could find her one—not fancy like this one, but something cute. I picked up the tray and walked out, smiling. It was a great present idea.

When I got back to the room, I traded the slide tray for Claire. I held her by the shoulders so she couldn't escape. It was time to leave. Claire talked nonstop all the way to our bike. The talking was fine, but her using the word "nifty" every ten seconds really bugged me. I was hoping that was going to wear off quickly.

As I was unlocking the bike, she said, "Miss Sato doesn't have a stomachache."

I cringed. What had Mr. Fred told her?

Claire smiled. "But she's getting better. Mr. Fred said she's going to love my cards. Do you know why?"

I put the lock and chain in my backpack and shook my head.

"Guess," said Claire. She jumped on the back of the bike. We put on our helmets.

"Is it because they're so beautiful?"

"Nope." She shook her head.

We were pedaling now, and it was harder to hear her.

"It's because she's like me," shouted Claire. "She loves goldfish!"

I nodded big so she could tell that I'd heard her. Somehow, that wasn't a surprise.

We got home pretty fast, even though for the last half of the ride I was the only one pedaling. Claire wanted to go to the VS Depot to see if Peter was back, but it was out of the way, so I said no. After that, in protest, she refused to pedal.

When we got home, Claire left me with the bike and stomped off into the house. She was trying to punish me, but really she was giving me a gift—more alone time. I told her where I was going and headed down to the basement. I pulled out the jar, took out a wish, and hid the jar again. If Mom came down to find me, I'd be safe. She wouldn't see the jar.

I sat down in the chair and opened the wish. As soon as I read it, I cringed and wished I'd picked a different one, but it was too late—I had to go. A second later I was gone.

I Wish I'd Never Met Ashley

"Black snake!" As soon as I saw Shue, I said it. I didn't know exactly what was going to happen, but I knew it was going to be bad. I forced myself to concentrate on what I was seeing, but it was hard not to worry about the trip home. It was going to be painful. Shue was up ahead of me, walking. We were on the street where I'd first met the girls. It was almost the same: Shue was walking toward Ashley, only this time Ashley had two other girls with her. I didn't know them, but somehow I already didn't like them. I ran up to Shue so I could see her face. She looked nervous. Ashley and the girls were talking and laughing. As they passed, Shue said, "Hi." Ashley mumbled back a "hi" and then slowed down. Was she going to stop? Was she going to talk to Shue?

"Who's that?" asked the girl on the left.

She was loud, one of those bossy types. Ashley didn't answer.

"She looks like she's twelve," said the girl.

"I remember when I was twelve," said the other girl. "I was such a baby!"

Both girls laughed. Suddenly Ashley was walking away fast. The girls next to her had to run to keep up. They were too far away for me to hear their words, but we could still hear their laughter, and somehow that was worse.

I tried to catch up with Shue, but she was fast, and I was fading away. Was she crying? Was she angry? Was she mad? And then I braced myself.

The zap was stronger this time. I wiped away my tears. But my tears weren't only for the pain; they were for something else. Something that made them hard to control, something that wasn't over in ten seconds—they were for Shue.

I sat in the chair for what seemed like an hour before I finally had the energy to get up. An hour of sitting gives you a lot of time to think. Ashley and Shue's story wasn't hard to figure out. They were best friends over the summer, and then when school started, Ashley dumped Shue. I tried to understand why Ashley had done this, but I couldn't. No matter how I looked at it, it didn't seem fair. I wanted their story to end happily ever after, but that wasn't going to happen. It was a tragedy. That kind of story is hard to watch. I had to drag myself up the stairs.

There was a lot going on in the kitchen. Claire was talking to her dad on the phone, Mom was making pasta sauce, and there was a postcard from Lucy sitting on the table. I sat down and read it. She had gotten the coconut! That made me laugh. Mom looked over, and I waved Lucy's card at her. I didn't want to explain the reason for my laughter, but I showed her the why. Lucy was having fun. I liked that she was finally telling me about what she was doing—not worried it would hurt my feelings. The coolest-sounding thing was a swimming obstacle course that had a rope swing and a trampoline, and they were both in the water. Only six more days to wait.

Claire finished the call with her dad just as I finished my postcard. Just like before, she was filled with energy.

"Guess what?"

Before I could guess, she was telling me.

"Daddy just got back from working at a circus, and he saw acrobats and three elephants. There were clowns too, but they weren't wearing their makeup, so they weren't funny." Claire was quiet. Was she thinking about the clowns? Disappointed for her dad? Whatever it was, she got over it and a few seconds later was back to her old self. "And when I go back home, we get to go there and watch the show."

I smiled and nodded. I hadn't thought about that, her being gone. Would I miss her? I was glad that she was happy, and clowns without makeup didn't sound disappointing at all. It was a bonus. It was nice that we both had something to look forward to.

The whole rest of the day was pretty uneventful. It gave me lots of time to recover. I didn't know why, but the wishes were different now. They were the opposite of Claire—they were sucking the energy out of me.

chapter thirty-three

Remember

Mom wasn't excited about me going down to the basement before breakfast. I had the notebook in my hand, but it wasn't working its usual magic.

Mom pointed to my chair. "Why don't you sit here with me and wait for Claire. We can have breakfast together."

I tapped my notebook. I was getting good at the lying, but was that something to be proud of? I tried not think about it and continued.

"I have some ideas I really need to get down. I'll come back up when Claire's awake."

Mom sighed and picked up her coffee cup. She'd

lost. I walked to the basement door, opened it, and then turned back.

"I'll try to be fast."

Was it another lie? I didn't know, but hopefully it made her feel better. As soon as I got to the basement, I pulled out the wish jar and picked out a wish. I studied the paper ball. More than anything I wanted it to be Anderson's. "Are you Anderson's?" Of course it didn't answer. I opened it and read it.

I Wish the Man Knew It Wasn't Us

The girls were in Ashley's room. Ashley was on the far side looking in her desk, and Shue was at the window. That was a good sign. Maybe this was about Anderson's—I smiled. I felt daring. I walked over to Shue and whispered in her ear.

"Emerald deer."

Shue gasped and shouted, "NO!"

I froze. She'd heard me? Could she see me? But she wasn't talking about me. She was pointing out the window. Ashley rushed over, but I couldn't move. My heart was still racing, and my feet were stuck. I tried to get over it. I listened to the girls.

Ashley moved closer to the window. "What's she doing?"

"She's pretending to be us!" answered Shue. "To

get us into trouble."

Ashley shook her head. "I don't know. Why would she do that?"

Shue put her hands up to her mouth. She looked upset.

Finally I felt normal. I walked over to the girls and looked out the window. It was the woman from the apartment—the one with the red shoes. She was standing at the back door of Anderson's, and she was doing exactly what the girls had done—putting her shoes into the man's boots. Shue was right. She was trying to get them into trouble.

Suddenly Ashley jumped up and danced around the room. "I was right. I was right. It's a love story."

Shue watched her, confused. "What do you mean?"

"You'll understand when you're older," joked Ashley.

Shue scowled and looked grumpy.

Ashley came back to the window. "Okay. I'll tell you." She waved her arms in the air, and gave herself a drum roll. "She's putting her shoes in his boots so she can talk to him again."

Shue shook her head. "That's dumb. If she wanted to talk to him, she'd just go talk to him."

Ashley shook her head and smiled. "It doesn't work that way. When people are in love, everything has to be romantic, and romance is complicated."

I could tell that Shue didn't believe her. We watched the lady hurry back to her porch. And that's when I noticed the purse—the goldfish purse. It was hanging over her shoulder. It was far away, but it looked like the same purse Miss Sato had—another weird coincidence? Or did it mean something?

Shue pointed to the lady. "What's she going to do now? Just sit around and wait for him to come out and find her shoes?"

Ashley nodded. "Exactly. It could take hours."

Ashley walked back to her desk and fiddled with some papers. Shue was torn. She probably didn't want to spend hours looking out the window, but she didn't want to miss anything either.

She put her hands on her hips and scowled. "Well, whatever happens, she's making us look bad!"

I nodded; she was right about that. I wanted to stay with Shue—see what would happen next—but I couldn't. I felt myself fading away. This time it wasn't slow and easy; instead it was blink-fast and painful—like touching an electrical fence. I felt it flow through every part of me, and then it was over. I looked down at my hands; they were like claws clutching the arms of the chair. I forced them free and sank back. What had just happened? If the first wish had been like this, would I have done another one? Why was it suddenly so painful? Was it the jar? I leaned over to pick it up, but it wasn't next to me. Instead, it was on its side in the middle of the floor, and the wish balls were scattered everywhere. I could hear Claire and Mom moving around upstairs. I cleaned it up as fast as I could.

When I got upstairs, Claire was eating a waffle.

Mom smiled. "She's trying something new."

I nodded. Claire held her fork up.

"It's nifty."

I rolled my eyes and pulled a bagel out of the bag on the counter. Fresh bagels—she didn't know what she was missing.

While we ate, Mom told us about the yard sale she was planning. She was doing it because it was on Claire's list, but it was a good idea. She really needed to clean out her junk.

"It'll be Saturday at nine," said Mom. "And Ash, I need you to go through your room and find some things for the sale."

I coughed and almost choked. Was she kidding?

Not that I was against cleaning my room, but really! With all the junk that Mom had, the stuff from my room wasn't going to make much of a difference. Mom looked at me and nodded.

"I know, I know. I have work to do." She put her hand over her heart. "I'm going to start today, in the attic!"

It was a declaration of war—Mom against the mess. I didn't say anything, but I was pretty sure she was going to lose.

Since Claire didn't have any old stuff to go through, she came to my room to help me. I didn't have anywhere near as much junk as Mom, but still, I had stuff I didn't use anymore. After about ten minutes, I wasn't so sure that having Claire help out was the best idea. Almost every time I put something in the yard sale box, she pulled it out and asked if she could keep it. Finally I just went downstairs and got her her own box and wrote her name on it. After about an hour her box was almost full, and my yard sale box had six things in it.

Mom was in the attic; I could hear her moving around. Every ten minutes she'd toss something down, and it would land in the hall outside my room. After a couple of hours the pile was almost as high as Claire's head.

I yelled up to her. "Are you close to done?"

Instead of answering, Mom came down the ladder and handed me a hat. It wasn't just any hat; it was my old adventure hat. Instantly my brain was filled with memories, all of them rushing back at the same time. Claire was staring at me. I knew I was smiling, but I couldn't stop. It felt great to suddenly remember things I hadn't thought about in ages. If Lucy had been next to me, all our sentences would have started with *Do you remember the time when . . . ?*

Claire tugged on my arm. "Why are you so happy?"

It wasn't easy to explain, but I tried.

"This used to be my favorite hat, and Lucy and I shared it. One day she'd get to wear it, and the next day I'd get to wear it."

Claire nodded—so far, so good.

"We called it our adventure hat, because whoever had the hat on got to make up an adventure for the day—things like an obstacle course, or a scavenger hunt—something like that."

Suddenly I remembered the time we'd gotten stuck in a tree, and Dad had to borrow the neighbors' ladder to get us down. I think that one had been my fault, but there were lots of stories. The hat was always getting us into trouble. That's why Mom called it the trouble hat. I smiled; I'd forgotten about that too. It was fun to suddenly remember everything.

"What's a scavenger hunt?" asked Claire.

Her question pulled me back to the now. It took me a second to adjust.

"Uh . . . it's kind of like a treasure hunt, only you have to find certain things. Usually there's a list, and you have to find everything on the list."

She pulled my arm. "Can we do that instead of a treasure hunt?"

I almost asked, "What treasure hunt?" but then remembered it was one of the things on her list.

I thought about it for a second and nodded. Sure, why not? It'd probably be fun to make one again.

"Can I try it?" Claire pointed to the hat.

I handed it to her. "Only for a few minutes. I want to mail it to Lucy."

"Are you going to write inside it?" She pulled the hat low on her head.

I shook my head. It didn't need any words. The hat was going to work for Lucy, just as it had for me. The minute she saw it, she was going to be on a trip down memory lane.

Claire came with me to the VS Depot. I wouldn't have been able to keep her away—she was desperate to see if Peter was back, and if he'd eaten the cookies we'd left him. I pulled up to the store and parked the bike. Claire jumped off and raced in. As soon as I opened the door, I saw him.

"LOOK! He's back!" shouted Claire. She was bouncing up and down. "He was gone because he had to go to a meeting."

I waved and smiled. I was glad he was back and happy to see him too.

"What are we mailing today? More cookies? I hope so, because those were delicious. Thank you."

Claire shook her head. "No, it's just a hat."

I pulled the hat out of my backpack and put it on the counter.

"No box, right?" asked Peter.

I nodded. Peter weighed the hat and stuck a stamp on it.

Before he had a chance to ask, I said, "I didn't read the book last night."

He looked disappointed. "Why? Are you not liking it again?"

I was trying to trick him, so I put my head down and pretended to be sad. And then, when I was sure that he was believing me, I looked up and said, "I'm loving it!"

Peter tried to act casual, but his smile was huge. I had totally tricked him. We talked about the book for another ten minutes. It was amazing; everything in the book was suddenly making sense—even the crazy story about the squirrel had turned out to be important. Peter knew the story even better than I did, but still he was interested in what I had to say about it. Most adults don't care what a kid thinks; Peter was different. He wasn't one bit like that. It was like a mini book club, and I loved it.

Claire was good about not interrupting us. Peter gave her some scrap paper and a pen, and as long as she could draw, she was happy.

Suddenly Claire stood up and waved her drawings in the air. "Can I mail these to the old people's home?"

I looked down; she was holding three new cards for Miss Sato.

I shook my head. "Let's wait until Friday, and you can give them to Mr. Fred again, just like before."

Claire shot me a scowling look and crossed her arms. "No, I want to mail them! You got to mail your hat; how come I can't mail my cards?"

I had two good reasons: one, I didn't have the address, and two, I didn't have enough money. But Claire was stubborn; she didn't care. Peter came to the rescue—he looked up the address and lent us money for the stamps. He was a nice guy.

Dad called after dinner and I talked to him for a whole fifteen minutes. I was surprised and glad when he said he was coming home in two days. How had I not been thinking more about that? Dad promised he would do something special with Claire and me before camp started. He wouldn't make any promises, but I was really hoping for a trip to the amusement park.

chapter thirty-four

Old

I set my alarm, and before anyone was awake, or even thinking of waking up, I was creeping down to the basement. It was five a.m. The plan was to do as many wishes as I could. I wanted to find the lady with the goldfish bag. Was she who I thought she was? The only thing that worried me was how painful the coming back would be. Was it going to be bad every time? Was pain the new normal? It was scary, but not enough to stop me.

I pulled out the jar, sat down, and picked a wish. As soon as I read it, I cringed. It was a bad one. I'd had it before. Maybe it wouldn't work? But it did, and a second later I was on my way.

I Wish Ashley Wouldn't Ignore Me

As soon as I saw Shue, I said my test words, "Gray penguin." I knew where I was. This was going to be the same as before—it was the first wish all over again. Everything was the same, the street, Shue, Ashley—only this time I knew who they were, and what was next. But it didn't make it easier. I couldn't watch Shue—I didn't want to see her cry. So I decided to watch Ashley.

The girls were walking toward each other; they were close now—almost passing. In a few seconds Shue would say hi. I studied Ashley; she was staring straight ahead, like she was the only person on the sidewalk—like Shue was invisible. But I saw her look left, just for a second, toward Shue. Did Shue see it too? Was that why she spoke? Ashley looked straight ahead and pretended like she hadn't heard her, but I knew that she had—I saw her flinch. And then I saw something that I hadn't noticed before, and Shue hadn't either—Ashley was crying. I hated her, felt sorry for her, and was disappointed in her, all at once. Why was she so weak? Why couldn't she stand up to her friends and be nice to Shue?

I felt myself fading away and braced for the pain.

Was it because I was getting better at being ready? Stronger? Braver? Or was the shock just not as strong? I couldn't tell, but whatever the reason, I was thankful that it seemed less painful than the last time. I reached into the jar and pulled out another wish.

I Hope They Get Married

Shue was walking on the sidewalk. At first I didn't recognize the street, but as we got closer to the corner, I recognized where we were—we were going to the candy store. When she got to the corner, Shue turned and walked toward it. We passed a store with photos of animals in the window; there was a cute panda in a tree. Suddenly I had my test words.

"Violet panda." I used my normal voice this time. Suddenly Shue gasped and dropped to the ground. She undid her shoe and slowly tied it again, and when it was tied she undid it again. I knew that trick—she was hiding from someone. I looked up. A man and a lady were walking toward us; it took me a few seconds, but I recognized them—not from their faces, but from their clothes—red shoes, a goldfish bag, and work boots. No wonder she was worried. Would the man recognize her? Shue kept her head down as they got closer. The man and the lady were joking, smiling, and holding hands.

"Those are nifty shoes," said the man, pointing to the lady's shoes.

"They helped me find you," she said.

"And find my notes," he added.

"But next time, I'll check my shoe before I put it on." The lady laughed.

They passed Shue without noticing her. She stood up, and a second later I was gone. This time I forgot to prepare myself for the pain, and it caught me by surprise. I screamed. It was sharp, but it was fast, and by the time Mom opened the basement door and called down to me, I had recovered. I jumped up and ran to the bottom of the stairs.

"ASH!" Mom shouted again. She started down the stairs. She stopped halfway down, suddenly seeing me. "Are you okay? I heard a scream."

"I was excited." I waved my notebook in the air. "I figured out something in my story—something important." For once it wasn't a lie. Well, not a complete lie. I hadn't written a story, but the figuring-out part was true—and my discovery was important. In fact, it was amazing and almost unbelievable. Miss Sato and Mr. Gripes were in Shue's wishes. And then, like a lightbulb suddenly flashing above my head, I knew the truth—there were no coincidences;

everything was happening for a reason. I didn't know the whats or the whys, but I couldn't think about that now. For now, just knowing it was enough. I smiled up at Mom.

Mom was confused. She glanced around the basement. From where she was standing, she couldn't see the wish jar. She sighed.

"Well, I'm happy it's going well."

I nodded and pointed to the chair. "I need more time."

Mom started back up the stairs. When she got to the top, she turned. "Just half an hour more, okay?" And she closed the door.

I wanted to scream but couldn't. I forced myself down and sat on the step. I hugged my knees in, pressing myself into a ball. Containing my excitement was hard—knowledge has energy. Miss Sato and Mr. Gripes were the man and the lady in Shue's wish. I couldn't believe it—these were real people, people I knew, and I'd seen them in some kind of time warp. The wishes were true! It wasn't just a fantasy. It was real life. And suddenly I was wondering: the magic, the wishes, and Sam—was it all supposed to happen? And to me? But mostly I was thinking about Ashley and Shue. Were they strangers? Or did

I know them too?

I walked back to the chair. I wanted to know more, do another wish, but at the same time I was exhausted and overwhelmed. I picked up the jar and held it in my lap. I looked down at the wishes; there were twenty, maybe thirty left. Suddenly it seemed like too much. Could I last that long? I picked one out and rolled it between my thumb and finger. Now I was wondering again, but this time it was different. This time I was worried. What if I found out something I didn't want to know? I opened the wish and held it on my leg, smoothing it out with my fingers—only feeling it—and then I forced myself to look down.

I Want to Play with That Girl Again

"Burgundy bear." I said my test words as soon as I saw Shue. I was getting tired of them, but should I give it up? What if it changed the wishes? What if I needed to say it to keep them working? Something had changed. I wasn't just watching a story—now I felt like I was part of it. Maybe what I did had power. Suddenly I felt more like Viola Starr, only poorly written and unprepared.

Shue was sitting on some front steps of a house—hers, I guessed. I could hear laughter and screaming coming toward us from down the street. Suddenly I recognized Ashley. She was holding a small brown bag in the air, keeping it away from a boy. It took me an extra second or two, but I recognized his shoes. It was Spencer. Ashley was taller, but Spencer was fast—he was going to get the bag away from her. Shue leaned forward and smiled—they were fun to watch. Suddenly Ashley saw Shue; a second later she called out to her.

"Hey, girl on the step! Come help. I'll throw this to you, and you throw it back to me!"

Shue hesitated; Spencer made a jump for the bag but just missed it.

"Help!" screamed Ashley.

Shue jumped up and ran behind Spencer. Suddenly the bag was in her hands. It was too much for Spencer—he was outmatched. He tried, but he couldn't compete. It was monkey in the middle, and he was forever going to be the monkey.

"Just one orange sour," whined Spencer.

Ashley shook her head. "No way! You ate your candy; this is mine."

Spencer tried for the bag one more time, but the girls were too fast. He scowled at Ashley and walked off in a huff.

Shue looked worried. "Is he mad?"

I could tell she was feeling guilty.

Ashley shrugged like she didn't care. She leaned to the side and looked behind Shue. "Is that your house?"

Shue nodded.

Ashley pointed down the block. "We just moved in. The brown house."

Shue nodded again. Ashley opened her bag. She looked inside and held it open for Shue.

"You can pick anything you want, just not the orange sours—those are my favorites."

Shue smiled. "They're my favorites too." She reached into the bag and pulled out a long string of red licorice. She smiled. "But I like this too."

Ashley picked out an orange candy and popped it into her mouth. She scrunched up her face. I guessed that was the sour part. She closed the bag, shoved it into her pocket, and walked down the sidewalk toward her house. Halfway there, she turned back and waved. I smiled; I liked this, knowing how they met. And then slowly I felt myself fading away. There was no pain, but I sat in the chair thinking about what had just happened. I'd changed my mind—I liked beginnings.

I didn't know how much time had passed. I was a little worried that it had been hours, but when I got upstairs, Mom smiled and said, "Oh, good, perfect timing." She and Claire were going through Mom's boxes for the yard sale and sticking on the prices.

Mom picked up an old rusty spoon and stuck a price on it. Who was going to buy that? Her hair was in her eyes and she looked tired. I had a feeling this yard sale was more work than she'd imagined. She looked over at me.

"Is your box ready? We're almost finished with these."

I nodded. I didn't have much in my box—Claire had taken most of it—but still, it was better than nothing.

When I got to my room, I collapsed on my bed. I wanted to rest, but my head was full of thoughts. Swirling and spinning and making me dizzy. I needed a break—fresh air. I grabbed the box and carried it downstairs.

I dropped it in front of Mom.

"Is that all you have?"

I nodded and told her about Claire. Mom looked in the box again, and then over at Claire. She was probably trying to imagine what Claire had pulled out. I didn't say anything, but Claire was like Mom—a junk lover. And Claire's room was starting to look a lot like the basement.

Mom pulled the box away from Claire. "Let's leave the rest for the sale."

It was crazy that Mom was worried about having enough stuff for the sale. This was going to be the biggest yard sale our neighborhood had ever seen.

Claire stood up. "Can we do my scavenger hunt now?"

She was always catching me by surprise, asking for things when I wasn't expecting it. There was an old page-boy hat in my box. She pulled it out, stuck it on her head, and turned it sideways—the girl definitely had a way with fashion. When she was sure that I was watching, she pulled it off and waved it at me.

"You can use this for the scavenger hunt," she said. Claire looked at Mom. "If you hide it, and I find it, I get to keep it."

Mom sighed and shrugged. She couldn't say no to Claire. I didn't say anything, but I felt the same way.

An hour later I was on my bike and headed to the thrift store. It was another new first—totally unexpected, totally not me, and one hundred percent because of Claire. It felt weird riding on my own—like I'd lost an appendage or something. It was faster and smoother, but I missed Claire being behind me. I parked outside the thrift store and locked up my bike. It was a secret, me coming here, at least from Claire. Mom had been shocked when I'd told her where I was going. I knew how she felt—I was shocked too! Can you surprise yourself? Absolutely.

Looking around the thrift store still wasn't my favorite thing, but it was better than I thought it would be. Having a mission helped. After about forty-five minutes I had everything I needed: a shirt, a vest, a dress, a skirt, a jacket, two scarves, and a belt. I wasn't sure how it would all work, but Claire was good at that—putting things together. I took everything to the counter and waited in line. There were two old ladies ahead of me. They were slow, but I didn't mind listening to them. Suddenly something on the shelf across from me caught my eye. It was staring at me, not blinking, and hard to ignore. It was a large plastic owl. That was Lucy's favorite animal! I had to get it for her. I grabbed it, but suddenly I was holding too much and things began to slip loose. The belt and the vest fell on the floor. I shoved the owl under my arm, shifted things around, and bent down to pick them up. And then, there in front of me, on the bottom of the shelf, were Claire's red shoes—the ones she'd been wearing around the store.

Should I get them? I grabbed them. Maybe she could use them for dress-up. I smiled—she'd be so surprised. It was a struggle to hold everything, but I made it to the counter without dropping anything else. This had gone even better than I'd expected. I wasn't a thrift store convert, but I got it. The thrill of the find was kind of exciting. And getting it all for seven dollars and thirty cents—well, that just made it even better.

When I got home, there was a postcard from Lucy on the table. I still missed Lucy, but it was different from before—not so desperate. The postcards had helped. Now I knew something new. Distance wasn't going to pull us apart. Lucy and I would be friends forever.

There was a lot about Claire—Lucy's Claire—in the postcard. I was surprised, but reading about them doing things together didn't make me jealous—not even a little bit. It was nice that Lucy had someone to hang out with. I wanted her to be happy.

While Claire and Mom watched a movie, I organized the scavenger hunt for the next day. It had a theme—fashion. My fingers were crossed that Claire was going to love it.

chapter thirty-five

Find

Claire woke me up super early. She was excited about the scavenger hunt and couldn't wait to get started. I was glad that I'd done the clues the night before—thinking of clue riddles at six in the morning would have been impossible. I made her go back to her room and wait, so I could get the clothes out of the laundry and hide them. I'd set my alarm to get down to the basement early, but that had been to do something completely different. Now there wasn't going to be time for wishes until after the scavenger hunt.

At the last minute I decided to not give Claire

the red shoes. I was bent down hiding them under the sofa when all of a sudden a new plan flashed in my head. Were the red shoes like my adventure hat? Could they do the same thing? For the right people some ordinary things had special powers—time travel powers; they could take you back in time. Maybe the red shoes could do that for Miss Sato and Mr. Gripes. Could seeing them remind them of how they used to be in love? They looked like the same kind of shoes from the wishes; maybe they would work.

It was crazy, but I wanted to keep my promise to Claire. Suddenly I could see how important that was. I ran upstairs and put the shoes away for later.

Claire screamed when I gave her the paper with the list of clues. I don't think I'd ever seen her so excited before. It felt good. Like her excitement was giving me a boost of energy and happiness. I was glad Mom was up; waking up to that scream would have been shocking. After about five minutes it was obvious—the scavenger hunt was too easy. Claire had no trouble figuring out the clues and finding all the clothes I'd hidden. At first I was disappointed, but then I decided too easy was probably better than too hard. At least she could do it by herself. Every time Claire found a new piece of clothing, she put it on. I had done a pretty good job with the sizes, and everything seemed to fit. The last thing she found was the second scarf, and she tied her hair up with it, just like Wendy, the girl at the VS Depot, had done. Mom got her camera and took a picture, which was good, because two seconds later it all came undone. I guess tying your hair up was harder than it looked.

When you get up early, you can get a lot done. By nine o'clock we were already on the bike and ready to ride down to the VS Depot. I couldn't find my backpack, so I used one of Dad's belts to attach the big plastic owl I'd bought for Lucy to my back. It was a strange way to transport it, but it worked, and Claire said she liked how it was looking at her while we were riding. I had to take the red shoes too, but that wasn't as tricky—they were small and not hard to carry in a normal plastic bag. I knew I wouldn't be able to get the shoes down there without Claire noticing them. As usual, she was full of questions.

"Why are you taking those? Are they yours? They look like the shoes I had in the thrift store. Can I try them on?"

I ignored her. There was no way to explain any of it so that she would understand. I just hoped she'd forget about them and get distracted by something else when we got to the store.

As soon as we got to the VS Depot, she jumped off the bike and disappeared inside. I followed behind. Peter smiled when I walked in. I dropped the owl onto the counter, and he picked it up and put it on the scale. I guess nothing surprised him anymore.

"So has the countdown started? How many days until camp?"

I counted them off in my head. I couldn't believe it. I held up three fingers.

Peter nodded. "Wow, that's soon."

We both looked at Claire. Were we thinking the same thing? Was she going to be sad when I left? She was staying an extra three days after I was gone. I had a feeling she was probably going to be lonely with only Mom and Dad to hang out with. Luckily, she was looking at something near the back of the room and wasn't paying attention to us. I changed the subject. "I finished the book."

Peter smiled but was quiet. He stuck a stamp on the back of the owl's head.

Peter looked up. "What did you think of the ending?" He put the owl headfirst into the bin behind him. It looked funny with its feet sticking up in the air.

I took a deep breath. "I loved it!" It was the truth.

I did. Even though I'd had trouble with it, in the end it had all been worth it. "I really like how everything came together." I thought for a second. "I don't usually like endings, but this was different—it was satisfying."

Peter grinned. "You mean it's all wrapped up, finished, no loose or uncomfortable ends sticking out."

I hadn't thought about it that way, but he was right—that's what I liked. It was all done—there was nothing left to worry about. I nodded. Plus it wasn't really the end—Viola Starr would be back in the next book.

I fiddled with a sign on the counter. "It's too bad that can't happen in real life." I was thinking about Lucy, and how different everything was going to be without her. That wasn't like the book: it wasn't wrapped up—there was still a lot to worry about.

Peter arranged the papers on the counter into a neat pile. "Sometimes it happens in real life, but it's rare—so when it does, it's pretty special."

I pulled the red shoes out of the plastic bag.

Suddenly Peter was surprised. "Two things today?"

I shook my head. "These aren't for Lucy. They go somewhere else, and I think I need a box."

While Peter walked to the back of the store to get one, I wrote down Miss Sato's name and the address of the hospital. When he came back, I was all ready. I slid the paper across the counter.

"Can I send it without my name and address on it?" I didn't want Miss Sato to know they were from me. That would raise lots of questions. It had to be anonymous. Peter looked at the paper and thought for a minute. "We could put the name of the store on it. Would that work?"

I nodded and put the shoes inside the box, and Peter taped it up.

I didn't have a lot of time. The box needed to get to Miss Sato as soon as possible. Mr. Gripes and Miss Sato had to fall in love in the next couple of days—it had to happen before Claire left. I knew that Miss Sato was sick, but if she could blink her eyes to answer questions, then maybe she could still fall in love. Love was an inside thing; she didn't need her body to be working for that.

"Can it get there tomorrow?" I tried not to sound desperate, but I was nervous.

Peter punched in some numbers on the computer and said, "Twenty-six dollars." I couldn't believe it. I didn't have anywhere near that amount of money.

"But it's not even out of town," I complained. "How come it's so expensive?"

Peter shook his head and held up the box. "Next day is always expensive. How much money do you have?"

I pulled out my money and put it on the counter. I had a five-dollar bill, and thirty-six cents in change. Suddenly I had the feeling that nothing was going to come together for me.

Peter picked up the money and said, "Let me see what I can do."

Claire had come up beside me. She held up the drawings she'd made and waved them in front of me. I tried to smile, but I was still thinking about the shoes. What would happen if they didn't get there on time? The answer to that was easy: nothing! I tried not to think about it. I nodded at Claire and smiled again but didn't do a very good job of it. I could tell she was disappointed.

Peter put his hands together and said, "Why don't you go out and unlock your bike. Claire and I are going to have a little talk. I'll bring her outside in a minute."

Claire was suddenly interested. "Is it a secret?"

Peter nodded. I was confused, but I left the store.

I couldn't see what they were doing, and by the time I was done unlocking the bike, they were at the door waiting for me.

"Well?" I asked.

Claire shook her head. "I'm only allowed to tell you when we're one block away." She got on the back of the bike and clamped her lips shut, so the secret couldn't come out before she wanted it to.

"Bye, girls." Peter waved and we pedaled off, but as soon as we were a block away, I stopped the bike and turned around to look at Claire.

Claire waved a five-dollar bill in the air. "Peter said we should have a snack with this money. It used to be yours, but now it was his, so you have to listen to how he wants us to spend it."

I smiled. Peter was full of surprises. "What kind of snack should we get?"

Claire decided in two seconds. "Cupcakes!"

When we got home, Mom was in a battle with the garage. She had stuff all over the driveway. She said she was enjoying herself, but she didn't look very happy. Maybe she was finally realizing it was all junk. Claire was excited about a pair of old stilts that were sitting by the door, so Mom said she'd watch her if I wanted to go inside and do some writing. I felt bad tricking her again, but the pull of the jar was too much. I couldn't stop myself. Guilt is a funny thing: you can feel it but still decide to do something that makes it worse. I left them, walked inside, and went straight down to the basement.

I pulled out the wish jar and sat in the chair. I was nervous, but excited too. I wanted to see Miss Sato and Mr. Gripes again. Now that I knew it was them, would it feel different? Would something special happen? I moved my hand through the wishes and picked one out. I was hoping for an Anderson's wish, and before anything could stop me, I opened the wish and read it.

Please Don't Let Ashley Be Dead

WHAT? I couldn't watch this! But it was too late to stop it. Suddenly I was back on the sidewalk where I'd first met Ashley and Shue.

I almost couldn't think of a test word, but then it popped out: "Fuchsia rat."

I said it quickly and quietly. Nothing had happened, but I was already worried and feeling sick. I wanted to know and not know what was going to happen, both at the same time. Knowing won. I kept my eyes open. Ashley was with her two friends—the ones from before, the ones I didn't like—and they were walking away from Shue. It looked like they had just passed each other. Ashley's group was crossing the street, and Shue was walking toward me on the sidewalk. Something shiny in the road caught my eye. Ashley had dropped it. It sparkled in the sunlight. She didn't notice and her group continued walking, but suddenly she turned, looked at the road, and ran back into the street. A second later there was a screeching of brakes, a thud, and then silence. And after that, yelling and screaming. I couldn't breathe—I felt dizzy. Everything swirled around me in slow motion: I was going to faint. I doubled over and covered my ears. I hummed loudly, blocking out everything. There was chaos all around me, but I couldn't hear it. I didn't want to see anything, but somehow after a minute or two I straightened up and followed my feet forward.

A car stopped in the middle of the road, and everyone was crowded around the far side of it. I looked down, and there next to the car, partially under the front wheel, was a silver necklace with a half-circle pendant on it. Ashley had been going back to get it. It was proof that she still cared. I heard someone next to me; it was Shue. She reached for the necklace and then stopped—if she pulled it, it would break.

We stood there, not moving, surrounded by

chaos, staring at the necklace. Paralyzed. I heard sirens in the distance. I didn't look up. I didn't want to see anything. I was scared, shaking, and beside me I could hear Shue crying. Suddenly she screamed, and I was gone.

The pain coming back was the worst yet. My blood felt like it was on fire, streaming through my body, burning me from the inside out. When I finally had the strength to look at my hands, I was surprised that they weren't red and raw. They looked perfectly normal. I forced myself to breathe in and out. The pain was over, but I was not okay. I closed my eyes, but suddenly I was afraid of the dark. I didn't want to be alone with my thoughts. Instead I focused on my hands, slowly relaxing my fingers one at a time until I was no longer gripping the chair. I leaned back and stared up at the ceiling and noticed for the first time the dark wood beams and spiderwebs above my head.

What I did next I can't explain. And if I can't, no one can, because I alone was responsible. I leaned forward, pulled out a wish, and read it. Just like that. After all the pain, and in the midst of sadness, that's what I wanted.

I Wish I Hadn't Gone to Ashley's House

I was still shaking from the last wish, but somehow seeing both Ashley and Shue standing together again helped. Shue was on Ashley's doorstep, and Ashley was in the doorway. The door was half closed like she was keeping Shue out, or maybe she was trying to hide behind it. This was before the accident. I wasn't sure how I could tell, but I could. I sighed and stepped forward. I hated these doorstep visits; they always ended badly. I said my test words, but without enthusiasm.

"Turquoise rabbit." I had a feeling it was going to be the only bright spot of the whole wish.

Ashley shook her head. "I can't come out."

Shue smiled and nodded. She took a step forward. I could see that she thought that she was going to be invited in. Ashley moved behind the door and closed it farther. This was unexpected. Shue stopped. Suddenly there was the sound of laughter from inside the house—girl laughter.

Ashley looked nervous. "Pam and Cathy are here. They're my high school friends."

For a few seconds neither girl moved or said anything. I was tired of this. I wanted to go up to Ashley and shake her. Tell her she was being stupid, and petty, and cowardly. Why couldn't she be friends with everybody? I noticed that Ashley was still wearing the necklace. Did Shue see it? It made me mad. She didn't deserve it—and then I remembered the accident. Maybe she was dead, and if so, it was because of the necklace. What did that mean? It was too much to understand. I closed my eyes for a minute. When I opened them, Shue was walking away, and the door was closed. Something had happened, and I'd missed it. I knew what was coming next. I closed my eyes and held my breath. It was like standing inside a furnace: it probably only lasted seconds, but it seemed longer, and then it was over. Painful and shocking, but not as bad as the last time. I sat back in the chair and rested my head on the cushion; a second later Claire was shouting.

"HE'S HERE! HE CAME BACK! YOUR DAD! HE'S HERE!" It was a proclamation—like something miraculous had just happened, and she couldn't believe it. It made me happy. It made me sad. But mostly, it made me feel lucky.

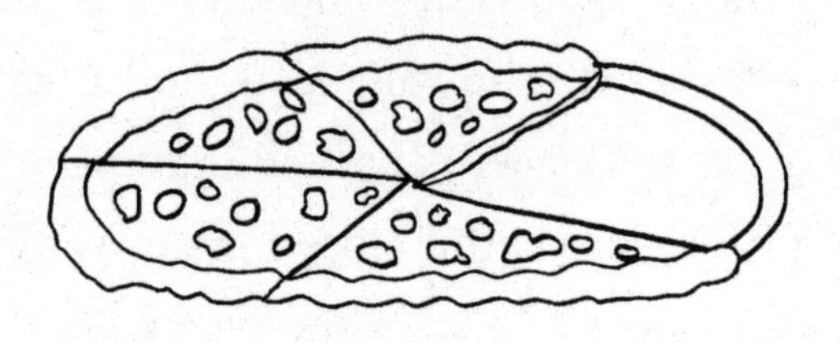

chapter thirty-six

Mess

The yard was a mess. Mom had stuff everywhere, and she wasn't handling it well. Junk out in the open is different from junk hidden away. It was how I felt too. Like suddenly there was too much of everything. And then Dad walked in and saved the day. Well, not really, but having him home changed things, and seeing him made me realize how much I had missed him. Mom seemed better with Dad around, too. That night we all went to Fannucci's, and it was a surprise; instead of it being awful, it was great—like it used to be. And the apple pie with ice cream was even better than I remembered it.

chapter thirty-seven

Magic

I slept late—later than normal. When I got up, there was only time for breakfast and to help Mom move a few things around in the yard. It was craft day at the old people's home, and the last one Claire and I would be doing together. When I went to get my bike, I was surprised by how big the garage looked. It was almost empty now.

Claire and I rode slowly up to the craft event. This was the last time we would do this together. The countdown had started; in two days I was leaving. It made me sad, but when I saw Sam's bike, I forgot about that and was happy again. This time Claire wasn't the first person going down the hall looking for Sam; it was me. He was in the room with the projector, and when he saw us, he smiled and jumped up.

"You'll never guess what happened."

"WHAT?" shouted Claire.

I patted her on the shoulder and told her to be quiet. The old people's home was not a place for loud voices.

Sam waited for me to finish talking to Claire, but he looked like he was about to explode. As soon as I was done, he started talking again.

"Mr. Fred said that yesterday a small man—and not just a little small, but *really* small—came to the hospital with a box for Miss Sato." Sam held his hand out at the height of Claire's shoulder to show us how small the man had been.

I knew exactly who he was talking about, but I kept quiet.

"Did Mr. Fred see him?" asked Claire.

Sam shook his head. "No, but the nurses did, and they'd never seen him before." Sam held up his hands. "But that wasn't the weird part."

Claire and I nodded, waiting for what was next.

Now Sam was almost whispering. "The weird part was what was in the box." He looked at us to see if we were paying attention.

We both nodded.

Claire leaned forward. "What was in it?"

Sam held a finger up in the air and then whispered, "Two red shoes."

Suddenly Claire looked at me. Her eyes were wide. She was about to say something, but Sam stopped her. He held his hand up.

"I know, it's confusing, but wait, I'll explain. Do you remember when I told you about Miss Sato saying *raishuu*?" Sam looked at Claire. "It's the Japanese word for yesterday."

I nodded.

"Well, it turns out she wasn't saying a Japanese word at all: what she was really trying to say was 'red shoe,' but because of her stroke it came out all wrong. She was trying to tell Mr. Gripes where she'd hidden the key to her safety deposit box."

Claire interrupted. "Why is that important?" She seemed disappointed.

I tried to explain. "It's where people keep important papers, and money and valuable stuff."

"And love notes," said Sam. "Miss Sato saved every single love note Mr. Gripes ever wrote to her. He used to put them in her shoes. Her red shoes. Isn't that weird?"

I nodded. I didn't know what to say.

Claire looked at me and then back at Sam. "Are they in love again?"

Sam shrugged his shoulders and looked embarrassed. "Mr. Gripes is reading the notes to Miss Sato, and she smiled for the first time yesterday."

Suddenly Claire ran over and hugged me. She was crying. I hugged her back. Now Sam was confused. He probably was thinking we liked Miss Sato a lot more than we did. He didn't know that the hug was for us, and all that we couldn't and didn't talk about.

It was for love that was broken.

Love that was weak.

Love that was hurting.

Love that was disappointing.

And love that was friendship.

It was for a lot of things.

The craft project itself wasn't my favorite. I'm not a fan of paper flowers, but that didn't matter, it was still a nice time. *Raishuu* and red shoes—I couldn't believe it. It was overwhelming; I could hardly keep it inside. Now it all made sense—the wishes, and Sam, and Miss Sato, and Mr. Gripes. I knew why it had happened. I had fulfilled my destiny. It was a relief. I tried not to think about Ashley; that was the loose end that still didn't fit.

Before we left, Claire invited Sam to the yard sale tomorrow. A week ago I would have been horrified, but now things were different. I was looking forward to tomorrow. I was tempted to stop by the VS Depot on the way home, to say thank you to Peter, but Dad said we had to be back by three thirty, and it was already past three. We'd have to wait until tomorrow. Maybe I could make him a thank-you card.

As soon as we got out to the bike, Claire asked about the red shoes.

"You sent them, didn't you? How did you know that was the right thing to send?"

I was ready for her question. "Do you remember the photo of Mr. Gripes and Miss Sato that Mr. Fred said was his favorite?"

Claire thought back and nodded.

"They were in love back then, that's why the photo was Mr. Fred's favorite. And in that photo Miss Sato was wearing red shoes. So I thought the red shoes might work like my treasure hat did for me. It might remind them that they used to be in love."

Claire stared at me, not saying a word. Now I was unsure about my explanation. Did it make sense? It wasn't the whole truth, but it was everything—except for the wishes. But I couldn't tell her about the wishes. Finally she spoke.

"You're a love detective." And she said it like she was believing it for the first time.

We got home superfast, both pedaling and excited about our adventure with Dad. I knew where we were going—Howling Hills. It was a huge amusement park—but for Claire it was a surprise. When she found out, she couldn't stop bouncing up and down.

The two best things about Howling Hills are the food and the rides.

The two worst things about Howling Hills are the food and the rides.

It's not easy to get the right mix of food and rides. I was doing pretty good until the funnel cake; after that I pretty much had to keep my feet on the ground. Dad tried to get me to go on the mini swinging chairs with him and Claire, but just looking at them made my stomach feel swirly. It was too bad, because it was the last ride of the day.

When we pulled up to our house, I hardly recognized it. Mom had been crazy busy while we were gone. There was stuff all over the front yard. She said it was too much to leave until the morning, so she had put the big stuff out now. The rest of it was piled in boxes in the driveway. It was a little hard to guess what Dad was thinking about it all. It was like he'd left town, and one kind of wife, and come back to an entirely different wife. He was probably still in shock.

It was late, but I still wanted to go downstairs. Mom was upstairs with Claire, and Dad was looking at his computer; no one would be looking for me for a while. Would I risk the pain again? What was the point? My mission was over, wasn't it? Maybe, but I still couldn't get Ashley out of my head. What had happened to her? Was she alive? Was she dead? And there were so many wishes left. Why? I turned on the light and started down the stairs. Halfway down I gasped and grabbed the railing. The basement was clean! The boxes were gone. I raced down to the workbench—my chair was still there, but everything else was cleared away. I dropped to my knees and looked under the bench. No boxes! No wish jar! NO NOTHING! It was all gone! My body was shaking. I could hardly breathe. This couldn't be the end. Mom had cleaned everything out, but it wasn't gone. It had to still be in the driveway. I ran up the stairs and raced outside. It was too dark to see. I had to get a flashlight. I ran back into the house and straight into Mom.

"Ash! What's wrong?"

She grabbed my arm and slowed me down. Suddenly I noticed I was crying. A second later I was inconsolable, head in my hands on the kitchen table. Mom tried to help. She was panicked. She patted my back and asked:

"Is it Claire?

"Daddy?

"Lucy?

"Me?

"Are you worried about camp?"

But I was like Miss Sato, unable to make her understand. I pointed to the door, to the driveway, but that didn't help. Finally I let her lead me upstairs and help me lie down. If she had her own theories about my sadness, she didn't share them. She stayed with me until I finally calmed down. I had a plan—as soon as she left I was going outside—but that never happened. I heard Mom leave, but when I opened my eyes again, it was morning.

chapter thirty-eight

Sale and Serendipity

I was lying on my bed, still in my clothes from yesterday, and someone had covered me with a blanket. My eyes felt swollen and crusty. I rubbed them, but they hurt. I staggered to the bathroom; the window was open and I could hear Mom and Claire talking outside. What time was it? Had the sale already started? Then I remembered the jar. I had to find it. I changed my clothes and raced outside. Claire was emptying boxes onto the tables, and Mom was writing down prices. As soon as Mom saw me, she stopped.

"Are you feeling better?"

I didn't know if it was true or not, but I nodded. I looked around. There was stuff everywhere. I'd never find the jar on my own. I had to ask. But how? Without giving myself away? I took a deep breath and tried.

"Did you see a jar with a nice label on the side of it? I think it said 'wishes.' I saw it once in the basement. I'd kind of like to have it."

I was hoping that sounded casual, and not like I was feeling—completely desperate. My hands felt clammy; I wiped them on my shorts. Mom didn't say anything. She studied me for a second, turned, and walked across the driveway. She pulled a box from a pile, looked in it, and held up the wish jar. I couldn't believe it. I wanted to run over and hug her, but I didn't. I forced myself to walk slowly.

Mom walked the last few steps toward me and handed me the jar. I took it from her and smiled, but then froze. The jar was empty—completely empty. The wishes were gone. Instantly my throat felt dry.

I pointed to it. "Wasn't there stuff in it?"

Mom waved her hand and moved back to the table with Claire. "Just garbage. I threw it in the disposal. It's a nice jar, though." She smiled.

I couldn't smile back. She had no idea what she'd

done. She'd thrown them away—my friends Ashley and Shue. Now they were gone—forever. It was over. I didn't want it to be over. I wasn't ready for it to be over. It was another loose ending. I felt sick.

"If you want to write for half an hour, Claire and I can handle this," said Mom.

I walked toward the house, not looking back. I was holding the jar like it was something precious, valuable, but it wasn't either of those things anymore. It was just an empty jar.

I went down to the basement, not even bothering with the notebook. I sat in the chair, but it felt strange with everything cleaned up. Too open, and unprotected. I twisted the lid off the jar. Instinctively my hand went into the jar, but there was nothing to pull out. It was empty. I felt empty too. We were one in our emptiness. I sighed, put the jar down, and dropped my head into my hands. This wasn't what I was expecting—this ending. I stared at the ground, at the lid, and then something caught my eye. I picked up the lid. I couldn't believe it. There, stuck on the underside edge of the lid, was one last little ball of paper. The last wish. I pulled it off and held it in my palm. Whatever it was, this was it. Would it tell me about Ashley? There was only one way to find out.

I dropped it into the jar, pulled it out, and flattened it out against my knee. I wanted to remember everything. How this was feeling. I counted slowly down from ten and looked down and read it.

I Wish That Boy Hadn't Seen Me Crying

Shue was running on the sidewalk. Her arms were filled with books. She was making a strange sound; it took me a second to figure it out—she was crying. Something about this seemed familiar. I looked behind me, and in the far distance I saw a figure walking away. Was it Ashley? Wasn't this the street where the girls always passed each other? I ran to catch up with Shue. All of a sudden she tripped and fell. Her books flew off in all directions. She lay in a heap in the middle of the sidewalk, not moving, and then groaned and sat up.

"Are you okay?" asked a voice.

It was a boy. I didn't recognize him. He wasn't one of Ashley's brothers. Shue nodded but didn't say anything.

"I'll help you," said the boy. He bent down and started to pick up the books. "I go to your school," he said.

Shue nodded again. She wasn't talking, but she had stopped crying. Together they picked up Shue's things, and when she had her arms full again, the boy turned to leave.

"Thanks," said Shue. Her hair was in front of her face, hiding her eyes. Did the boy know she'd been crying? He walked down the street ahead of her, then turned and shouted, "I'll see you later."

She half waved back, and I slowly faded away. This time was not like last time—there was no great pain, just a slow, uncomfortable tingle, like the last drizzle of something unpleasant. I sat in the chair and waited—for what, I don't know. It was hard to believe this was the end. It was disappointing. It hadn't been the wish to end all wishes. I still didn't know about Ashley, and now I'd never know. I thought back to the wish and went over it. It had no relevance. I'd forgotten to say the test words, but that didn't matter now. Everything was over. Suddenly Claire was calling down to me. I shoved the wish into my pocket and went up; the yard sale was starting.

From the minute it opened, the sale was a success, and I had the feeling that Mom had found a whole new thing to love—yard sales. She couldn't believe how much money she was making, but more than that, she was excited that her junk was making other people happy. My job was easy: help sell stuff and keep an eye on Claire.

I was pretty easy to bargain with. If someone said, *I'll give you twenty cents for that*, even if the price was a dollar, I'd say okay.

"How much is this?" Claire shoved something yellow in my face.

It was too close to see. I pushed her hand away. I was right in the middle of helping two other people, one with books and the other with cups. We were busy, and there were too many people asking questions. I caught Claire's eye and held up my hand.

"I'm helping this lady. I'll be with you in a minute."

"Can she have it for ten cents?" asked Claire.

I almost nodded but changed my mind and looked over to see what she was holding.

"It's ugly," said Claire.

She was talking to the little girl standing next to her.

"Are you sure you don't want something else?"

I gasped. It couldn't be. But there it was, right in Claire's hand—a duck statue, just like the one in the wishes. The one that Ashley and Shue hid in each other's rooms.

"Where did you get that?" I was almost yelling.

The little girl took two steps back and looked around. I was scaring her.

I snatched it away from Claire. "I'm sorry—this isn't for sale." I held it tight, as if they would try to pry it away from me.

Claire looked surprised and then she scowled. She took the little girl by the hand and led her away.

"Come on, let's find you something even better, and you can have it for free."

Where did she get this? I looked around, but it could have come from anywhere. Suddenly Mom was standing next to me.

She pointed to the statue. "What are you doing with that?"

Maybe she knew? Maybe she could point me to the right box. Maybe it would be a box with clues. Maybe even clues about Ashley.

I held it up. "A little girl had this. Do you know where she got it? Which box?"

Mom shook her head.

"It's not from a box." She took it from me and smiled. "It used to be mine, but I don't need it anymore."

I wanted to say something, but suddenly I was numb. I couldn't talk. It belonged to Mom? THIS

WAS MOM'S DUCK? Another coincidence? Mom put the duck down on the table and looked at me.

"Are you okay?"

It wasn't easy, but I made myself move my head up and down. She smiled, turned, and walked over to help some people looking at a set of dishes. As soon as she was gone, I grabbed the duck and ripped its head off. I gasped again. There was a slip of paper inside. This was the duck! The duck from the wishes. I pulled the paper out and read it. IT WAS ASHLEY'S HANDWRITING! My legs felt wobbly. I held on to the table for support. The note had eight words on it. And they were the perfect words for Shue. "I am sorry for being a bad friend." Wait, the right words for Shue? Did that mean the right words for Mom?

Was Mom Shue? Then who was Ashley? Was that who I was named after? The maybe-dead girl? I felt sick, and dizzy, and suddenly the world seemed distant and quiet, and then I was gone.

The first face I saw was Mom's. She was calling my name and touching my head. I hadn't noticed it before, but she had Shue's voice. Not exactly the same, but now that I knew what to listen for, I could hear it. After what seemed like twenty questions about what hurt and what didn't, she finally let me sit up. She was really worried. "Are you okay? Do you feel sick? Does your head hurt?"

I shook my head and smiled. She was Shue. Mom was Shue! I was grinning like crazy, I couldn't help it. I hadn't lost Shue; she was right here standing over me.

Mom looked at me and frowned. "Are you sure you feel okay? Why are you smiling?"

Suddenly I heard another familiar voice—Sam. I tried to jump up, but Mom made me get up slowly. I let her hold my arm. Seconds later Claire was introducing everyone. I couldn't stop looking at Mom. It was like seeing her for the first time. She was the same Mom, but now things were different—completely different.

Mom pointed to Sam's hand. "Did you bring that for the sale?" Sam put his hand behind his back.

He looked embarrassed. "No, it's sort of for Ash."

He was having trouble talking in front of Mom. Mom noticed too, because she suddenly pointed to the far side of the driveway and said she had to get over there and help out. That was nice of her. When Mom was gone, Sam held up what was in his hand. It was the clown tray from the thrift store. I was shocked. I didn't know what to say.

Suddenly Claire noticed it too. "Hey, you found another one!"

Sam shook his head. "It's not another one. It's the same one from the thrift store." He looked at me, and back at Claire. "Ash forgot it the day she was there." He handed it to me. "But it's probably too late to send it to Lucy."

I took it and smiled. He'd bought it for me. I couldn't believe it. I'd never have thought I'd be happy to hold the clown tray, but I was. I couldn't stop smiling.

"Thanks—I can still send it. We'll do it today."

It was true. Claire and I had one last trip to the VS Depot later today, to say good-bye. The tray could be my last present for Lucy. And it was strangely perfect, because it was the start of the story. And I was going to tell her everything. I'd decided this morning. It was too much to keep to myself.

Sam hung around the yard sale for most of the afternoon. He didn't buy anything, but we had fun selling things together. Before he left, he gave me his address, and I promised to send him at least three postcards. He seemed happy, and that made me happy too.

When the sale was over, I found a Sharpie and wrote a note to Lucy on the back of the tray. I wanted to write something intriguing, but I couldn't think of anything. All I could come up with was "I have a story to tell you." When I was done, I decided that creepy clown on the other side made it seem mysterious—not in the way I'd envisioned it, but it was better than nothing.

The day was moving faster than I'd planned. I had a million questions for Mom, but I couldn't just ask them. I had to do it right. Why was her name Shue? What happened to Ashley? Was I named after Ashley? I wasn't sure I wanted the answer to the last question. Who wants to find out you're named after someone you don't like?

chapter thirty-nine

Good-bye

Claire and I were rushing to maneuver the bike past all the remnants of the yard sale. Mostly it was empty boxes, but still it was kind of like an obstacle course. The VS Depot closed at five, and it was already after four. Just before we left, Claire leaned over and handed me something. It was the yellow duck. "You dropped it when you fell," she said.

She pointed to the head. "I put it back on."

I took it, pulled off the head, and looked inside; the paper was gone. For a moment I was disappointed.

"Did I do it wrong?" Claire looked worried.

I smiled, pushed the head back on, and put it in

my pocket. "No, it's good. And thank you for saving it for me." I was glad to have it.

We got on the bike and were off. The tray was too big for my backpack, so I had to use Dad's belt again. This time Claire wasn't happy about the eyes looking at her while we were riding. Clown eyes weren't as friendly as owl eyes. Halfway there I had to stop and turn the tray around so the clown face was next to my shirt. I couldn't blame her. It was creepy. When we got to the VS Depot, she jumped off the bike, but this time she didn't run in; she waited for me. I was surprised, but I didn't say anything. Maybe she was like me—recognizing that this was the last time we'd do this together. As we walked into the store, she took my hand and held it. At first we didn't see Peter. There were two men in the store, and they were behind the counter working on something. When we got closer, I could see that they were taking the ramp apart. All of a sudden I shivered, but it wasn't cold—it was sadness.

"Hi, girls!" It was Peter. He caught us by surprise; he was standing off to the side of the front door. I wasn't used to him not being on the ramp, so seeing him short felt a little strange. I was used to looking at his face, not at the top of his head. But I tried to act like I didn't notice anything different. I smiled and held up the tray. Peter walked over to the counter, and we followed. He said something to the guys working on the ramp, and they left. I was glad. I wasn't used to having other people around, and I wanted our last time together to be the same as it always was—just us. I didn't notice it at first, but Claire hadn't said a word since we'd walked in. I looked at her but couldn't tell anything.

I put the tray on the counter, clown side up. Peter took one look at it and jumped back. Claire laughed.

Peter scowled. "I don't like clowns."

I thought he might be joking, but he was serious. I turned the tray over. He shook his head and pushed it onto the scale. He didn't say anything else until it was stamped and in the mailing bin behind him. Claire and I were quiet too, like there was some clown curse on all of us to be silent. When Peter turned back to the counter, he was his old self again.

He winked at us and said, "I have things for you." He bent down under the counter.

Suddenly I was feeling bad; I was going to make him a card but I'd totally forgotten. Claire didn't have anything for him either. We looked at each other, not saying anything but probably feeling the exact same way—guilty. When Peter popped up again, he had three packages for Claire and two for me.

Claire was excited about her presents. She got the giant goldfish poster from the wall, a book of blank postcards, and a secret thing that was in an envelope that she said she'd show me later. She seemed extra excited about the secret thing, but I didn't have time to wonder about it, because Peter had just handed me something amazing that I was not at all expecting. It was a book, but not a regular book—it was an advance reader's copy of a book. I'd seen that kind of book before; the librarian at school sometimes got them. I read the name on the cover and screamed. It was *Willow's Wondrous World*, by PJ Walker. It was the new PJ Walker book, and I was holding it before it was even in the stores.

"This is amazing!" Now I was like Claire, full of questions. But Peter held up his hand and opened the book to the title page. There was an inscription: "For Ash, Believe, Trust, and Hope, PJ Walker." At first it was exciting, but a second later I recognized the handwriting. Now it was unbelievable. It was the same handwriting that was all over the store. Could it be? My friend was PJ Walker? I looked up at Peter, and he nodded. I wanted to say thank you, but instead tears were suddenly streaming down my face, and I couldn't control them. Peter patted my hand and pushed a box of tissues toward me. After a few seconds he and Claire started talking again—that helped, hearing their voices. When I was finally calmed down, and after I had used up most of the tissues, Peter handed me the second package. I opened it. It was a notebook with lined paper, some writing paper, and a bunch of stamped envelopes. I don't know why, but we didn't say anything more about the book. Somehow I knew we weren't supposed to talk about it. We both knew the truth, but to anyone else it was a mystery. I smiled; I was good at secrets now.

Peter pointed to the notebook. "Claire told me you like to write stories." He patted the envelopes and the writing paper and winked at Claire. "And if you ever want to write to anyone, here are the supplies."

"They're for writing to me!" shouted Claire. I nodded.

Suddenly the two guys were back, and it was time to go. Peter walked us to the door. Claire gave him a hug, but I felt strange about that. Peter offered me his hand, and I shook it—that felt better. He watched us get on the bike.

It felt weird, this good-bye forever. Was this it?

Were we never going to see him again?

Claire must have been thinking the same thing, because she said, "Can we do this again next summer?"

Peter thought for a minute and nodded. "And until then, if you want to, you can write to me at the shop." He pointed to his store.

Claire looked at me.

"Do you promise?"

It was a big promise to make—three weeks next summer—but I only had to think about it for a second.

I put my hand over my heart, looked her straight in the eye, and said, "I promise." I made another promise too, but this one was not for Claire; it was to myself. And even though it was silent, I knew I would keep it. I had to. *No more lying.*

We waved at Peter one last time, and we were gone, pedaling home.

As soon as we got home, we showed Mom our presents. She was impressed, but not as excited as me—PJ Walker wasn't her favorite author.

Dad took Claire out for dinner so Mom could help me pack. It was a good idea, and I was glad to have some time alone with her. I pulled the duck out of my pocket and put it on my dresser. It was going to be my prop—the way to ask Mom questions without her getting suspicious. When she brought my suitcase down from the attic, I was ready.

I pointed to the duck. "That used to be yours, right? Where did you get it?"

For a second Mom didn't say anything, then she smiled. "You're not going to want to keep it when I tell you."

I shrugged my shoulders. "That's okay. Just tell me."

Mom looked at me one more time and shook her head. "I found it in a Dumpster, with my friend Ashley."

She was expecting me to be shocked, but I wasn't, and I couldn't fake it. I had to smile. It was so cool. I knew exactly what she was talking about.

"Is it the Ashley I'm named after?" I crossed my fingers. Would she tell me what I wanted to know? Did Ashley live? Or did she die?

Mom nodded and looked sad. I covered my mouth. Oh, no, Ashley had died! I wasn't expecting that. Suddenly it all came back to me—the way I'd felt at the accident. I turned away from Mom, picked up a shirt, and tried to fold it. I couldn't let her see my face. Mom reached over and put her hand on the shirt. I stopped folding.

"I should have told you this before, but my friend Ashley was Claire's mother."

What? My body froze as my brain tried to understand what she was saying, and then I was relieved.

"She didn't die!" I blurted it out without thinking. If Ashley was Claire's mom, that meant the car didn't kill her.

Mom shook her head. "No, she died."

Suddenly I realized my mistake, but it was too late to take it back. We sat there for a minute in silence, Mom waiting for me to look up, and me getting more confused. It didn't make sense. Claire's mom was the Ashley from the wishes? Claire hadn't said her mom's name was Ashley, and I knew Claire—that was something she definitely would have mentioned.

Finally Mom sighed and said, "When Ashley was fourteen, she changed her name to Alex. She was in a car accident." Mom paused for a moment. "We had some problems. We weren't as close after that."

Mom didn't say anything more. I nodded like I understood, but I didn't. I couldn't. Even though I'd watched it happen, I didn't know how she felt. I'd never lost a friend like that. Lucy was leaving, but it was different—I wasn't losing her; she was just going to live somewhere different. It wasn't the same; we were still going to be friends. Distance wasn't going to pull us apart.

Mom was upset. She was folding my socks, and socks don't need to be folded. I should have helped her, changed the subject, talked about something else, but I couldn't. I had one more question, and I had to ask it.

I picked up the folded socks and put them in my suitcase.

"Why did you name me after Ashley?"

Suddenly Mom was smiling.

"Ashley's a beautiful name. I've always loved it. And it was in memory of her—my very first best friend. That summer together was special, almost magical. It's hard to explain, but it was a turning point for me—like suddenly I felt brave and the world made more sense."

I nodded, not because I understood what she was saying, but because I didn't want her to stop talking. I wanted more.

She stopped folding my underpants and stood up. "Ashley and I had a lot of fun. She even gave me a nickname."

"What was it?" I tried to sound casual, but I needed to know. What did Shue mean?

Mom shook her head.

"Maybe some other time. It was just a silly prank I came up with." Now she was smiling. She handed me my folded underwear. "Don't forget to pack a pair of scissors. You never know—you might need them."

It took only a second, but then I got it—the reason for Shue.

Mom started to walk out of the room, but she stopped at my dresser. She picked up the yellow duck and pulled off its head. I must have looked shocked, because she said, "Don't worry, it's not broken." She pointed to the inside of the duck body. "There's a message in here."

I stood up. How had I missed it? When Claire gave it to me, it was empty. Mom put the head back on and set the duck on the dresser. As soon as she was gone, I ran over, grabbed it, and yanked off the head. There was a slip of paper inside. I pulled it out and read it. "I'm so happy you're my daughter." I recognized the handwriting. It wasn't Ashley's, it was Mom's, and the message was for me.

chapter forty

Going

I knew it wasn't going to be easy, saying good-bye to Claire. It was silly, but I had my special ASH LUCY shirt on, and somehow, I felt like it was giving me power. We'd all gotten up early, because it was a three-hour drive to camp, and I had to be there by ten. Dad was driving me and Mom was staying home with Claire. Claire's dad had called last night, and he was coming a day later than planned, so she'd be there four more days with just Mom and Dad. Mom did a great job of making plans for when I was gone. She had a whole list of things to do that Claire was excited about.

Claire and I were standing outside by the car.

Mom and Dad were in the house, so it was just the two of us. I had something special for Claire, something Mom had given me last night. She'd said it was for me and Lucy, so we could remember each other when we looked at it. But now I'd changed my mind. Lucy and I didn't need a reminder; this last month had proved it—we'd be friends forever. But Claire was different. She needed something.

I smiled and held out my hands—each one a closed fist holding a treasure. "I have something for you."

Claire held up the envelope from yesterday. She had something for me too. I motioned to my hands.

"Pick one."

She pointed to the right hand. I opened them both at the same time. Each was holding the same thing—a silver half-circle pendant on a silver chain. I handed one to her, and we put them on together. I felt like I should say something, something important but not cheesy, but I couldn't concentrate. All I could think of was Ashley and Shue sitting on the roof, and the full moon from the trampoline. A moment later Claire was hugging me. I hugged her back—it was better than words.

"Now my turn," she said.

She took a step back and handed me the envelope. Inside was a photo of her smiling behind the counter at the VS Depot.

"So you can remember me," she said.

It was a great photo; Peter had done a good job. Right on the wall, almost directly over Claire's head, was a sign. I hadn't noticed it before. I looked closer; it had something to do with printing—there were strange words printed all over it, but two of them caught my eye. Right there on the first line were the words "Roman Helvetica."

"What's wrong? Don't you like it?" Claire sounded worried.

I looked up and made myself smile.

"Nothing's wrong. I love it!"

My brain was a jumble—thoughts spinning and swirling. I tried to put the pieces together. Claire's story about her mom wasn't true. She didn't run off to be with Roman Helvetica; they were just words. Something she'd seen on the wall at the VS Depot. Claire was wounded; she was like Percy—needing a story to soften the truth. And this picture was a message, the last piece, so I could understand everything. And then I had it—clarity—it was like the zap back from time travel. Only it wasn't painful; instead it was enlightening. It was time to make a promise, another promise to the universe.

Claire was holding my hand now, tighter than

ever before. Like she would never let it go. We walked around the car.

"Remember that story I was writing?"

She nodded.

"Well, I'm going to write it for you, and every week, I'm going to send you part of it, in a letter."

Claire looked up. "Like you did for Lucy?"

I nodded. "Exactly, and maybe I'll even send you strange things—things from the story."

We stopped walking.

Claire was watching me, serious. "You never forgot to send them. You did it every second day."

I nodded. "I never forgot."

She let go of my hand and bounced up and down. Suddenly she was back to normal, back to being a little kid, and excited like she'd just won something amazing.

But it wasn't anything amazing, it was only me. It was less than she deserved, but maybe it would help.

After a lot more hugs, and a few kisses, Dad and I were in the car and ready to go. Good-byes were exhausting. I was glad to have three hours to rest, plus we'd stop for a snack—snacks were good. We drove through town, and I watched the familiar and the unfamiliar pass by my window. When we got to the highway, Dad looked back at me.

"Are you okay? Do you want to tell me about your time with Claire?"

I shook my head. I didn't have the energy. It was too complicated.

Dad tried again. "Is there anything you want to talk about?"

I thought for a minute and smiled. "Tell me about the first time you saw Mom, and what she was like in high school."

Dad laughed. "Well, your mother says she doesn't remember the first time I saw her, but it was a few years before high school. She was sitting in the middle of the sidewalk crying, and her books were all over the ground. Her hair was everywhere, messy, but I got a peek at her face. She had nice eyes. I helped her pick everything up." Dad paused. "You'd think a girl would remember something like that, wouldn't you?" He looked back at me through the rearview mirror.

I nodded, too stunned to speak. While Dad talked, I leaned back, listened, and closed my eyes. If this were a movie, the camera would sweep in for one final shot—a close-up of my face. There wouldn't be words, but my smile would give away the ending. I was happy.